CL SE
protection

CL🞉SE
protection

EDEN VICTORIA

GALLERY YA
SIMON & SCHUSTER

London New York Amsterdam/Antwerp Sydney/Melbourne Toronto New Delhi

GREEN FAMILY MANSION

BASEMENT

GROUND FLOOR

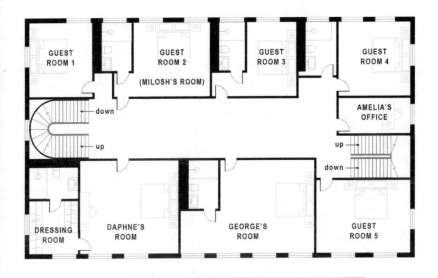

1st FLOOR

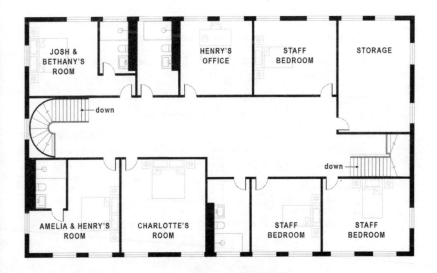

2nd FLOOR

First published in Great Britain in 2025 by Gallery YA,
an imprint of Simon & Schuster UK Ltd

1 3 5 7 9 10 8 6 4 2

Simon & Schuster UK Ltd
1st Floor, 222 Gray's Inn Road
London
WC1X 8HB

www.simonandschuster.co.uk
www.simonandschuster.com.au
www.simonandschuster.co.in

Simon & Schuster Australia, Sydney
Simon & Schuster India, New Delhi

The authorised representative in the EEA is Simon & Schuster
Netherlands BV, Herculesplein 96, 3584 AA Utrecht, Netherlands.
info@simonandschuster.nl

A CIP catalogue record for this book is available from the British Library.

ISBN 978-1-3985-3968-6
eBook ISBN 978-1-3985-3970-9
eAudio ISBN 978-1-3985-3969-3

Typeset in the UK by Sorrel Packham

Printed and bound by CPI Group (UK) Ltd, Croydon, CR0 4YY

To everyone who believes they don't deserve
princess treatment, newsflash . . . you do.
Oh, and BookTok? You're welcome :)

1

'Blue or grey?'

'Huh?'

'Blue or grey, your tie for tonight. I need to know so I can plan the rest of your outfit,' I explain as I close the door and go to sit down on the chair facing my father's desk.

'Daddy, are you listening to me?' I continue when he doesn't respond.

The rising annoyance in my voice prompts him to lift his head and focus on me instead of whatever on his screen was causing him to frown.

'I'm sorry, Daphne, I wasn't listening. What were you saying?' He exhales, removing his glasses and rubbing the bridge of his nose.

'It's fine, Daddy,' I soften, placing the tie options on the mahogany desk in front of me. 'But I need you to listen to me, please.' I pause until his eyes come to meet mine. 'Tonight we have Camilla's engagement party and I don't trust you to pick out your own outfit.' I gesture to his current ensemble – navy trousers and a blue house shirt underneath a camel knitted cardigan.

'When Amelia told me you wanted to see me in your study before breakfast, I assumed we'd be going over what I picked out for you, hence the ties.' I pick them back up and watch him patiently as he stares down blankly at the material.

'So . . . blue or grey?' I encourage, giving the ties in my hand a little jiggle.

As if a lightbulb turns on, my father's eyes illuminate with understanding, only to dim with confusion seconds later.

'Camilla's engagement party is tonight? I'm sorry, darling, I completely forgot.' He sighs.

My father is a brilliant man. As CEO of Greenway Discoveries, he has to be. But even with all that intellect he somehow always fails to be organized.

Amelia, our house manager, takes care of the staff, their routine and the general running of the house but her role has never extended to keeping my father's diary. Thanks to Julie, his assistant, he normally remembers all my extracurricular competition dates and kept up with our scheduled phone calls when I was at school in Switzerland, but when it comes to social events, his lack of organization is obvious. I mean. Julie can only prompt him so many times.

But ever since I returned home from school he's been different.

Scattered.

Quiet and distracted. Even more so than usual.

'Daphne, I'm sorry I've left it till the eleventh hour to tell you this, but we can't go to Camilla's party.'

'What do you mean we can't go?' I ask as I rise from the chair, unbidden irritation crawling across my skin. 'We RSVP'd "yes" months ago. It would be improper to just not turn up.'

In the last two weeks since I've been back, my father has been constantly locked away in his study, only resurfacing to eat or sleep. Yes, we've been having dinner together each night, but his attention has been elsewhere, most accurately on his laptop that he seems to be glued to.

The man who's a stickler for etiquette has his laptop at the table. Ironic, isn't it?

Amelia said his work has been stressful recently, but it's been stressful before and he always made time for me then. So what's so different about now?

'Yes, it will be rude of us to cancel, but things have changed, Daphne, which is actually why I asked Amelia to call you in.' He's clearly nervous, which is not at all like him. Letting out a long sigh, he turns off his computer monitor, offering me his full attention. 'There's something I need to discuss with you. Come, sit back down, please.'

I move away from the door and settle into the uninviting leather chair, the air trapped in the cushion slowly dispersing as I sink into it.

'Is everything okay, Daddy?'

'Daphne, darling, you may have noticed that I've been a little preoccupied since you came back from school. You've been nothing but patient with me, so I thank you for that.' I give him a small smile as he places his hand over mine from across the mahogany desk. 'The reason I called you in is because there has been a security breach at work. Someone tried to break into my office – and the lab – a couple of weeks ago now. He got away before the security team could stop or ID him but the issue was dropped when they realized he wasn't able to get in. However, two nights ago he tried again. Only this time he succeeded.' I feel my father's hand tense over mine for a moment before he swiftly releases it, turning his monitor back on and angling the screen towards me.

It illuminates with CCTV footage, the image grainy and distorted. 'He didn't take anything, thank goodness, but he was clearly looking for something specific. And evidently he has experience doing this, as he knew how to avoid the cameras completely.' I can't tear my eyes off the screen as I watch the man move. He is tall and well built, with his broad shoulders straining against his black hoodie, but Daddy is right, it's impossible to make out his face.

We both watch silently for a moment as the man closes the door behind him with a gloved hand, moving through the office with ease as if the layout is already familiar to him. Opening and closing drawers swiftly and decisively.

'What is he looking for?' I ask, looking up.

'We're not sure, but clearly he doesn't find it,' Daddy responds, shifting his weight, not taking his eyes off the footage.

On screen, the intruder resorts to a different method.

Within seconds, he trashes everything in sight. Papers go flying, the computer monitor is smashed and thrown to the floor and all the desk drawers are yanked out. He's getting desperate.

He grabs my father's lab chair and throws it into the Perspex screen protecting the chemical room inside the lab. I flinch as the chair bounces off the window. Seeing that didn't work, he resorts to attempting to kick down the door, the force knocking his hood off to briefly reveal a buzz cut and a short full beard before he harshly tugs it back into place.

Realizing his kicking is pointless, he stalks over to Daddy's desk and effortlessly flips it over. How that action was supposed to break the lab window I don't know, but hey, no one ever said criminals were smart.

But then my breath halts as he pulls out a gun.

A real-life gun.

As in, shoot-and-you-die gun.

He swiftly loads it and releases the safety, firing at the door. The thumbprint lock explodes, causing the electricity to short out and the door to open. He proceeds to look through all the serums and mixtures my father has in there before pulling out his phone and calling someone. The footage has no sound so I don't know what he's saying, but clearly he's telling them what he's found, or not found. After thirty seconds he nods, puts his phone back in his pocket and walks out the way he came.

'I don't want to frighten you, sweetheart,' Daddy says, pausing the video and turning the screen back around. 'But I wanted to show you just how violent this man is so that you understand why I now need to take measures to ensure your safety. What if they have our address and what they're looking for is in this very study?'

'Do you know what they're looking for?' I ask, surveying the room, feeling my stomach lurch.

As the children of Hezekiah Green, the founder of the Greenway Group, my father and his siblings have had multiple security scares over the years, so have always taken the necessary precautions to ensure their safety. With large security teams at their offices and smaller ones at their respective homes, I've always felt safe. Even the schools me and my cousins attended were highly secure, so I never had anything to worry about.

Until now.

None of this makes any sense. What in this study could they possibly want?

My father heads up the Greenway Discoveries division of the Greenway Group, which specializes in chemical engineering and new inventions. From what I know about his job, nothing confidential leaves his office and when he works from home he uses codewords when speaking about confidential projects so nothing can leak.

So what would they want from here that they couldn't get from his work office?

'Honestly, I don't know,' he responds, sighing as he rubs a hand down his face, looking back over to the screen. 'A couple of other offices were ransacked as well, so at least I know they weren't solely focused on me or what was in mine But that doesn't mean that I won't take extra precautions when it comes to you.'

'Okay, but how did the security guards at work not hear the gunshots?' I question.

'They were in the middle of a shift change so there was no one on the top floors. Which means whoever these people are, or whoever they work for, they've been watching this building and everyone in it for far too long to just give up when they don't find what they're after.'

My stomach drops as I try to come to terms with the facts.

Bad man with gun.

Works for even worse man who has been planning this for a while.

Bad man didn't get what he's after. Now, bad man *with said gun* is angry he didn't get what he wanted.

See now, that's not ideal.

'Hopefully there is absolutely nothing to worry about,' my father continues, snapping me back to reality, 'but I can't take that risk, not when I have you to protect. So I've increased the security around the house, and I've also hired a close protection officer to stay with you until we can be sure this is over. His name is Milosh Petrov,' he blurts out.

'You've hired a *close protection officer* to watch me?' I reply slowly. 'Like a bodyguard?'

'Yes, exactly like a bodyguard.' Daddy eyes me carefully,

almost bracing for impact as if I'm a bomb that might detonate.

'So let me see if I'm understanding this correctly,' I say, my voice as soft and measured as I can get it. 'You saw that security footage, and instead of, oh, I don't know, *calling the police,* you thought the best course of action would be hiring a random guy to follow me everywhere?'

'Daphne, of course I've taken the necessary steps to report what happened. The house is completely safe, I'm sure of it, but this is just an extra step. I am a concerned father, give me this.' He smiles softly. 'You're all I have, darling. I need to keep you safe.'

Before I have the chance to respond, there's a soft knock on the door and Amelia pokes her head round with a friendly smile. 'Sorry to interrupt, George, but Milosh Petrov is here.'

'Wait. I'm sorry, the bodyguard is here? Now?' I ask, appalled by the lack of notice.

'Yes, he is,' my father confirms. 'I'm not wasting any time when it comes to your safety. Thank you, Amelia, please send him in.' Amelia gives me an apologetic glance as she closes the door behind her.

'Daddy, I can't meet him now. I'm in my pyjamas first of all,' I look down at my pink silk nightdress and robe revealing my long brown legs and bare feet. The only saving grace is that I flat-ironed my hair last night and it looks fantastic.

'Oh, that doesn't matter, darling. He's going to be living with us anyway so I'm sure he'll see you in much more unfavourable conditions than this,' Daddy says in an oddly chipper tone.

'He's what?' I practically shriek. But before I get the chance to continue, the door opens and Mr Milosh Petrov walks in.

Well . . .

This should be entertaining.

2

MILOSH

Opulent, *grand* and *stately* are the words I would use to describe the Greens' estate. 'We don't have time for a tour now, but I'm sure Daphne will show you around after your meeting,' Amelia says softly as she guides me down the hallway, her sensible loafers clacking on the light oak flooring.

I mentally run through the list of facts I've memorized about Amelia, from the initial background check I ran on her when I got this assignment:

- Aged thirty-four. House manager
- Graduated Durham University with a bachelor's degree in Business Administration and Management followed by a master's in Finance
- Has worked for the Greens for ten years, during which time she met Henry Harris, head of home security
- Married for six years. No kids

Background checks don't tell me everything I need to know about a person, but from what I've seen so far, Amelia seems fine. From the brief conversation we had when I first arrived and the communication prior to that she seems to genuinely care for Greens. As long as that continues, she'll be an asset in keeping Daphne Green safe.

Daphne Green.

When I did a background check on her I wasn't surprised by what I saw:

- Aged seventeen. Only child of George Green
- Graduated Le Rosey boarding school three weeks ago, top of her class. Attending University of York in the fall. Studying Midwifery
- Well liked amongst her peers and faculty

The people's princess.

What the background check failed to mention is that she's almost definitely a spoiled, entitled daddy's girl, who has never heard the word *no*. This girl is the only child of one of the richest men in England. There's no world where I wouldn't expect her to be a brat.

I can already feel my spine tensing at the impending encounter as we pass picture after picture of her at various competitions, always holding the first-place trophy or medal. But I knew what I was signing up for when I accepted this assignment.

The only upside to cases like this is that they're almost always low risk and blow over quickly, so it should be a quick in and out.

As we continue the walk to George's study I think back to the meeting I had a week ago with him.

'Mr Green, great to meet you,' Andy drawls in his thick, Tennessee southern twang. 'I'm Major Andy Davis and this is Special Agent Milosh Petrov.'

From the pictures I've seen of George Green, I expected him to be shorter. In the photos I guessed his height at 5'10", but standing close to him he's only a few inches shorter than me, putting him at roughly 6' or 6'1". He's a friendly-looking black man with his hair cut short, slightly greying around the edges and a light moustache sharing the same greying qualities. His fitted suit showcases a strong, relatively muscular build which I couldn't see in any of his pictures. Clients with a good strong build are always helpful. One less person to worry about.

'Good to meet you, Mr Green,' I say, shaking his outstretched hand.

'You too, gentlemen.' He gestures for us to sit down. 'Now, I'm sorry to be blunt, but what is this about? I have a lot of work to get back to.'

Andy nods, taking a seat. 'As I mentioned on the phone, me and Special Agent Petrov are part of a joint task force with the military, the FBI, Interpol and the NCA working to shut down an international organization called Daveeno. We've been monitoring any movements that may be connected to them and when we got word from the NCA about your break-in, given that you worked with MI6 in the height of their Daveeno . . . affliction, we believe that the break-ins to your office may be connected.'

George goes still. 'Why would you think that?'

'You used to work with MI6 but left after your wife was murdered by a Daveeno member. And now nine years later there's a break-in at your office and they stole one of your old work journals? I know it may sound far-fetched but there's a chance there could be a connection.'

George shifts in his seat. 'All right, so what exactly do you want from me?'

Andy continues, 'We would like to place Special Agent Petrov in your home to keep an eye on things. His main task would be providing protection for your daughter, but he would also be looking out for any potential Daveeno threats.'

George frowns, looking over to me. 'You're not a qualified close protection officer. Why would I trust you to keep my daughter safe?'

'Sir, Special Agent Petrov is one of the best young

agents we have. He joined the military younger than most, at sixteen, and served for two years before moving on to a special operations unit. He protected seven US congressmen, ensuring their safety when they came under fire, every one of them remaining completely unscathed. I assure you, he's more than qualified to protect your daughter.'

George sighs, nervously tapping his pen on the table. 'Fine. You can stay, but do not tell my daughter who you are or why you're really here. I don't want her to worry.'

I nod. 'Of course, sir. To her, I'll just be a close protection officer you hired as a precaution.'

$$\oplus$$

'Wait here one moment while I inform Mr Green that you've arrived.' Amelia's words bring me back to reality before she continues down the hallway towards a heavy-looking wooden door. She knocks, and sticks her head around the jamb.

After some inaudible conversation she closes the door and returns to where I am standing in the hallway. 'Go on in, Milosh,' she says with a kind smile, gesturing towards the door.

As I walk in, I automatically do a quick survey of the room – a large fireplace and seating area takes up the left side with floor-to-ceiling Georgian windows lining the back, looking out on a backyard. To my right I notice an extensive book collection with what looks like too many first editions to count.

The room is decorated with a variety of striking paintings and stately furniture. If money had a smell it would be this – musk and worn leather. As I go to close the door behind me I notice a painting of Miss Green hanging on the wall. She looks significantly younger here than in any of the hallway pictures but her air of regality is still the same.

In the centre of the room George sits at a sturdy mahogany desk, with an oddly eager smile on his face.

Opposite him with her back to me, sitting on what looks like a very uncomfortable chair, is a feminine figure. Daphne Green.

'Milosh, hello! Great to finally meet you,' exclaims Mr Green, standing up to greet me as he starts the charade. I'm not completely happy lying to his daughter, but, hey, she's not my kid.

'Good to meet you, Mr Green,' I say, closing the distance between us to shake his hand.

'Oh, please, call me George,' he insists, gripping my hand firmly. 'Come, sit down, we have a lot to talk about. This is my daughter Daphne who you'll be guarding. Daphne, this is Milosh Petrov.'

As I go to sit down in the empty leather seat across from George's desk I turn to my left and lock eyes with Daphne Green. Just like George's, her picture didn't truly capture what she looks like in person. However, unlike with

George, this discovery is wildly inconvenient.

Brown skin, slender physique, with deep chestnut eyes and pillowy lips. Her raven hair softly cascades down her back, which is held impeccably straight.

In the pictures she had a regal presence. In person it's almost overwhelming. Even though I'm wearing street clothes and she appears to be in her pyjamas, I somehow feel underdressed just sitting next to her. 'Miss Green.' I nod, as I offer my hand to shake.

'Mr Petrov,' she replies, her voice honeyed and gentle. As she encases her soft, slender hand within mine, a look of deep confusion comes over her face. 'I'm sorry,' she enunciates slowly. 'You'll have to forgive me, but I don't quite understand. You . . . you're the bodyguard?' She turns to face her father. 'He's the bodyguard?'

'Close protection agent,' George corrects. 'And, yes, Milosh is to be your protection detail for the foreseeable future.'

'Forgive me, and absolutely no disrespect Mr Petrov, but you look rather young to be a qualified bodyguard,' Miss Green states. 'I mean, don't get me wrong,' she continues, giving me a once-over, her eyes briefly landing on my forearms, 'You look very capable. I'm just slightly puzzled as to how you're the best person to protect me.'

She turns back to George before continuing, 'Because if

this threat is as big as you think it is, surely I need a team, or at least someone with more experience.'

'Milosh has plenty of experience, Daph. From what I remember, he served in the US military for two years before joining a special ops team. He protected a group of US congressmen, keeping them safe when they came under fire, earning him a medal of honour. And all that before turning twenty. He's practically an American hero. Does that about cover it, Milosh?' George sits there looking pretty pleased with himself, although I can't understand why. It's not like he was there with me.

'Pretty much, sir,' I respond.

'So, to answer your question,' George continues to his daughter, 'I hired Milosh because he has a proven track record of being discreet, and he's more than capable of protecting you. And, as a plus, because you're close in age, if you go out his presence won't draw attention. I want this situation to affect you as little as possible. You need to be out there enjoying your life.'

'Sorry, sir, you mean for Miss Green to go about her daily life as normal during this time? While the threat hasn't been properly understood?'

They both look at me, Daphne clearly more horrified than her father. Mr Green silently studies me, his tone is slightly more guarded as he adds, 'Within reason, of course.'

Daphne shifts and huffs silently under her breath. Mr Green doesn't see it, but it's the kind of thing I've been trained to notice as her weight shuffles from thigh to thigh and her eyes dart around the room, pleading for an out.

She doesn't protest like I thought she would. If I'm honest, I thought there would be a tantrum or something by now. The congressmen acted more entitled than her. After a few deep breaths, she looks up and smiles at me.

'Well, thank you, Mr Petrov. I've appreciated hearing more about your credentials. I look forward to us working together.'

She sounds like an accountant in her mid-thirties, with a mortgage to pay and kids to feed. But better that than a whiny six-year-old. 'Milosh is fine, Miss Green.'

She smiles politely, gives a curt nod and then proceeds to completely ignore what I just said. 'Well, *Mr Petrov*, as introductions seem to be over I'll leave you to talk to my father while I have my breakfast.' She rises from her chair and leans over the desk to place a kiss on her father's cheek before retreating towards the door.

As soon as the hinges click shut George starts speaking again, his cheerfulness immediately evaporating. 'Just a reminder, Mr Petrov, I don't want my daughter to think this is anything but an overprotective father trying to keep his daughter safe. She doesn't need to know about the journal.

She doesn't need to know about the ins and outs of any of this. Understand?'

'Yes, sir.'

'Brilliant. Now let me introduce you to the rest of the team.'

3

Daphne

'He's young.'

'You're young,' Amelia says, briefly looking up from her laptop as Josh, one of our cooks, places my breakfast in front of me.

'Thank you, it looks lovely.' I direct my words to Josh, with a smile, then glance back over to Amelia. 'Yes, I'm young but I'm the protectee. I don't need to be old.'

'Protectee?' Amelia laughs. 'Is that even a word?'

'He's the protector, which therefore makes me the protectee by extension. It makes perfect sense.' I shrug. I'm sitting in the main kitchen atop a bar stool in front of the island while Amelia is bent over the other side, eating a snack while finishing some work. Normally I eat my breakfast in the dining room by myself, but after that meeting I didn't want to be alone with my thoughts so I came to the kitchen to talk to her.

'What's the actual problem you have with him, Daph?' Amelia queries as she closes her laptop, turning all her attention to me.

'I don't know,' I groan. 'The thing is, I get why Daddy is doing all of this, I really do. But I just don't want a bodyguard, Meelie.' I take a bite of my eggs. 'And I mean, I know that sounds bad, but for the foreseeable future I'm going to have someone *I don't know*,' I really stress that point, 'following me around everywhere. And I didn't want to tell Daddy any of this because, well, have you seen the man's face recently? He looks like he's in a constant state of stress from the moment he wakes up to the moment he goes to bed. I can't be a brat about it if this will bring him some peace of mind.'

'Hey, Josh, any breakfast for me?' Henry asks as he walks into the kitchen, grinning when he spots Amelia.

'Why couldn't I have had Henry?' I ask Amelia as he comes up behind her and gives her a kiss on the neck, wrapping his strong arms around her waist.

I've known Henry since I was five and Amelia since I was seven. A lot of my friends have staff as well, but they don't really interact with them as much as I do. Since my parents were always working when I was younger I spent more time with Henry, Amelia and the others, so we've got very comfortable together over the years.

'Ah, we talking about Daph's new bodyguard?' Henry enquires, moving from Amelia over to Josh, plate in hand.

'Yeah.' Amelia giggles. 'Hen, can you please tell Daphne this is a good idea, and to stop worrying about all of it?'

'Yeah, Daphne, it'll be fun.' Henry smirks, coming to sit down next to me. 'Stop worrying about it.'

'Have you met him yet?' I ask, completely ignoring both of them.

'Yeah, George just introduced me to him. He's with the other guys now.' When I first met Henry, he was our only security guy, but over the years he's become the head of security and now manages three other men – one daytime and two night-time security guards.

'Okay . . . Well, what did you think of him?'

'The question isn't what *I* thought of him.' Henry looks up from his food, that same irritating smirk on his face. 'It's what *you* thought of him, Daphne.'

'I thought he seemed . . .' I trail off, thinking back to moments ago when I was sat in Daddy's study as Mr Petrov walked in. He was taller than I expected, with dark brown, almost black hair, longer on the top and shorter on the sides. Gently tanned, with green eyes, thick dark eyebrows, a strong nose and an even stronger jaw, dressed in black cargos, boots and a black short-sleeve tee, he stepped into the study with an air of dominance and assertion. His voice was deep, with an American accent that had a hint of something else, something Slavic maybe. He didn't say much, but when he did speak, he spoke with such conviction and purpose. '. . . professional.' I finally settle on, before clearing my throat and bringing myself back into the current conversation. 'He seemed professional.'

'That's it?' Henry probes, his cockney accent shining. 'Just professional?'

'What exactly do you want me to say, Mr Harris?'

'I want you to tell me how you really feel, not do your calm, collected and mature thing.'

'In my opinion, Daph,' Amelia cuts in, smiling softly, 'I think he seems nice. Well-trained and discreet. And those are two of the most important attributes you need in a bodyguard.'

'Yes. I agree,' Henry adds. 'Well-trained and discreet is great. And I mean, it doesn't hurt that he looks like a young Captain America with the broodiness of Bruce Wayne.'

'I'd have to agree with that, but I was thinking he's more of a Clark Kent.' Amelia nods thoughtfully.

'Wait, are we talking ability or physical appearance?' I ask.

Hey, if you can't beat 'em, join 'em.

'I don't know,' Henry cocks his head. 'What do *you* think, Daphne?' Both Amelia and Henry have the same irksome look on their faces. I can really see why they're married.

'I think my father hired Mr Petrov for his ability.' I look pointedly at both of them. 'Not his physical appearance.'

'Yes, that's true, but your father also hired Henry for his ability and not his physical appearance, and now look where we are.' Amelia gazes at Henry and all of sudden I feel like I'm interrupting something.

Henry and Amelia met when she joined the household two years after he did. From the moment Henry laid eyes on her, he's looked at her with adoration that never falters for a second. After what seemed like an age of constant flirting with stolen glances and lingering and very unnecessary touches they decided to go on a date, and they've never looked back.

Watching their love grow and deepen over the years, seeing the way Henry treats her, I've resolved to never settle for less.

If it's not like Amelia and Henry Harris's love, I don't want it.

'It was the best decision I ever made, taking this job.' Henry's eyes soften as he reaches over and tugs on Amelia's arm, gesturing for her to move next to him.

'I agree,' Amelia whispers as he cups her face, pulling her in for a kiss.

With Amelia being 5'6" with lovely hazel eyes, tanned skin and soft light brown hair and Henry a solid 6'3" with chiselled features, strong arms – one with a tattooed sleeve – and fluffy brown hair, they make an absolutely stunning couple. But that's no excuse for the constant PDA. You'd think he'd just come back from war with the way the two of them continuously carry on.

I do *love* love and all that, but I could do without it being shoved in my face constantly.

I get up and swiftly leave the kitchen, signalling Josh to perhaps do the same, when I collide with a warm wall.

'Miss Green.'

'Oh, Mr Petrov, apologies, I didn't see you.' I right myself quickly as he stands there, hands in his pockets, looking everything but impressed. 'Have you finished with my father?'

'Yes, he told me to find you or Mrs Harris to show me to my room.' I look down to see his duffel bag in his hand then look back into the kitchen to see Amelia still wrapped up with Henry.

'Amelia's a little . . . preoccupied right now, so I can show you to your room and give you a tour of the house if you like. Do you have any more luggage?' I ask. His duffel bag is small . . . and black . . . and sad. It looks like it could barely fit everything I'd need for one night away.

'No, this is it.'

'Really? Everything you need for the foreseeable future is in that bag?'

'Mm hmm.'

'Oh.' I pause, glancing back down at the bag. 'Are you sure? That's an awfully small bag.'

'Yes, Miss Green, I'm sure,' he drawls, his eyes briefly perusing my body.

'Well, all right, then.' I smile politely, clearing my throat and standing taller as I pull my robe a little tighter, trying not to wither under his gaze. 'Follow me and we'll start on the first floor.'

4

MILOSH

'We have four floors in total,' Daphne states as we begin walking up the large staircase, her hair swishing behind her as she turns to look at me. 'Basement, ground floor, first floor and second. Live-in staff have rooms on the second floor, while mine, my father's and some of the guest rooms are on the first.'

'I'm gonna need a layout of the estate, any blueprints and access to all security cameras, codes and keys,' I tell her. 'I also need a list of people who have access to this house, all the staff and the frequency with which they come in and out.'

'Amelia can get all of that for you. I'll show you where her office is in a moment then you can stop by later and she'll sort it out.'

We stop short at the top of the stairs as we approach the first set of rooms. Just as Daphne goes to open what I presume to be her room, a mousey-looking woman comes out of the door opposite, holding a basket full of cleaning supplies.

'Morning, Charlotte.' Daphne smiles warmly.

'Good morning, Miss Green.' She smiles back, her eyes darting between me and Daphne. 'I'm just setting up this guest room for our visitor per your father's request. I'm almost finished. I just need to get some towels and remake the bed, then you can show him.'

'Oh.' The shock in Daphne's voice is prevalent but she quickly recovers. 'Okay, thank you, Charlotte, that's great.' She turns to me. 'I'll show you my bedroom first, while she finishes up. Then you can go and unpack your things.'

She opens a door to reveal a large, clean, feminine room, with cream-coloured walls, light furniture and large windows looking out to the driveway at the front of the house. Her bed is pristinely made, with too many pink-and-cream decorative pillows to count and a bedside table on either side. A bouquet of white roses stands on one and the other houses a few books and an alarm clock. In front of the windows is a small cream sofa with even more pillows.

Who needs that many pillows?

What would you even do with them?

'The dressing room is through here,' Daphne says as she opens another door and crosses the threshold. I walk behind her into a slightly smaller room, neatly packed with a ridiculous amount of clothes, shoes and bags. The vanity along one wall is painstakingly organized, with an expensive-looking perfume collection meticulously displayed on a tiered stand to one side and an elegant cushioned jewellery box on the other. We move into her bathroom which connects to both her bedroom and her dressing room. It's the largest en suite I think I've ever seen and it has the same light pink theme as the other two rooms – classy, sophisticated and clean.

She's wearing pink pyjamas, she has loads of pink clothes in her dressing room and there are pink decorative accents everywhere.

She likes pink. Got it.

'How do your windows open?' I ask as we walk back into the bedroom.

'Um, by the latch at the bottom. You just have to twist and push.' She goes to sit on the end of her bed while I check the sturdiness of the glass and latches.

'Do any of these doors have locks?'

'Yes, the bathroom locks from the inside and the door to my room has a key, but the dressing room doesn't have a lock apart from the door to enter the bathroom.'

'I'm gonna need a copy of the keys to your main bedroom door,' I say as I turn back around to face her. I watch her as she gently pulls out the bedside table drawer furthest from me, her hair momentarily falling into her face before she delicately sweeps it back behind her ear.

'Here you go,' Daphne says, placing the brass key into my palm. A small shock passes between our hands as her fingers brush mine, which she clearly feels too, as she draws back swiftly.

She looks away, slightly flustered. 'It's the carpets.'

'Excuse me?' I ask.

'The electric shock. They're caused by the static in the carpets.'

'Hmm.' I nod, as I slip the key in one of my pockets. My eyes scan down her face, onto her neck, stopping at her collarbones, where I can see the rise and fall of her shallow breaths. I look back up at her only to find her eyes on my mouth. My tongue darts out to wet my bottom lip and she looks up, meeting my eyes. She's parts her lips, about to say something before we hear a gentle knock on the door. We both turn to look as mouse-girl Charlotte leans her head around the door.

Her eyes glance between me and Daphne again, before offering a shy smile. 'The guest room's all ready, Miss Green.'

Great. Thank you, Charlotte. Daphne smiles. Charlotte nods once before closing the door, which leaves just me and Daphne again. I watch her as she slips on a pair of slippers that are at the foot of her bed before looking back to me. 'Let me show you to your room, Mr Petrov.'

'Milosh,' I correct.

When we cross the hallway to the guestroom, Daphne twists the door handle, using her weight to push it open. When it doesn't budge, I walk up behind her, placing my hand on the wood just above her head, and give it a shove to help her out. The door swings open, but for a moment we remain in the threshold, frozen. This close, I can smell her sweet, innately feminine scent. She smells like a mixture of orange blossom and marshmallows.

Great.

So not only does she look like a princess and talk like a princess, she even smells like one.

Recovering from my very obvious brain malfunction I clear my throat to refocus and walk past her into the room.

Placing my duffel on the plush footstool in front of the bed, I do a quick survey of where I'll be staying for the foreseeable future. This room's a lot more neutral than Daphne's, with cream walls, brown and beige furniture and deep wooden accents. There are a few pieces of art hung on the walls, and the heavy floor-to-ceiling curtains are pulled back to reveal large windows looking out onto the Greens' huge backyard. The bed features crisp white linens and a copious number of neutral-coloured pillows. Not as many as Daphne has, but still more than necessary.

'The en suite is through here.' Daphne motions, walking

gracefully into the bathroom. 'Extra towels are in the wardrobe. They're replaced every second day. Just leave them on the hook here and Charlotte will collect them.'

I nod as I take in the bathroom. It's smaller than Daphne's but bigger than anything I've ever had. Both this room and the bedroom have the same vibe as the rest of the house. Classic and elegant mixed with small modern touches. The whole house screams money without trying too hard, including the people living within it.

The thing is, I've seen money before. The congressmen I protected were wealthy, but they were nowhere near Green wealth. I wouldn't be surprised if one of those ridiculous throw pillows cost more than my outfit.

Move on from the pillows, Milosh.

Focusing back on safety, I check the windows for sturdiness and look around for anything that could be used as a weapon if needed. Happy with my assessment I turn around, finding Daphne in the doorway with her head cocked, a curious expression dancing on her face.

'Where would I find the keys for the wardrobe and the door?'

'Room keys are normally stored in one of the bedside tables,' she answers after a beat, turning on her heel and walking over to check the drawer closest to her. Once she retrieves the keys, her soft hand finds mine and places them in my palm, just as her chocolate eyes lift to meet my gaze. A crazy part of me wants to run my thumb across her plump bottom lip, just to see if it is as soft as it looks, but I hold off and settle for slipping the keys into another pocket, keeping my hand there to prevent myself from doing something stupid. She watches the fluid movement, her eyes tracking up my arm and settling on my bicep. After a few moments of silence, I clear my throat.

'Would you, um, like to unpack now or do you want to do it after we finish the tour?' she breathes, looking back up at me. I smell a fresh waft of that orange blossom and marshmallow scent of hers and instantly make up my mind.

'I'll do it later. Let's finish the tour.' I need to get a handle on myself and get this tour over and done with. The quicker I'm done with the tour, the quicker I can create some much-needed distance.

Jeez. I've only known the girl two hours.

Wildly inconvenient indeed.

5

Daphne

As I sit down at my dresser to get ready for bed, I realize I haven't checked my phone all day. I scroll through notification after notification and settle on opening all the unread messages from my Cousin Isabella.

Isabella

12:42 p.m.

Important question: what dress are you wearing tonight? I'm thinking of wearing my white Zimmerman dress, or is that too casual?

12:43 p.m.

Wait, I can't wear white to an engagement party 💀
Okay, I'll just wear the blue Alexander McQueen maxi with the silver Rene Caovillas.

7:15 p.m.

Cam seated us together, by the way, we're on table three. For when you get here x

8:03 p.m.

Blue was definitely the right idea, Cam is the only one wearing white, ahaha

8:57 p.m.

Camilla's asking where you are so I told her you're running late, when do you think you'll get here?

9:45 p.m.

Hello, Earth to Daphne . . . where are you? Did something happen?

10:03 p.m.

Oh my gosh, DAPHNE.
Auntie Harriet's WATERS JUST BROKE.
IN. THE. MIDDLE. OF. THE. SPEECHES.

Me
10:45 p.m.
STOP.
NO WAY!

Isabella

10:49 p.m.

Yeah, they left about twenty minutes ago. I don't know how Uncle Jonathan stayed so calm, Grandma was a mess 😭

Me

10:51 p.m.

Agh, I'm so annoyed I couldn't be there 😣
I wanted to go tonight but Daddy cancelled last minute.

Isabella

10:55 p.m.

Wait, so you're not coming at all? I didn't know if you were planning some weird fashionably late thing lol.
Why did Uncle George cancel?

My fingers pause over the phone keypad, wondering what I should say. Do I tell her about Milosh? Do I tell her about the break-in at Daddy's office? Even though Bella is my closest cousin, she's terrible at keeping secrets, and my better judgement tells me this is too important to share. My phone vibrates again but I place it face down on my dresser, overwhelmed by the whole situation.

I unclip the clasp of the necklace that I've kept hidden under my clothes all day, and place the locket in the palm of my hand. The dull gold glimmers and the ornate filigree design shines as it catches the light. I instinctively open the locket, revealing faded pictures of me alone on one side, and me and my mother on the other.

Somehow over the years this has become my nightly routine: skincare, change my clothes, morbidly obsess over a piece of jewellery that once belonged to my mother, read a few chapters of my book, then go to bed.

I open one of the drawers in my dresser, revealing something close to a shrine made from her belongings and old family photographs.

Following my routine, I place the necklace in a gold dish next to all her other jewellery, and pick up her old perfume bottle. Lifting it to my nose, the fragrance takes me back to the time when she was still here. Her smell was always so distinctly her. Warm but fresh, clean but sweet.

She smelled like my memories. Cosy yet distant.

After she died, Amelia used to spray her perfume on my pillow at night to help me sleep. When it started to run out, I began searching for a replacement. I couldn't find it, so I took a small sample to a perfumer to have it recreated but it never smelled the same. So for the last few years I've been rationing the remainder of her perfume, not wanting her memory to fade away with the scent.

I pick up my favourite picture of us as a family and smile weakly. It was my fifth birthday, and we were at my fancy-dress party. I was sitting at a table blowing out the candles on a cake that was almost as big as me, with my parents stood behind me. My mother was dressed as Princess Tiana, I was Sleeping Beauty and my father was Robin Hood, as if he's not the very man Robin Hood would most likely be stealing from.

I hear a faint knock at my main bedroom door so I shut the drawer, quickly hiding the memories of my mother, and look at my watch. 11:04 p.m. Charlotte already turned down my bed an hour ago, so who in the world is knocking so late?

Turning the lock on the drawer, I walk out of my dressing room and open the main door to find my father standing there, looking exhausted as per usual, but smiling warmly at me nevertheless.

'I just wanted to say goodnight, darling,' he says, hovering in the doorway.

'Yes, that's definitely the only reason you're here.' I smile, opening the door wider to let him in.

'I wanted to check in to see how you're doing after today?' He walks over and collapses onto the plump reading chair next to the window as I sit on the end of my bed to face him.

'I'm doing fine, really.'

He raises an eyebrow.

'It'll just take some getting used to, that's all,' I try instead.

'Think of him as another Henry around the house, just closer to you in age.'

'And proximity,' I mutter under my breath.

'I know it's not ideal but it has to be done. I'm sure I'm just worrying for nothing and this will blow over shortly,' he reasons. 'Hey, did Isabella tell you what happened tonight at the engagement party?'

'Yeah, Auntie Harriet's waters broke! How crazy is that?'

'I told her to stay at home but of course no one wants to listen to me.' He faux-sighs.

'To be fair, Uncle Jonathan was probably saying the same thing.' I shrug, laughing lightly.

'I'm truly sorry you had to miss it, darling. But, hey, if it makes you feel better, I can buy one of those labour simulators and we can try it out on me and Henry to see who can last the longest?'

'Oh my goodness, YES. Buy immediately.'

We both laugh, and I think it's the first time I've seen my father relax in weeks. But it's short-lived, as after a moment, his shoulders sag again and his face turns serious and a little sombre.

'Daphne, honey. I'm sorry to ask . . .' He pauses, evading my eyes. I wait for him to finish the question, tension crawling up my spine.

What now?

'I was wondering if you've seen a necklace anywhere around the house?'

'I have a lot of necklaces, Daddy. I need you to be a bit more specific,' I prompt, knowing full well which necklace he's referring to.

'Of course, of course,' he says, slowly becoming flustered. 'It's a gold necklace with a locket.'

'Are you talking about Mother's old locket?' As the word 'Mother' comes out of my mouth, he flinches slightly.

'Yes,' he replies meekly. 'That's the one.'

'Why? Is it lost? I didn't realize it was valuable to you,' I say curtly.

We never really talk about my mother any more, but not for lack of trying on my part. I had just turned nine when my father came into my room, sat on my bed, and emotionlessly relayed the news that my mother had drowned in the lake near the house. At that age, I understood the concept of death but I didn't really grasp its consequences. It took me months to accept the fact my mother hadn't just gone on a long work trip, she had left us for ever.

After that conversation, every time I brought her up Daddy would deliberately change the subject. Rather than helping us both confront our grief, my father pushed me into even more extracurricular hobbies and ensured I had extra swimming lessons, so I wouldn't fear the water. I know everyone deals with grief in a different way but it hurts to only have Amelia to talk about her with. And I can't even do that well because Amelia had only known my mother for a short while before she died. In an attempt to keep her memory alive, I've taken things of hers over the years: clothing, jewellery, photographs, which would explain the drawer. I wish I could talk freely about her to my father, but every time I try, he shuts me down. And every time he shuts me down, my resentment grows.

'It is,' he says, sensing my rising frustration. 'Lost, I mean. I think.'

'Oh, well that's an awful shame.'

'Uh, y-yes. Yes, it is.' He shuffles in his seat, avoiding eye contact.

'And when exactly did you realize it was lost?'

'Um, w-well,' my father stutters, at a loss for excuses. 'You know, about two weeks ago.' He finally looks into

my eyes. 'Around the time you got back from school.'
Now I know he's lying.

When I was eleven, I was messing around in my
father's study while he was with the personal trainer in
the basement. I was opening and closing all the drawers
in his desk when I noticed that one drawer moved
differently to the others, and had a much darker bottom.

I took all the contents out, opening it up fully to reveal
a fake bottom hiding a bunch of documents and a small
velvet box. Opening the box I saw my mother's gold locket.
Days, evenings, workouts, weddings, my mother would
always be wearing that necklace. It unlocked a memory of
her that I had long forgotten. I placed the necklace in my
pocket, carefully returning everything else to how I found
it, and I've kept it ever since.

'Daddy, stop lying. It's been missing for years, so why
do you need it now, huh? Why the sudden interest in
Mother's belongings? Before this you couldn't seem to run
fast enough any time I so much as mentioned her, let alone
asked to see her things.'

'You have it? You have the necklace?' He looks at me
with a weird mixture of panic and relief. Completely
ignoring everything I just said, of course.

'Nope.'

'Daphne, come on. Be reasonable. Just give me the

necklace,' he says, his temper rising.

I can't help but laugh. 'So, let me get this straight. You can't share memories of my mother with me, or even talk about her, but it's fine for you to come into my room and demand I give you something of hers, something that *I don't have*,' I enunciate, 'when you clearly couldn't care less about it for the last six years?'

'You did take her necklace, Daphne. That's obviously how you know so much about it.'

'You're right. I took it.' I shrug. 'But I lost it two years ago.'

'What? You lost it?' His eyes widen in horror as his volume increases.

'Those are indeed the words that came out of my mouth, yes.'

'How?'

'What?'

'How did you lose it? Where did you lose it?' he says, his expression starting to make me nervous.

'Remember when I fell off the new horse at the stables? I was wearing it then and it landed in the mud. I looked but I couldn't find it.' Now that part was true, but what I failed to mention is that I did eventually find it after having a minor breakdown.

'Oh, great,' Daddy mumbles as he gets up and starts

pacing the length of my room.

'Daddy, what is so important about the necklace? Why are you so concerned about it?'

'It's not for you to worry about, Daphne.'

'Well, clearly it is, if it's causing you to stress and pace.' I stand up to try and get him to look at me. 'Daddy, please, just tell me wha—'

'I SAID, DON'T WORRY!' he roars in my face.

I recoil, stumbling back, hitting the back of my legs on the bed.

I'm shocked.

My father rarely loses his temper, least of all with me.

Yes, I did push him but I don't understand why he won't include me in anything. My mother, his work, whatever is causing him stress. I could help him, talk through everything with him, but he just won't let me.

'I think it's time for you to leave,' I whisper, my eyes starting to water.

'Daphne, I—'

'When you're able to have an adult conversation,' I interrupt, walking to the door, 'and respect my boundaries enough to not shout in my face, you can come and talk to me. But for now I'd like you to leave.'

'Daph—'

'Goodnight, Father.' I open the door and close my eyes,

willing the tears not to fall until he's out of the room. I wait until I hear him leave my room and retreat down the stairs. As soon as he's gone, I open my eyes and the tears come, instantly blurring my vision. I go to close the door only to see Milosh Petrov across the hall.

Perfect timing, Mr Petrov. Just impeccable timing.

He's holding a manilla folder and is about to enter his room when he sees me. He stops, momentarily pausing by his door.

Ugh, I can only imagine what he must be thinking right now. He's probably appalled by my tears and lack of decorum. I know I would be if I could see myself. Not meeting his eyes, I shut the door, get into bed and proceed to cry myself to sleep.

6

I gasp awake and check the clock beside me, 2:42 a.m. *Right on time.*

I sit up and grab my sleep log notebook to write down the nightmare. I've had a lot fewer these past years, but every time it's always the same one, over and over again.

I check my surroundings and go through my routine of reassurance.

'You're fine. No one is trying to hurt you. No one's in the basement. You're okay,' I mumble as I climb out of my bed and slide my slippers on.

Over the years, I've developed somewhat of a routine when I get this nightmare – wake up in a delightful pool of sweat, affirm to myself that it was just a bad dream and go to the main kitchen to get a glass of water and some blueberries. Tonight, said sweat was even more delightful than usual, so I decide to change out of my nightdress and into a fresh long-sleeved two-piece set. I rip off my silk headscarf in the process, allowing my hair to cascade down my back and breathe, before it starts reverting back to its curly state.

Feeling miles fresher, I finally make my way downstairs.

I choke out a gasp when I turn to enter the kitchen and see Milosh standing there, pouring milk into a bowl of bran flakes in the dim lighting.

Of course he likes bran flakes, they're the blandest cereal out there.

'Mr Petrov, you frightened me,' I say, clutching my hand to my chest.

'Apologies, Miss Green,' he drawls, his voice deep and cold with indifference. He didn't even so much as flinch when I rounded the corner. He just kept his eyes on the bowl as he continued to pour the milk.

As I walk to the fridge to get out what I need, I give him a once-over. He's still wearing his black cargos and a black short-sleeve T-shirt, but his hair is now slightly tousled and messy, as if he's been continuously running his hands through it.

I wonder what it would feel like to run my hands through it?

Yeah, no. We're not doing that.

Shaking off that thought, I focus on looking for the blueberries.

'What are you doing downstairs so late?' I ask, my

breath catching as he comes up behind me to return the milk to the fridge.

'Couldn't sleep, so I thought now would be a good time to look through the documents Mrs Harris gave me,' he says, his arm brushing mine as he reaches past me to grab an apple. This close, all I can smell is him.

And it's intoxicating.

Whatever fragrance he's wearing is the perfect mix of freshness and pure masculinity, without trying too hard.

'Why couldn't you sleep? Is there something wrong with the bed?'

'No. Just couldn't sleep,' he states as he returns to the pile of documents strewn across the island counter, apple in hand.

'Oh, okay. Well, good.' I close the fridge, grab a bowl and start sorting through the blueberries. 'Does your work normally keep you up at night?' I ask, trying to keep the conversation going.

'Depends,' is his one word answer.

'Depends on what?'

'Whether I'm working military or . . . private.'

'Which one do you prefer?' I ask, moving over to the sink to rinse my fruit.

'Both have pros and cons, but there seem to be a lot more perks with going private.' I turn back to look at him only to find his eyes already on me.

'Oh.' I clear my throat, suddenly feeling a rush of heat throughout my body while the ghost of a smirk graces his lips as he looks back down at the paperwork in front of him.

'Why were you crying?' Milosh asks after a few moments have passed.

'Pardon?'

'Why. Were. You. Crying.'

'Oh, um . . . My father and I had a little disagreement, that's all.' I smile sadly.

'He made you cry?'

'No, the situation made me cry,' I correct, attempting to keep my expression soft. I'd rather not be talking about this right now. Least of all with a guy I only met yesterday.

'Why?'

'Why what?' I ask, trying to keep my tone level, but failing when I hear a hint of exasperation slip through.

'Why did the situation make you cry?'

I stop for a moment, trying to think of the best way to answer that question whilst still painting my father in a positive light. 'Well, sometimes talking about my mother can unearth some pretty unpleasant emotions for my father.'

His eyes drink me in as he processes my answer. I turn my back to him and walk over to the cupboard to get a glass, only to find they've all been put on the highest shelf.

Of course they have.

Trying to make myself tall, I reach up but they're still well out of my reach. All I wanted was to get some blueberries and water and go back to bed, why am I being punished?

'Miss Green, what are you doing?'

I huff. 'I'm trying to get a glass down.'

'Stop it, you're gonna hurt yourself.' His bored tone at complete odds with his concerned words.

I turn around to look at him, his face suddenly vexing me. 'Mr Petrov, if I could magically grow an inch I would, but I can't, therefore I shan't.' I turn back around to face the cupboard and, after trying again, I settle on taking a mug off the bottom shelf instead. That'll just have to do.

As I reach for it I feel a warmth envelop me and that distinct clean, masculine scent invading my nose. My gosh, he smells good.

So good.

I keep my eyes forward as Milosh reaches up with ease, my breath dipping when I feel his chest brushing against my back as he takes out the glass I was reaching for. He sets it down on the counter, but he doesn't move. He lingers with his front still brushing my back as his arms cage me in.

'Don't let anyone speak to you that way again. Yes?' he commands, voice low and authoritative. A set of unwanted goosebumps erupt across my skin when I feel his breath fan out against my neck, my eyelids closing as I revel in his closeness.

'I'm sorry, what are you talking about?' I breathe after a moment, my mind misty.

'I don't care if he's your father, don't let anyone shout at you. Do you understand me?' All I can do is nod in response.

'Good.' He drops his arms and walks away as if nothing ever happened, while I try to collect myself, gather my things and make sense of it all.

'G-goodnight, Mr Petrov,' I say after filling up my glass and heading for the door.

'Mmm,' he hums in response, not looking up from his documents.

As I walk out of the kitchen, towards the stairs, I hear a shuffling sound coming from Daddy's study. *Why is everyone up so late tonight?* I think, stopping short of the door. But as I reach for the handle the door swings open, revealing a tall man dressed head to toe in black.

'Hi, princess,' the man says, a sinister smirk spreading across his face.

'I'm sorry, who are you, and what were you doing in

my father's study?' I ask, looking around for a quick out if need be. I'm sure he's a new member of staff that Amelia hasn't introduced me to yet, but there's something eerily familiar about him, and I just can't shake the gnawing feeling that something isn't quite right.

'I'm the new night guard,' he says, stuffing his leather-gloved hands into his pockets.

There are no new night guards. The only new security is Milosh. So why do I recognize him?

Then it clicks.

The buzz cut. The tall build. The short full beard. The gloved hands.

He's the man from the CCTV footage.

He's the man that broke into my father's office at work.

My heart drops as he cocks his head, letting out a little chuckle.

'You figured me out, huh, princess?' I go to run, but he grabs me by my waist before I can get anywhere. 'We can't have you running off to call Daddy now, can we?' he says, yanking me towards him.

The impact of my body crashing into his causes me to drop the mug and bowl. They smash, scattering berries, glass and ceramic fragments across the now-wet floor.

'Now why'd you have to go and do that?' he sneers, removing one arm from my waist and grabbing me by the neck, locking my head in his tight grip.

'Please,' I wheeze, the word barely audible. He wraps his other gigantic, suffocating arm around the back of my neck, securing the hold as I try to scratch at his eyes.

'You can try all you like, princess, it ain't gonna change a thing,' he hisses.

My vision starts to blur as I open my mouth to scream, but fades away until all I see is black.

7
MILOSH

The first sign that something was wrong was when I couldn't hear Daphne's footsteps on the stairs, but I didn't think too much of it because this is such a large house. But, when I hear what I assume to be her bowl dropping and smashing, I get up to help her clean the mess, only to find her being strangled by a guy twice her size.

White-hot rage runs up my spine as I see Daphne in such a vulnerable position, but I swiftly damp it down. This isn't the time to lose control.

Because of where I'm standing neither of them can see me, giving me an advantage. As she quickly loses consciousness I run through my options.

With the lighting so dim, using my gun wouldn't be safe for Daphne so that's out. From this angle my knife would only wound the guy and probably make him more angry, likely leading him to take that frustration out on her, so that's out too.

I survey the kitchen, quickly considering what else could be used, then it comes to me.

Quietly rushing to the cabinets, I open up the pots-and-pans drawer I saw Josh, their cook, go into earlier, and pull out a large cast-iron skillet. Stalking over to the kitchen entrance, I stop abruptly as I remember the secret door leading from the kitchen straight to George's study from the schematics I was just studying. I look around, trying to locate it, before spotting it at the far end of the kitchen. Walking over, I open the door quietly, and briskly walk through the room to get right behind the man.

'Honestly, choking you would've been pretty hot under different circumstances,' the guy says to the nearly unconscious Daphne. 'But hey, maybe next time, yeah? When you're tied up in my—'

Unfortunately, he doesn't get to finish his perverted sentence because I strike him over the head with the pan. He drops to his knees in the doorway, releasing Daphne in the process.

'If a girl has to be unconscious for you to get her into bed,' I spit, thrashing him with the pan again, 'I think you need to ask yourself if you're the problem.' I deliver a blow to his airway, following it up with a few kicks to his back to make sure he's down before dropping the pan and rushing over to Daphne who is lying among the shards of glass and broken ceramic on the cold, wet floor, unconscious.

I drop down next to her and begin assessing her injuries. Placing two fingers on the side of her neck, I feel a steady pulse. Then I look for any glass shards that may have been caught in her skin, checking to see if any had been wedged anywhere lethal. Confirming none are life threatening I brush them off her, then wrap my hands around her jaw and tilt her head back to feel for breath. 'Daphne? Daphne, wake up.' Feeling my panic rising, I drop one hand to her arm and gently shake her.

'Come on, Daphne,' I whisper, 'wake up for me.'

She starts stirring and her eyes flutter open slowly. 'Milosh?' she whispers.

'Daphne? You okay?'

'Gu—' she groans.

'What?'

'Gun,' she says, catching her breath. 'Milosh, he has a gun.'

I turn around and see that she's right.

The intruder is on the floor, stretching towards a gun that must've fallen out of his pocket and is now in front of him, just out of reach. I pull out my knife from my right pocket and throw it towards his hand. It rips through his flesh and pins him between the floorboard and the door of the study, leaving him screaming, and temporarily immobilized. He's so loud I'm shocked George doesn't immediately come running down the stairs.

'Wow,' Daphne gasps. I turn back to her, only to find her staring in shock at the knifework I suddenly feel pretty good about. 'How did you do that?' she asks, searching my eyes for the answer.

'Training, Miss Green.'

'Agh!' the intruder cries. 'You stabbed me, you prick.'

Ignoring him, I scan Daphne over. She's sitting up now, but still looks a little out of breath. 'Can you stand?' I ask, walking away from her and over to the large inconvenience who's currently staining the floor with his blood.

'Um . . .' She gets up slowly, testing her balance, wobbling for a second but righting herself almost instantly. 'Yeah, I'm good. What do you need me to do?'

'Go and get some cable ties and tape, and I'll secure him.'

'I think there's some in the laundry room downstairs,' she says as she starts walking towards the basement.

'Wait.' I shake my head. 'Don't go down there; I don't know if he came in alone.' She stops abruptly and walks slowly back to me. I drop to my haunches and unbuckle my belt, yanking it swiftly out of the loops. This'll have to do for now.

'Go and have a look in your father's study to see if there's anything else I can use to tie him up.' I instruct her, keeping

66

the guy still as she walks past him. I know no ones in the study and from here I can still see her.

With my boot-clad foot holding down his free hand, I lean over and fasten my belt around his feet, tying a little tighter than necessary. I look back into the study to check on Daphne who's filing through her father's desk drawers. In my peripheries I see the intruder straining to look into the study, smiling when he see's Daphne.

'I bet she'd look real good freshly fu—'

Before he can say another word I bring his free arm up towards me and twist it the wrong way, breaking his wrist with a loud crack.

He screams out in pain. 'You bastar—'

'Shut your mouth,' I spit, 'or I'll break each finger individually.' I lean closer into him. 'And that's not a threat. It's a promise.' And just like magic, guess who stops talking?

I keep grasping his broken wrist with one hand, adding just a little bit of pressure to discourage the guy from doing anything stupid, and search his pants and jacket pockets, finding a burner phone and a wallet. I put the phone on the floor and open up his wallet. 'Stefan Mikelson, age thirty-four.'

'Good for you, you know my name,' he remarks.

The man has the sass of a Chihuahua.

'I thought I told you to shut your mouth,' I respond,

snapping his thumb back, offering a right hook to his jaw. Leaning over, I pick up his discarded gun, take the blunt edge of the handle and smash it into his temple, knocking him out before he has a chance to make any more irritating quips. With his head turned, in a very uncomfortable position, I see a faint tattoo on his lower neck. Moving his sweater down, the full tattoo comes into view. It's a skull, with the eyes in the shape of letter *D*s, and a chess knight set atop it.

The Daveeno tattoo.

'Is this okay?' Daphne comes up beside me, slightly breathless, before offering me the duct tape.

'Yeah, this can work.' Dropping the gun I take the tape from her, ripping off a piece and covering his mouth.

'Is his hand supposed to bend that way?' she asks, her delicately arched eyebrows drawing together in concern as she chews on her plump bottom lip.

'Nope.'

'Huh,' she murmurs, looking up at me. 'Maybe you really are as good as they say, Mr Petrov.'

'Just doing my job, Miss Green.'

She searches my eyes with such intensity that I feel my blood start to heat. My gaze falls to her mouth as it parts, as if she's about to say something, before we're interrupted by the sound of the front door opening.

'Do you think that's one of his friends?' Daphne whispers,

looking nervously over to the unconscious nuisance in front of us.

'I don't know. Stay here.' I grab Stefan's gun from the floor in front of me and quickly cock it, moving slowly towards the door, pausing when I hear talking and . . . moaning?

'Shh, you don't want to wake everyone.'

Is that . . .?

'Everyone's asleep, gorgeous, it's just you and me.'

Yup.

I turn the corner, only to be met with the sight of Henry pushing Amelia against the front door as they make out. I put the safety of the gun back on and clear my throat just as Henry starts kissing his way down Amelia's neck. Her eyes open slightly at the sound of me, and the haze quickly leaves them as she comes to her senses and swiftly pushes Henry off her.

'Milosh, oh my goodness!' Amelia breathes, pulling her dress down briskly. 'What are you doing up so late?' Upon hearing Amelia's voice, Daphne turns the corner, and at the sight of her bruises and the bloodstains on her pyjamas, the Harrises quickly jump into parental mode.

'What happened?' Henry demands, any trace of desire or humour gone. I simply pocket the gun and lead them towards Mr Inconvenience so they can see for themselves.

'I'll call the police,' Amelia declares, taking in the scene.

'No.'

'What?' Both she and Daphne look at me as if I've told them I decided to take up knitting as a career.

'No police,' I instruct again. 'This guy –' I give him a little kick, just because I can – 'clearly wanted something here that he couldn't find at George's work. Me and Henry will search the house to make sure he didn't come with a friend. Then we'll wake George, question *him* and go from there. But for now, no police.'

8

MILOSH

'You all right?' I ask, walking into the snug where Amelia told me I would find Daphne. She's sitting on the floor in front of the fireplace, covered in a white fluffy blanket, clutching a hot chocolate.

'Miss Green?' I prompt when she doesn't respond.

'Huh? Oh yeah, sorry.' It comes out rushed. 'I'm okay, thank you.' She looks up at me with a weak smile.

I go to sit beside her and we both stay quiet for a moment, watching the flames dance in front of us.

'I just don't get it,' she says softly after a beat, wrapping herself a little tighter. 'Why was he here? How did he even get in? Why did he have to hurt me?' A single tear rolls down her face and it's the most heart-achingly beautiful image I've ever seen. She even cries with poise.

Cupping her cheek, I turn her face to look at me and wipe the tear away with my thumb. 'Don't cry over him. Once he's conscious again we'll get the answers we need. Okay?'

'Yeah, okay.' She nods.

'Good.' I wipe away the last of her tears and draw back my hand, turning to face the fire again, needing some distance from her.

People cry all the time, so why am I so affected by her tears?

'That knife thing you did was pretty cool,' Daphne says, a small smile creeping across her face.

'Oh yeah?'

'Mm hmm.' She nods, biting her lip.

'Want me to teach it to you?' *What the hell am I saying?*

'What?'

'I can teach you, if you'd like.'

'You'd teach me how to throw knives?' She looks at me, her big brown eyes filled with scepticism.

'That, and maybe how to protect yourself . . . If that's something you'd want?' *What am I doing?*

She contemplates for a moment. 'I never want to be in that situation again, but if I am, I want to be able to protect myself.'

'All right, good.'

'You'll really train me?' She looks at me like I've just hung the moon, and boy, if it doesn't make me want to do everything in my power to protect her, task force be damned.

'Yeah.'

'Milosh?' Henry calls, as he opens the door.

'Uh-huh?'

'Stefan's awake,' he says, voice cold. He looks over to Daphne, concern and guilt enveloping his face. 'Daph, how you doing, sweetie?' I can tell he feels guilty and somewhat responsible because he wasn't there to stop all of this, but Daphne's been trying to reassure him it was fine. She's told both him and Amelia at least twice already that they don't live to serve her and they deserve a date night once in a while. It just so happened that their date night coincided with tonight's attack.

'I'm fine, Henry, thank you for checking up on me.' She smiles sincerely.

'Okay,' he responds, clearly not convinced. 'Call me if you need anything, I'm gonna get Meelie to keep you company.' He closes the door behind him, leaving me and Daphne alone again.

'Tomorrow,' I tell Daphne as I get up and head for the door. 'We'll start tomorrow.'

'Milosh?' she whispers. I stop short of the door and turn around when I hear my name, hating how good it sounds when it rolls off her tongue.

'Yeah?'

'Thank you.'

I nod and close the door behind me quickly.

Trying to shake off whatever happened in there, I focus on the task at hand as I walk back towards the study. My phone rings so I pull it out to check the caller ID.

Major Andy Davis.

'Sir?'

'Petrov, we did a search for Stefan Mikelson and can confirm his movements line up with Daveeno,' Davis's Tennessee drawl fills my ear.

'Who is he, sir?'

'Stefan Mikelson. Age thirty-four. In and out of prison over the last fifteen years for petty theft, breaking and entering, drunk and disorderly conduct, arson, robbery – the list really does go on,' Davis recites. 'We believe he was recruited into Daveeno five years ago, after he finished his third stint in prison. I've sent someone from Interpol and the NCA to come and collect him so we can do a thorough questioning.'

'All right. He didn't have many personal belongings with him but he did have a burner phone. I did a general check and couldn't find any immediate red flags, but I'll give it to the team so someone in tech can take a look.'

After ensuring Stefan Mikelson was secured in the study, me and Henry swept the house. When we confirmed it was clear, Amelia took Daphne away to get checked over by

Josh – who, yes, is the Greens' cook, but also used to be a doctor – Henry went to wake up George and I called Davis. I gave him the report of what happened and sent him the security footage of Stefan entering the house. It was during the night guards' shift change so he entered undetected, picking the lock of the front door effortlessly. He entered just before I came downstairs so that explained why I didn't hear him entering.

I explained the Daveeno tattoo I recognized to Davis, and that I believe this is the same man that broke into George's work office. Davis agreed that I might be right so went to get more information on Stefan and organize discreet transport telling me he'd call back once he had more.

'Understood,' Davis replies. 'While the team is on their way I want you to press for any information you can get. But not just from Mikelson, from George as well. We need to know what they want from him. Is it all a coincidence or is he hiding something too?'

'Got it.'

'Okay, call me with any updates. Oh, and Petrov?' He pauses. 'How's the girl?'

My jaw clenches at the memory of Daphne lying unconscious on the floor. 'She's fine. The Greens have a cook who used to be a doctor so he checked her over and all her cuts and bruises should heal quickly. I'm gonna start teaching her self-defence too, so she doesn't feel so helpless if this situation arises again.'

'Good idea. If you need any training equipment let me know and I'll get that arranged. The team are also bringing an updated security system for the Green estate so there'll be more surveillance and evidence. See if you can talk to the head of security about hiring more help. I can't spare any more men right now but I'm sure they have reliable contacts for this.'

'Copy. How quick can you get equipment here?'

'I can have it to you end of day today.'

'Great. I'll send you a list.'

'All right, talk soon. Good job tonight.'

'Thank you, sir.'

I hang up and walk the rest of the distance to the study where George, Henry and Amelia are standing outside.

'Major Davis is gonna have someone from Interpol and the NCA come and detain him,' I explain once I reach them. 'It's confirmed he works for Daveeno but we don't know what he's after.'

Henry's nostrils flare and George shifts from one foot to the other.

'The team should be here soon so we only have a short time to ask him any questions. After he's gone I may get a few updates but overall it's easier to just try to get the information we want out of him now.'

'Well, then, I'll leave you to it,' Amelia says, giving Henry's hand a gentle squeeze before walking off. 'Oh, and Milosh.' She stops abruptly, looking back at me, water pooling in her eyes. 'Well done for tonight. I dread to think what would've happened if you hadn't been down here.'

'Just doing my job, Mrs Harris.'

'No, she's right, Milosh,' Henry adds. 'You really stepped up, and you've only been here a day.'

'I just can't believe this happened to Daphne, of all people,' George says, guilt coating his voice. 'She doesn't deserve it.' He looks down when tears start welling in his eyes. 'She doesn't deserve any of it.'

'Sir, you need to focus,' I cut in. We really don't have contemplation time right now. 'She's safe and that's all that matters. Before we go in I need to ask, do you know what these guys are after? They've targeted you three times now, taking it to the extreme of breaking into your house and hurting your daughter. They're clearly after something.'

'What was in that journal they took from your office at work?' Henry enquires, crossing his arms and leaning against the wall.

'I honestly don't know,' George replies. 'It was an old work journal I had lying around in my office. I think there were some formulas for antidote serums I used to work on with MI6 in there. But I don't understand what else they would want. If the antidote formulas are what they were after, they got them.'

'Hmm,' Henry hums in agreement. 'I suggest we go ask Mr Mikelson.' He turns to look at me. 'How did you wanna play this?'

'I'm happy to observe while you take the lead.' I direct my words to Henry. 'Me and George will take a back seat so he doesn't get strung up on power dynamics. If need be I'll step in, but I think you'll do fine. Use whatever methods you want.'

When I see the glint in his eye I specify, 'Within reason.'

The background check I ran on Henry Harris showed that he was ex-army. I'm not entirely clued up on British Army methods, but from what I understand he should've been given basic interrogation training.

'All right, that sounds like a plan.' George nods.

'Great. Let's see what Mr Mikelson has to say for himself.'

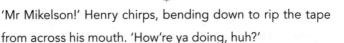

'Mr Mikelson!' Henry chirps, bending down to rip the tape from across his mouth. 'How're ya doing, huh?'

Stefan just glares at him, spitting some leftover blood onto the floor. Henry tracks the movement, a sly grin emerging on his face. 'Feeling better now?'

'Go to hell.'

'Nah, I'm all right,' Henry replies, before drawing a long

sigh and straightening back up. 'I have a few questions for you, Stefan. Now, if you give me the answers I need we won't have a problem, but if you don't I'll start by breaking your other wrist, then your shoulder, then your knees. And I'll continue until there are no unbroken bones left in your body.'

Stefan is sitting in a sad old wooden chair, hands bound behind his back with cable ties. I can tell that they're cutting into his skin and agitating the wrist I cracked earlier. George and I are standing near the door, leaning against the wall, watching the scene unfold.

When I first walked back into the study and got another look at this guy, my blood burned with fury. But my anger simmered down once I saw much pain he was in.

There really is nothing better than making a grown man cry.

'Now, Stefan,' Henry continues. 'Out of all the stupid things you've done in your lifetime, attempting to strangle that girl was by far the stupidest.'

'How is the little princess doing?' Stefan retorts, closing his eyes. 'I see why you're all so protective of her. Those muffled screams and that soft skin.' He lets out the most disturbing noise and George pushes off the wall, going to move in on him. It takes all my strength and discipline not to join him, but instead I reach out and grip George's wrist, shaking my head. *Don't give him what he wants.* 'I'd do it all over again if I could, but I'd really savour it this time. Maybe I'd get her down on her knees and—' He doesn't get to finish that sentence because Henry backhands him across the face so hard one of his teeth fly out.

Well, that was awfully satisfying.

'Imma stop you right there, Mr Mikelson.' I can feel Henry's rage permeate the air. With every word he says, his cockney accent becomes clearer and stronger. 'See, you've just crossed a line into the no-limits zone. You crossed it earlier, too, and you've got all your injuries to show for it. You talk about that girl again and I *will* kill you. It'll be slow, and painful, and I'll really enjoy watching the life drain out of your eyes. So, let's get back to the topic at hand, yeah?'

I look back over to Stefan to see his face pale and sickly, any trace of amusement long gone.

'I'm going to ask you this one time, and one time only. Why are you here?'

Stefan looks between me, George and Henry, clearly weighing up his options. I put myself in his shoes for a second, wondering what he must be thinking. There are now three tall, bulky men staring down at him, and somehow he's managed to piss each and every one of us off. We'll get the information out of him one way or another. Whether Interpol takes him out in a body bag or not is really up to him.

'Read the note in my wallet,' is all he says.

Henry looks over to me and George, and I leave to get Stefan's belongings. I check his wallet, my eyes settling on a crumpled receipt stashed at the bottom. I snatch it out and head back into the study, opening the note on my way.

Just give us what we want and this will all go away.
D.

The D must be for Daveeno, but what do they want? They already have the journal with all the antidote formulas. What else do they need? What else is George not telling me?

I slam the door on the way back into the study, shoving the note into George's hand as I pass him to reach Stefan.

Reaching behind him, I take his broken wrist in my hand and contort it, pressing down on the bone with my thumb.

He yelps in pain as I calmly drop to my haunches. 'What does Daveeno want with George?'

'I don't know what Daveeno is,' he cries.

'You have their insignia on your neck. Maybe be a little more discreet with your tattoos next time.'

I let go of his wrist, stand back up, then deliver a swift blow to his stomach before leaning down with a hand on each arm of the chair.

'Now. I'm going to ask again. What does Daveeno want with George?'

He coughs and splutters for a moment, so I step back and wait for him to gather himself. After a minute, he swallows then looks directly at George.

'You have something they want.' He shrugs. 'And they'll stop at nothing to get it. Including hurting your daughter. They've taken your wife away from you so they have no problem dealing with the girl as well.'

'What do they want?' George seethes.

Stefan doesn't answer. He just smiles. 'Wouldn't you like to know.'

George storms past me and punches Stefan in the jaw. 'What. Do. They. Want.'

Stefan smiles, his mouth full of blood. 'I'll let you find that out by yourself.'

Henry's radio buzzes and one of the security men calls in. 'Sir, I believe Interpol and the NCA have arrived.'

Stefan laughs. 'Looks like you're out of time, boys.'

'Mr Mikelson, I assure you, this was a walk in the park compared to where you're going. I suggest you wipe that smile off your face because by tomorrow you'll be wishing we'd killed you.'

9

'Mr Petrov, in the nicest way possible, get out.'

'No.'

I hear him walk across my room and pull open the heavy curtains, causing soft beams of light to seep in through my eye mask.

In the last forty-five minutes I've been greeted by the dreadful noise of an alarm I don't possess, waking me up at 4:30 a.m. in the morning. Said alarm then proceeded to go off every five minutes until I unplugged it. Then, Amelia came in and tried to wake me up. And now I have a grumpy bodyguard invading my personal space.

'Up.' Milosh says as he pulls my eye mask from my face.

'Please explain to me why I need to get up at –' I look over to my personal clock that's set for the reasonable time of 6:30 a.m. – 'five-fifteen in the morning?'

'You said you wanted to learn self-defence.'

'I do, but not at five-fifteen in the morning.'

'Now or never, Miss Green,' he starts, heading towards the door. 'Be outside in sixteen minutes,' he finishes, before promptly walking out of my room.

'All right, Troy Bolton, calm down,' I mumble, dragging myself out of bed to throw on some clothes.

'What are you wearing?' Milosh asks, looking vaguely disgusted as I walk out of the back door onto the patio, the crisp summer morning air greeting me instantly.

'All my other coats are at the dry cleaner,' I reply, looking down at myself. I fully understand his reaction. It's abnormally cold today so on top of my light-pink leggings with a matching short-sleeve top, I'm wearing a long brown fur coat. Meanwhile, Milosh is wearing black joggers, a black hoodie and a black puffer coat.

'How exactly do you suppose you're going to train wearing that?' Milosh asks, and to be honest that is a very fair question. I really hadn't thought that far ahead when I pulled this on. I just knew I was cold and this was all I could find quickly.

'You know what, Mr Petrov? I really don't know,' I sigh, looking at him. 'Do *you* have any suggestions?'

He stares at me blankly for a moment before proceeding

to shed his puffer coat, throwing it onto the chair with deft precision, then pulling off his hoodie in one swift motion. It may have been swift, but time stood still when his T-shirt lifted ever so slightly and I caught sight of a sliver of abs.

'Take off the coat, and put this on,' he says, holding his hoodie out to me. His bewitching green irises track my every move as I slip off the coat and follow his instructions. The hoodie completely drowns me, engulfing me with that strong, clean, masculine scent of his. It's huge, but offers a lot more mobility compared to my coat.

He nods his approval before turning around to grab something off the patio table. 'I'm gonna teach you the basics of self-defence. We'll study boxing, weapons training and Muay Thai to establish a base, then we'll build from there. Until this . . . situation with your father is sorted out we'll meet every morning and train together for a couple of hours.'

'Okay,' I breathe in a daze, slightly taken aback. It's almost overwhelming how authoritative he is, and not just with his words but with his presence and character. He exudes control and assertion, standing tall and strong, with eye contact so acute it could burn my retinas.

He takes a new skipping rope from its packaging, handing it to me briskly before sitting down on the chair and shrugging his coat back on. 'Let's start with a warm-up.'

'Mr Petrov, what you're not going to do is sit on that chair and watch me *skip* for the next ten minutes. If I'm warming up, then so are you,' I say, matter-of-factly, as I neatly fold up the rope and place it gently onto the table. 'Now, seeing as there's only one skipping rope I suggest we go on a light jog to warm ourselves up.' I give him a polite, mildly satisfied smile as he gets up, but it dims gradually with every step he takes towards me.

Smirking, he licks his lips, stopping with his face only inches from mine. 'Miss Green,' he drawls, his voice low, 'thank you for your concern, but in the hour it took you to come downstairs, I already warmed up.'

'If you're expecting a cookie, Mr Petrov, you're not going to get one.'

'Maybe not.' He shrugs, slipping his hands into his pockets. 'But what I will get is the sight of you jumping that rope while I. Sit. And. Watch.'

I smile lightly, ignoring how rough and unfortunately sexy that sentence just sounded coming out of his mouth. 'No.'

'Miss Green, usually when I say something is going to happen, it does,' he says softly, those emerald eyes piercing my soul.

'Well, that's lovely, Mr Petrov. However, this is not

going to be one of those times.' I meet his eyes, my gaze dipping for a moment, catching a barely-there smile that's gone so fast I half believe I imagined it. 'I very frequently get my way, Mr Petrov, so please stop trying to force otherwise,' I whisper, taking a step towards him. We're so close now that our breathing is synced.

He offers a low chuckle and my eyes involuntarily close, revelling in it. 'Fine, Miss Green. No rope. But I won't be joining you on your run.' He walks away, creating some much-needed distance and goes to sit back on that vexing chair. He pulls out his phone and starts typing something, paying me absolutely no mind. I guess that's the conversation over then.

Well, I can just feel the time flying by.

10

Daphne

'Punch me.'

I falter. 'Pardon?'

'Punch me, hit me, kick me,' Milosh responds. 'Act as if I'm the guy from last night.'

We're standing on two of my old gymnastics mats that have been put down to cover the hard stone floor of the patio.

After my delightful warm-up, I've shed his hoodie, hot for more reasons than one, and am now wearing pink boxing gloves.

Pink.

Pink boxing gloves that I didn't own before today.

Which means Milosh ordered me boxing gloves and purposefully bought the pink ones.

How . . . nice . . . of him.

Milosh raises his hand, holding it out for me to hit the

boxing pad attached to it. I swing, my fist clenched inside the glove and my stance wide. I try it a couple more times before Milosh starts calling out different combos for me to try. After a while he begins to include kicks as well as punches. 'All right, good. Now we've established you can throw a punch towards my hands, I'm gonna teach you the basics of self-defence. From what I've seen so far, your arms are pretty weak and your form is off, but you're fast and your legs are strong. Speed and agility are gonna be your best friends if you're trying to take down someone bigger than yourself.'

He walks over to the shed and pulls out a free-standing boxing bag I was completely unaware we had, placing it down on the mat with ease. 'Take off your gloves, we're gonna try freehand now.' He goes to grab a wicker chair, pulling it up alongside where I'm standing in front of the boxing bag, then takes a seat. 'Punch it whatever way feels natural,' he instructs. I punch again, but without the gloves on, my wrists sting upon connection with the bag.

'Your lower body needs to move with the swing.' He gets up off the chair and stalks towards me. 'Right now you're only moving your arms, but once you let the power of the punch, hit or slap come from your legs and hip rotation you'll get a much better result.' He comes over to the boxing bag and demonstrates slowly a couple of times. He starts talking me through his motions, but the sound of his voice gradually starts to fade away, getting more distant every time his arm extends and his bicep ripples. His hand clenches into a tight fist, the veins in his forearms bulging, becoming more prominent every time his knuckles meet the bag.

'All right, now you try.' He steps back to observe, while I try to recall the steps he just showed me. I widen my stance and punch back into the bag, not moving it nearly as far as he did when he wasn't even trying.

'Make a fist for me.' He comes up next to me, so close I could run my hands through his hair if I wanted to. 'Let me see your nails.' I re-extend my fingers to reveal my medium-length, light-pink nails. 'Create a fist again for me.' Milosh then takes my hand, analyzing it as if it's a completely alien concept to have pretty, well-manicured nails. 'Your nails are a bit too long to have in a complete fist, that's why you're not punching properly. Hold them like this instead and try again. Also remember, not too wide on your stance. Your legs should be shoulder width apart.'

I take my hand and replicate his fist, leaving my fingers a little straighter and placing my thumb on top of my pointer finger, and punch again.

'Better,' he nods. Something warm flutters inside me in response to his praise but I quickly damp it down. 'This time, remember to rotate your hips to give you more power.' I try again, feeling the improvement myself this time.

'That was good, but your hips are still too straight on. Twist them a little,' he says, taking the stance and demonstrating the twist. I try to copy him again, but this time my lack of co-ordination on this particular task gets in the way.

'I don't get it. If I'm right-handed, which foot is in front? And do my hips face the same way as my shoulders?' I say, distractedly switching the position of my feet. I inhale sharply when I feel his warm hands come down onto my hips as he moves them to face the right way. He's behind me so I can't see him, but I sure can feel him.

'Left leg comes out,' he instructs. Distracted, I put the wrong leg in front, meaning Milosh then has to place the right one into the correct place, moving it in front of me. I lean into him, trying to regain my balance, feeling his firm front against my back. 'Better,' is all he says, righting me before he stalks off back to his chair, as if the heat of his hands and body hadn't just seared invisible scars into mine.

'Mr Petrov, we have been out here for three hours. I'm hot, I'm hungry and I want a shower. What more could you possibly have to show me?' Before I get to finish my sentence the man pulls out a gun that has apparently just casually been sitting in his back pocket this whole time.

'Mr Petrov,' I breathe as calmly as possible, plastering on a polite smile, 'why is there a gun in your pocket?'

'There's not a gun in my pocket,' he counters. 'There's a gun in my hand.'

'And what exactly are you planning to do with this gun?'

'Hand it to you.'

'And what do you expect me to do with it?'

'Shoot it,' is his oh-so-simple answer.

'Absolutely not,' I reply. 'I'm not a big fan of firearms.'

I know I said I wanted self-defence training but right now I'd give up my Rose Sakura Birkin 25 just for a chance to go and eat some breakfast.

'Wait here,' Milosh commands as he stalks off towards the house. He returns three minutes later holding the shotgun I use for my clay shooting competitions. 'You mean to tell me you're okay using this,' he asks, holding it out, 'but not *my* gun?' He looks down at the shotgun in his hands. 'This is double the size, Daphne.'

He's only said my first name a handful of times, but

every time my name leaves his mouth I have a visceral reaction. His deep voice, with his American accent and its distinctive Slavic tinge, just sounds so good. Don't get me wrong, the whole 'Miss Green' thing is nice, sexy even, but when he says my actual name? It's the sweetest sound I've ever heard.

'I'm okay with shooting at clay disks. That,' I point to his gun, now lying on the table, 'is used to kill people. Whereas that,' I point to my gun, still in his hands, 'is used in competitions. How did you know I shoot, anyway?'

'Miss Green, this house is filled with pictures of you and your hobbies. They're everywhere. It would be very hard to miss the dozen or so pictures that line the shelves in your father's study. Let alone the ones that hang on practically every wall in this house.'

He places the gun into my hand and jogs off to the end of the garden, where he lines up different targets. Catching his drift I go over to the outdoor storage cupboard, take out some shotgun shells and load the barrel. 'Okay, let's make a deal,' I say, once he's back on the patio. 'I hit all the targets and we're done for the day. For each one I miss, that's another ten minutes you've got me outside.'

'No.'

'What do you mean, no?'

He plucks the shooting gun from my hands. 'I know

you can shoot with this or you wouldn't have all those trophies. What I don't know is if you can transfer those skills to a different gun. You're not always going to have a weapon that's tailored to you. That's why it's important to train with multiple weapons so it's easier for you to transfer your skills if need be.'

'And when exactly do you suppose I'm going to need to use a gun, Mr Petrov?'

'The man who broke into your house had a gun. If you'd been able to disarm him, and turn the gun back on him, then it would've given you the upper hand. I don't know how deep this all goes, or what your father's got himself into. Unlike the majority of my other assignments, I honestly don't know what you're up against, so you need to be prepared for anything.'

What my father's got himself into? What does he mean by that?

Before I can question him, he raises my shotgun, which is way too short for him, and fires at the empty cans he's set up in the distance. He hits every target effortlessly, reloading with ease, as if this is something he's done since he was a child.

'The only reason I was able to do that is because I trained in a myriad of different environments, using a variety of weapons. The best and the worst. So my skills are not dependent on my equipment.' He turns to look at me, placing the gun down. 'Now, if you're able to hit every one of those cans with my gun, we'll stop for the day. If you can't, then we'll keep on going.'

'Fine.' He hands me his gun and it's a lot heavier than I expected. I run my fingers across the length of it, memorizing its grooves and texture, appreciating how innately *him* it is. It's matt black, with sharp edges and a strong centre. The weight is evenly distributed as I pass it from one hand to the other.

I wonder what this gun has seen − or rather, who has seen the barrel of this gun.

Holding it up with both hands, preparing to shoot, I call back the image of Milosh cocking it yesterday. I copy his movements until I hear a satisfying click and aim it at the new target Milosh has prepared. Focusing, I let my breath ground me as I do with clay shooting, my sight locked solely onto the target. I usually aim towards moving objects, so I struggle to fix my eyes on the right spot when I fire off the first shot. I nick the side of the target, slightly off centre. 'That still counts,' I say, turning to Milosh with a satisfied grin. He simply nods and looks back over to the next target.

Now that I've got an understanding of the reverb the gun gives off I hold my body slightly differently, moving my arm down and squaring my shoulders. I fire off the next round, hitting the can target dead on this time. Without pausing, I turn to shoot the next three, not even stopping to watch them as they fall, until there's only one left.

'Mr Petrov, one thing you'll come to learn about me is that I excel at everything I put my mind to,' I say, just as I shoot off the last bullet, hitting the can dead in the centre. I turn around to look at him, pulling back on the safety and placing it in his hands.

'I don't doubt that you excel at most things,' he says as he starts to re-cock his gun. 'But you missed two.' We both turn to look at the targets, and he's right. I went too fast and missed, blowing the targets down as the bullet passed by.

'What you've done is impressive,' he admits, holding one arm out and shooting straight into the un-shot sideways can. 'There's a lot of men I know who can't shoot like you, even after years of practice.' He looks into my eyes as he shoots off the next bullet; another clean shot. 'You did good, Miss Green, but not good enough. Now, let's start with how to reload.'

11

'So how's it going with Milosh?' Daddy asks, before stuffing a forkful of venison into his mouth. I always find it funny how the man who wanted to send me to finishing school has the manners of a graceless fish.

'Fine,' I answer bluntly. Even though it's been two weeks since our disagreement, this is the first time we've been properly alone. I haven't really seen much of my father, as for the past few days he's been locked up in his study, even eating in there, and I've been going to bed earlier in preparation for my morning training sessions with Milosh.

When I bumped into him on my way downstairs yesterday he was quiet and evasive when I tried to make peace with him and start a conversation. I've always been raised to be polite and kind, and I do like those characteristics about myself, but I like mutual respect more. I don't take kindly to being shouted at and then ignored for a week. If it weren't for Amelia practically forcing me in here tonight with the promise that she and Henry would join us, I would've eaten elsewhere.

'Daphne, how long are you going to keep this up, huh?' my father asks, dropping his cutlery and turning to fully look at me. 'What do you want me to say? You want me to say sorry?'

'Sorry would be a start,' I quip before popping a slice of carrot into my mouth and turning to look at him. 'I don't want you to say sorry just for the sake of it, I want you to mean it.' He rolls his eyes and scoffs in response just as Amelia and Henry walk through the door.

'Good evening, Green family, how are we doing today?' Henry enquires cheerily, pulling out a chair for Amelia then taking the seat next to her. I go back to eating my food, and I guess my father does too because Henry doesn't get an answer to his question.

'I asked Milosh to join us too tonight,' Amelia says warmly, trying to break the tension. 'I thought it might be nice for all of us to eat together.'

'That was very thoughtful, Meelie, thank you.' I offer a small smile and go back to focusing on my food. The quicker I eat, the quicker this meal can be over.

'Great choice for dinner today, gorgeous,' Henry says,

focusing solely on Amelia.

'Thank you, Hen,' she replies, blushing profusely when his hand disappears under the table.

'You want me to say I'm sorry and mean it?' Daddy says, pretty randomly. Amelia, Henry and I all turn to look at him when he starts laughing. 'You want me to apologize for your wrongdoing?'

'Daddy, what are you talking about?'

'The necklace, Daphne. The necklace.' He takes a swig of scotch and looks at me blankly. 'You took – no, stole – the necklace and then you went and lost it. It didn't belong to you but you didn't care, you took it anyway.'

'I was eleven and missing my mother,' I say, then take a deep breath. There's no need to get worked up over this. My father's clearly just stressed and is acting like a petulant child.

Does this happen often? No. But when it does you've just got to ride it out and wait till he comes to his senses. The alcohol definitely isn't helping matters, though.

'No, you were a stupid brat who couldn't keep her hands to herself.'

'Woah, George, that's not necessary,' Henry chimes in, his face serious. 'It was an honest mistake Daph made when she was a kid. How about you apologize and we can all move on and enjoy dinner?'

'Mr Harris, if I need your help, I'll ask for it,' Daddy responds. 'And did I ask for your help? No. So don't give it.' He takes another swig of his drink and goes back to eating, just as Milosh walks in. He takes the empty seat next to me as Josh brings round his plate.

'What's wrong?' Milosh asks quietly, looking at me.

'Nothing,' I whisper, offering him a tight smile. He nods and picks up his fork, stabbing a carrot and bringing it to his mouth.

'Listen, Daph, I'll apologize for getting in your face. That was uncalled for,' my father says after a beat. 'But I'm not going to apologize for shouting at you.' At that, Milosh halts his fork mid-air before placing it down to hear what wonderful insult my father has for me next. 'Frankly, you deserved it for stealing. Do you know how much more difficult you've made my life by losing that necklace?'

'No, I don't, because you never tell me anything,' I say softly, once again trying to collect myself as I place my cutlery together, finished with my dinner and this conversation. 'You hardly talk about Mother at all, and when you do it's only if you need something. You never let me in and always push me away instead, as if that's going to help matters. I'm sorry that I caused so much turmoil for you, Daddy, I really am, but none of that makes any of this okay.'

'Oh, shut up with the sob story, Daph,' he scoffs, rolling his eyes once again. 'I'll shout at you if I damn well want to, because this is my house.' I feel Milosh shift next to me before pushing out his chair and walking over to my father.

'Get up,' he says curtly.

'Mr Petrov, I advise you to sit back down,' my father says, reaching for his scotch glass.

'I'm only gonna say this once more, Mr Green.' Milosh moves the scotch out of my father's reach and stares down at him as if he's a parent and my father his irritable child. 'Get. Up.'

'Or what?' Daddy sneers.

'George, maybe you should lie down for a bit and sleep off some of the alcohol,' Amelia suggests, trying to diffuse the situation.

'Oh, shut up, Amelia,' snarls Daddy. 'This really isn't the time for your stupid peacekeeping antics.'

'Okay,' Henry huffs, standing up. If there's one thing I've learned about Henry over the years it's that you can make fun of him all you like, but as soon as you say anything less than positive about his wife, you and he are going to have a problem. And Henry is not the kind of guy you want to rile up.

'Hard way it is,' Milosh says, grabbing Daddy's arm

and hauling him up with ease. 'I suggest you treat your daughter with a little more respect, Mr Green.'

'Let go of me, Mr Petrov. I'm warning you,' my father slurs, his stern tone spoiled by his obvious inebriation. Clearly Milosh doesn't care for threats, as in response to this he shoves my father up against the wall, trapping him there with his forearm. Amelia and I both gasp with horror as the room disperses into complete silence and tension.

'You can threaten me all you want, George, it ain't gonna change a thing. Don't. Disrespect. Your. Daughter. It's really that simple.' Milosh shrugs. 'Now, Henry is going to take you upstairs, you're gonna sleep this off and tomorrow you're gonna come downstairs and apologize to Daphne and Amelia for your behaviour. Understood?'

Henry walks over to them and starts guiding my father upstairs, leaving me and Amelia to stare at Milosh in disbelief. I don't think my father has ever been spoken to like that, let alone by someone he employs.

Did I enjoy seeing my father threatened? No, of course not.

However, did something warm settle in my stomach knowing someone was threatening him for my sake? To defend me? Yes.

Without question.

'How often do things like this happen?' Milosh asks as he returns to sit next to me, picking his fork back up as if it's just a regular Thursday.

'Not often, just when he's really stressed or upset,' Amelia answers. 'He's not a big drinker, and he does know how he gets when he drinks, but I think he's just concerned that's all. I'm sure he'll be ready to apologize tomorrow.' Amelia gives me a sympathetic look before turning her attention back to her dinner.

I look over at Milosh to find him gripping his fork awfully tight. 'What you did was a little . . . unhinged,' I start, shifting slightly so I can see more of him. 'But, thank you. I appreciate it.'

He looks at me, really looks at me, almost as if he's seeing me for the first time, taking in my statement. 'My job is to protect you, Miss Green,' he responds. 'That includes protecting you from a potentially volatile situation. No matter who or what is the cause.'

12

MILOSH

'Miss Green?' I say after a few unanswered knocks. It's 5:30 a.m. and after just over two weeks of daily training, starting promptly at 5:15 a.m., I'm surprised she isn't up yet. That girl is a stickler for punctuality if I've ever seen one.

'No.' The word sounds faintly through the door.

'Miss Green?' I say again, knocking a little louder this time.

'Stop, please stop,' she says, sounding distressed.

'Daphne?' I get the spare key to her room out of my pocket.

'Get off!' That's all I need to hear for me to wrench the door open, my heart racing a mile a minute. I haven't even been here a month and this girl has already caused me a near-heart attack one too many times.

So much for a simple, easy case.

I do a quick survey of the bedroom and its connecting rooms, but can't see an intruder or any signs of forced entry.

I stalk over to her and see that she's having a bad nightmare. Her sheets are strewn about her bed and her eye mask and headscarf have been ripped off.

'No, no, no, stop,' Daphne begs, a tear rolling down her face, still completely fast asleep. Even though it's just a dream and no one is actually hurting her, it doesn't stop the pang in my heart or the ache in my lungs at the thought of her in pain, whether real or not.

What the hell is happening to me?

'Daphne, wake up.' Kneeling down, I gently shake her arm, trying to ease her out of the dream. I know it's not a good idea to wake someone mid-nightmare, but I can't bear the sound of this any longer, or the sight of her crying. Again. 'Come on, Daphne, wake up,' I whisper.

Her eyes jolt open and she grabs my forearm.

'Milosh?'

'Are you all right?'

She blinks a couple of times, adjusting to her surroundings. 'Y-yeah, it was just a bad dream.'

I clear my throat, stand up, and settle my face into a look of relative indifference. 'All right, well, get dressed and come downstairs. You're late and we have a lot to cover.' I walk out of her room without looking back and make my way downstairs, needing to assess the situation I've gotten myself into.

I don't get it. I've been at this house for under a month and I've already broken so many of the unspoken boundaries I put in place when I'm working. Granted, this isn't a protection detail for middle-aged congressmen, or a military tour. But that doesn't change the fact that I'm slipping. Last night I literally shoved George against a wall and threatened him, all because he was disrespecting Daphne. That has nothing to do with Daveeno, so why did I get involved? As much as I think no woman should ever be disrespected, I've never felt the need to be so direct in enforcing that belief. Somehow I've gotten a little too invested, but that stops today.

To Daphne, I'm just an employee.

To me, Daphne is a job. Just a job.

At least that's all she should be.

Job. Her.

Employee. Me.

Walking into the backyard and pulling out the equipment I need for today, I refocus on the task at hand: teaching Daphne how to defend herself. I just need to focus on training her, maintaining professional boundaries and minding my business and we'll be fine.

'Good morning, Mr Petrov,' I hear from behind me as I stomp on the base of the free-standing target, fixing it in place. 'What delightful task do you have for me today?' As I walk back towards the patio, I see Daphne chewing on some blueberries, her eyes roaming over the row of knives I've placed on the table. Any trace of her earlier distress is long gone.

Her slick, straight hair is pulled up into a neat ponytail, and her face is void of any tear marks or puffiness. She's wearing pink leggings again, with the hoodie that I never got back after our first day of training. I'm not mad, though. She wears it better than me. It practically drowns her, coming down to her mid-thighs, but she has the sleeves rolled up so she still has range of motion. The black is a stark contrast to her usual pink or white variety of gym wear, giving her a just-rolled-out-of-my-boyfriend's-bed-and-needed-something-to-put-on look.

Why do I kinda love that?

Boundaries, Petrov. Boundaries.

'You wanted to learn knife throwing. Today I'm gonna teach you.' She looks up at me with an unexpected smile on her face, which slowly morphs into a fully-fledged grin.

'Finally, something fun.' I resist the urge to chuckle at her endearing eagerness, remembering what I just told myself about keeping my distance.

Job. Her.

Employee. Me.

Blurring the lines would be a really stupid decision.

I pick up a knife and throw it at the target, hitting the

centre with ease. 'The goal is for you to be able to do this after a couple of lessons. But, before you even touch a blade – ' I pluck the knife that she's just picked up out of her hands and place it back on the table – 'you need to learn the basics, so you don't hurt yourself. Let's warm up first.' I hand her the jump rope that she's actually come to like and walk to the shed to retrieve the mats.

'I didn't know they teach knife throwing in the military,' she says, opening up the rope and starting to jump.

'They don't.'

'Oh . . . so where did you learn it?'

'I was in a children's home when I was a kid. The older boys taught me.' I cringe at my words. She doesn't need to know that. No one does, but most of all her.

'You were in care?' she asks, abruptly pausing her skipping, a look of concern on her delicate features.

'Yes. Keep skipping.'

'That must've been hard for you. I'm so sorry,' she says, beginning to skip once again. I know I shouldn't look at her but my gaze catches hers anyway. The peaceful sincerity in her voice makes me want to hit a wall. Not many people know I was in the system, and those who do have never sounded as genuinely caring as she just did. Something about this girl makes me want to sit down and tell her my life story. Every single rough detail. But I will never subject someone as pure as she is to something as dark and dirty as my past.

'It was fine.' I walk past her and drop the mats on the floor, lining them up, nodding towards them once they're in the right place. 'Push-ups now.'

Daphne stops skipping and comes to the mats to start her push-ups, still breathless from the skipping. 'You must've been living in a rough area, if the older children were teaching you how to throw knives.'

'Keep your lower back down,' I say, ignoring her implied question. I crouch down beside her and push gently down on the base of her spine, correcting her form. I really shouldn't be this close to her.

From here I can feel the heat radiating from her body. I can smell her marshmallow and orange blossom scent and hear her quick, shallow breaths, taking my mind to places it really shouldn't be going.

'Do you not like talking about your time in care?' she digs, breathless.

'No.'

'Oh, okay . . . well, if you ever need someone to talk to, I'm always here to listen.' She sits up and places her hand on my forearm with a soft smile. After a beat, she removes it, standing up. Creating some much-needed space.

This girl is too kind for her own good.

'Thank you, Miss Green, but that won't be necessary.'

'Everybody needs somebody, Milosh,' she says softly. 'I'm not saying I have to be your somebody, but I can listen, if you'll let me. I want to be the same kind of help to you that you were to me last night.' She holds her slender brown hand out towards me. 'You help me and I help you. Deal?'

I shouldn't do it. Boundaries, Petrov. Boun—

'Deal.'

Well, that was stupid.

I encase her hand in mine and they mould together like a sculptor's dream. Heat pools in my stomach at the sensation of her touch and I see her mouth gently part, as she takes a small breath. I look from her pillowy lips to her warm, chocolate eyes, trying to read her expression.

Job. Daphne.

Employee. Me.

I snap out of my trance and let go of her hand, taking a step back for good measure.

'Let's get started with your stance.'

⊕

Walking back into the kitchen to grab some water after training, I run into George.

'Mr Petrov, could you join me in my study for a moment?' he says, disappearing out of the kitchen door. I haven't seen him since last night, and judging by his tone I'm guessing he wants to talk about what happened.

I quickly finish my drink and walk into his office, taking a seat opposite where he is now sitting behind his desk.

He doesn't pay me any mind as I sit down, continuing to type away on his computer for a few more minutes before turning to look at me.

'Mr Petrov, your behaviour last night was unacceptable and unprofessional.'

I mean, he's not wrong. I say nothing, waiting to see where exactly he's going with this. 'I have never been spoken to like that by anyone in my own home.' He makes a dramatic pause as if we've got all the time in the world.

'That being said, I understand your actions. I was confused and angry, and I'd had too much to drink, leading me to take my frustrations out on the wrong people. Normally if anything like this had happened, you would've been fired without a second thought. However, you don't work for me. You're in my house to help me and you've already shown that you are vital to my daughter's safety, and I was out of line last night, so I'm not going to ask you to leave.'

Oh yippie.

'All I'm going to say is this: don't ever physically threaten me again. And . . .' Cue another dramatic pause. 'I'm sorry. I truly am sorry.' He looks down at the papers on his desk, awkwardly shuffling them around.

'I'm not the one you should be apologizing to, sir,' I state simply.

'Yes, I know.' He looks back up at me with sincerity in his eyes. 'I apologized to Amelia and Henry this morning, and now you. Daphne's last on my list.'

'She should've been first.'

He looks back at me, a blaze of fire briefly clouding his eyes. 'I know, Mr Petrov.'

'Good.' I stand to leave.

'Anything you'd like to add, Mr Petrov?' he probes.

'If you're expecting an apology, sir, you're not gonna get one. I'm here to keep an eye out for any Daveeno movement and protect your daughter. It just so happened that last night the person she needed to be protected from was you.'

Guilt.

Guilt and shame are all I see on George Green's face.

Good.

I turn to leave, but stop short at the door. 'Sir, your daughter loves you. It's obvious she loves you very much, but if you continue down this path you will lose her. My advice? Stop lying to her and blaming her for everything. None of this is her fault. Just take the time and explain things to her. You'll be surprised to see how empathetic she can be.'

He hangs his head. 'You're right.'

I watch him for a moment. 'Sir, I know you told us that you

don't know anything about what Daveeno wants from you, but have you had any more ideas of what it could be?' He's not telling me something. I don't know why but every time I've brought up Daveeno he's shut the conversation down, as if that's not the sole reason I'm here.

He glances back up at me, an odd, unreadable emotion crossing his face. 'I've been thinking about it and perhaps I know what they're after.'

I walk back over and take a seat before he continues.

'Around nine years ago, I was working with MI6 on an antidote formula for a toxin called serum 627. Me and my lab assistant were working tirelessly trying to create it, but we failed. We made the situation even worse. Somehow we managed to concentrate the effects of the serum so that it would not just kill spies painfully and slowly but also leave no sign of foul play. The new serum we created made it look like the agent died of natural causes rather than poison. Not only that, but once they took the serum they would be more susceptible to interrogation as it removed inhibitions, which means that no one had to torture their victim, they could just feed them the serum, get all the information they needed and leave them to die and no one would suspect a thing.'

I take my time and fully process everything George just said before asking, 'What happened to the formula?'

'I destroyed it. I was there to make antidotes, not

weapons. And with MI6 having a big double agent problem I couldn't trust anyone, so I got rid of it and all the evidence that went along with it. I don't know how but I think Daveeno have found out what I created and want the serum for themselves, but I don't have it.'

'All these years later? When you haven't worked with MI6 for nearly nine years? Why would they want it now? How would they even know?' I'm asking these questions out loud to myself, but George answers.

'I'm wondering the same things. It doesn't make sense but that's the only plausible explanation as to why they're after me.'

I sigh, my brain mulling through all the possibilities. 'All right, I'll inform Major Davis and we'll see what he says. With this intel he may be able to get something out of Stefan Mikelson. He's still in their custody after the home attack.'

'Okay, that's a good plan. Thank you, Milosh.'

I nod, rising out of my chair and pulling my phone out of my pocket. 'Sir?' I turn back at the door.

'Yeah?'

'I know this is a very stressful situation but don't take it out on Daphne. Maybe you should tell her the truth about all of this?'

'Thank you for your opinion but I'll deal with my daughter the way I see fit.'

I walk out of George's office to find Daphne waltzing down the stairs in a pretty floral dress, bag in hand.

'Miss Green.' She turns at my voice, her previously relaxed expression now becoming tight and constricted.

'I'm going shopping, Mr Petrov,' she says, though I really didn't ask. 'You're welcome to come with me, but I'm going whether you like it or not.'

Oh joy.

13

'No.'

'Yes.'

'No.'

'Yes.'

'No.'

'I've really got all day, Mr Petrov,' I sigh, opening the cupboard door and taking my car keys off the hook.

'You're not going,' he replies, finality in his tone as he snatches the keys from my hand and walks towards the kitchen.

'I need an outfit for the charity gala in a few weeks, and you definitely need to be fitted for a suit if you insist on joining me.' I pout, following him into the kitchen. 'Plus, I haven't left this house in an age.'

I'm not normally a whiner but, hey, desperate times.

'I don't care if you've been in this house since birth,

you're not going,' he says, sliding my keys into his back pocket and heading for the fridge.

'But why not? You're okay with me going to the gala in two weeks but not this?'

The Greenway Group hosts an annual summer charity gala, supporting a different cause every year. It's invite-only and is one of the highlights of my summer. Everyone dresses in extravagant ballgowns and tuxedos, there's great food and I get to meet up with a lot of my family and friends that I don't see when I'm away at school. This year the Greenway Group are supporting the British Deaf Association.

'The gala has tight, well-monitored security, an exclusive guestlist and well-vetted staff. Whereas the mall has hundreds of unknowns, thousands of people and no screening process.'

'Well, I think . . .' I turn at the sound of Daddy's voice as he enters the kitchen from his study. We haven't spoken since dinner last night and on instinct I tense up, ready to call it a day and head back up to my room to avoid another argument. '. . . you should go.'

'I'm sorry, what?' I say, not bothering to hide the surprise in my voice. Normally when my father and I have a disagreement we have a cooling-off period then go back to normal. But whatever's been happening recently has caused that cooling-off period to lengthen. It continues to be extended with every new disagreement we have. And lately, that's been a lot.

'I think you and Milosh should go out. You've been through a lot recently and it's only fair you have a little fun.' He comes to stand on the other side of the island to where Milosh and I are. Facing me, but still keeping his distance, with a conflicted look on his face.

'Daphne, darling, I'm really sorry about the way I've been acting lately,' he continues. 'First in your room, and then last night. This whole break-in thing has caused me so much stress and I've really taken it out on the wrong people . . . well, person. I don't want to cause a rift between us, especially at a time like this. You don't have to forgive me now, or at all, but I just wanted to get that off my chest.' He looks everywhere but at me, fiddling with his hands like someone just gave them to him.

'Oh,' he adds, 'if it helps, shopping is on me.' He reaches into his pocket and pulls out his wallet, handing me his credit card.

'Daddy, shopping was always going to be on you, but thank you for the gesture,' I say, meeting his eyes and giving him a small smile. 'And thank you for your apology, I appreciate it.'

He retreats to his study with a hesitant small nod, and I turn my attention back to Milosh who's been leaning against the counter silently watching the scene unfold.

'See, Daddy says we can go.' I hold up the card, walking over to stand in front of him. 'He even sponsored the event.'

'No, Daphne.'

It's really hard to be annoyed at him when he says my name like that.

Deep, gruff and strong.

I move closer to him, settling my hand on his forearm to draw his full attention to me. 'Please, Milosh, only for a couple of hours?' I blink up at him as he slowly takes a gulp of his water, eyes never leaving mine.

I hold his eyes, running my nails up his arm ever-so gently, making gentle patterns against his skin.

'Two hours. That's all you get.'

My eyes light up at his answer and I give his arm a gentle squeeze. 'Thank you!' I swipe the bottle from his hands. 'You can drink that in the car, come on.'

Milosh follows me out of the door that leads to the garage. 'Which one's yours?' he asks, gesturing to the line of cars that fills the space. Most of the staff who drive to work park along the private street, so the cars in here belong to either Amelia and Henry, me or my father.

In front of us right now are Amelia and Henry's Audi, my light-pink custom-made Sharpay Evans-inspired Greenway Motors estate, two of Daddy's sports cars – one

Greenway Motors and the other McLaren – the Bentley our driver uses and the family Rolls.

Yes, my Uncle Jonathan runs the Greenway Motors side of the Greenway Group, but that doesn't mean all of our cars have to be Greenways.

'Take a wild guess, Mr Petrov.' I smirk. His unimpressed expression amuses me as he unlocks the car, slipping into the driver's seat. I don't argue because honestly, I hate driving, and I slip into the passenger seat beside him. I watch as he buckles his seatbelt, mirroring his actions as I soften my voice.

'Thank you for agreeing to this, by the way,' I say sincerely. He studies me for a second before nodding curtly and starting the car. 'I really do appreciate it,' I finish, placing my hand gently on his as he puts the car into drive.

'It's no problem, Miss Green. Let's just get in and out quickly. I'm guessing you want to go to the Greenway mall?' I nod and lift my hand off his, as we pull out of the driveway.

My grandfather, Hezekiah Green, founded the Greenway Group when he was a teen. Since then it's grown into a pretty large conglomerate, splitting off into four groups, each with one of his children in charge. Daddy runs Greenway Discoveries, Uncle Leo runs the

Greenway Hotel Group and Properties, Uncle Jonathan runs Greenway Motors and Auntie Emily runs Greenway Aviation. There's recently been talk between the cousins about a fifth Greenway sector opening up, but nothing's been confirmed. All of the grandchildren – me included – have been groomed since birth to take over their parents' sectors and while some of us love it and are eager for it, others aren't. I'm in the latter category. I've decided to go a different route and study Midwifery.

Now that's a *real* sore point for my father, so I bring it up as little as possible.

Bored of the silence, I ask the question that's been bugging me since Milosh arrived.

'What exactly are you, Mr Petrov?'

'What?'

'Where are you from?' I specify. 'I know you lived in America, but your voice and your surname suggest you started out somewhere else.'

He glances over at me, catching my eye, a look of conflict passing through his own for a split second before he responds, 'Bulgaria. I moved to America when I was ten.'

'Why did you move?'

'Because I had to,' he states blankly. I look back at him and consider his odd, vague response, noting the tight grip he now has on the steering wheel. I know his past is a bit of a touchy subject yet I can't help wanting to know more. He has such a hard exterior but I know that there's something softer under that. I've seen glimpses of it over the last few weeks.

Pink boxing gloves.

Waking me from my nightmare.

Standing up to my father for me.

The fact that he didn't raise his voice with me just now, even though he was clearly uncomfortable, speaks volumes.

'I'm sorry, I didn't mean to pry. I just wanted to know a little more about you,' I say, as we reach a red light. He looks at me with hair-raising intensity, scanning my features as if he's trying to commit them to memory.

'I moved to America to live with my aunt after my parents were killed. I lived with her for a year, learning English slowly, before she died. Then, I moved to a children's home where I stayed until I was sixteen, when I joined the military.'

Ah.

So *that's* why he doesn't like to talk about his past.

'I thought you had to be seventeen to join the military in the US?'

'You do, but I saved a boy who was getting beaten up, and it turned out he was the son of a lieutenant and an admissions officer so they let me in early as a favour.'

'Did you only join the military to get away from your children's home?' Now he's actually letting me in, I can't help but keep asking questions. This is the most he's opened up since I met him, so yes, I'm going to ask until I can't ask any more.

'Yes and no. I hated that home, but it taught me some valuable lessons. I joined the military because I wanted to help people.'

'That's why you started doing close protection work too?'

He goes silent for a moment. I look at him but his eyes are focused on the road. 'Something like that.'

I don't know what happened, but there's a distinct shift in the air. Attempting to keep the mood light, I continue. 'Thank you for sharing that with me. You didn't have to but you chose to anyway and I appreciate that.' I look over at him, but he keeps his eyes on the road, only dipping his head in acknowledgement.

'Since you've shared something, is there anything you'd like to know about me?' I suggest, rolling down my window, closing my eyes as I revel in the warm breeze against my skin. Milosh stays quiet for a moment, and I assume he just doesn't want to know anything more about me, until he shocks me by speaking again.

'Your nightmares.' I can hear the hesitation in his voice, but I keep my eyes closed, waiting to hear where he's going with this. 'You had one the first day I got here, didn't you?'

'Yeah,' I answer weakly. I know I told Milosh to ask me anything but I'd rather eat my left big toe than go through this with him.

'Do you eat blueberries after every bad dream?'

'Yeah.' I scoff lightly. If there's one thing about Milosh Petrov, it's that he's a heck of an observant guy.

'Do you get them often?'

'They started when I was young, and would come once a week roughly. They stopped when I was at school, but as soon as I came back home for the holidays they would start up again. Since the break-in, they've got worse, though, coming more frequently and vividly. But it's always the same dream over and over. That never seems to change.'

We turn into the shopping centre car park and pull into a space. Killing the engine, Milosh turns to look at me. 'Thank you for sharing that with me.'

One thing I've come to appreciate about Milosh is that even though he's rough and assertive with his words, he always speaks to me with respect and relative kindness whether he's irritated with me or not.

'You help me, I help you.' I smile gently, shrugging as

he gets out of his side, coming around to open the door for me.

We walk towards the entrance in comfortable silence for a moment before Milosh changes the subject to the task at hand. 'When you go shopping, do you often see people you know?'

'Most of my friends live in other countries so I never really see them here, but some of my extended family live nearby, so I've run into them on occasion.' I hear a car door slamming in the distance and I flinch, letting out a sharp gasp. Milosh looks down at me with a puzzled expression as he presses the button to call the lift.

'I've been a little jumpy since the break-in,' I explain.

Understatement of the century.

I've not just been jumpy but paranoid too. Since the break-in, I haven't been able to go downstairs at night and even got scared of the wind lightly tapping on my bedroom window as I got ready this morning.

After the break-in, all Henry told me was that the man was looking for something to do with Daddy's work and he hurt me so he could escape without any problems. But I just don't understand what he could be working on that's so important someone would strangle me to get their hands on it. Nothing has been normal since I got back from school so I need to make this shopping trip count. Because until they catch the man that guy was working for, I still remain at risk.

'On the off-chance we see anyone you know,' Milosh says, taking me out of my head and back into the conversation, 'they ideally shouldn't know I'm your . . . bodyguard.'

'Why?'

'Because normally when you let someone know that you − a regular person − have a bodyguard, people start to worry, then they start to ask questions. Questions that neither of us want to answer. So it's easier if you introduce me as your friend or something.'

'Mr Petrov.' I gaze over at him. 'I mean this in the nicest way possible. No one would believe that you and I are friends.' It's not that I don't have male friends. It's that I have no male friends that look or act remotely like him. Where Milosh Petrov is sharp, rough and direct, my male friends are preppy, book-smart and not athletic in the least.

'Fine, then introduce me as your boyfriend instead.' He sighs.

'Okay, if no one would believe you're my friend, why would they believe you're my boyfriend? Have you seen the way you dress, Mr Petrov?' He looks at me with the most bored expression a person could make as we walk into the lift.

I step back and try to look at him objectively, as if I were one of my friends seeing him for the first time. I take in the combat-style boots, black cargos and black T-shirt. The dark hair and the sharply structured facial features. He stands with authority and dominance, physically and metaphorically taking up the space he enters. 'You're a literal walking Pinterest board for the bodyguard aesthetic. The whole army brat thing is not the look I traditionally go for.'

'And what is? Cable knits and dickies?' Amusement dances in his eyes as he presses the button for the first floor.

'No, I'm more of a quarter-zip and gilet kinda girl.' I try to picture him in the outfit of a man I would typically go for.

Yeah, no, I can *definitely* work with that.

'Okay, so if we're really gonna sell this we're gonna need to get you some new clothes.'

'Absolutely not.'

'Mr Petrov, you said that I shouldn't tell people you're my bodyguard, but I won't have to if you're wearing that.' I gesture to his ensemble. 'So if you're going to play the boyfriend role, you need to look the part.'

'Believe me, Miss Green.' He dips his head until his mouth is hovering over my earlobe. 'If I'm playing the role of *boyfriend*, it's not the clothes that will convince them.' I shake off the involuntary shiver that runs through my body and focus. 'But it's your shopping day, so I'll humour you. Where to first?'

14

'Goodness, no. Take it off.' I sip my water and look around the shop again, hoping something else will jump out at me as Milosh goes back into the changing room. 'How many tops do we have now?' I ask the sales associate next to me.

'We have four tops, two pairs of trousers and one jumper so far.'

'Thank you,' I reply with a smile. 'We just need a quarter-zip and a gilet, then we're good to go,' I call out to Milosh.

He appears a minute later wearing dark-wash jeans, a navy quarter-zip jumper with a navy blue gilet over the top and some loafers.

He looks good. Really good.

'Much better.' I smile, walking over to him so I can take a closer look at the fit. 'And everything fits you really well!' I was slightly concerned that we'd have trouble finding something to fit his broad shoulders while also being long enough, but this jumper moulds perfectly to his body. 'Do you have this outfit but in black?' I ask the sales associate.

'Let me go and check.' She walks off, leaving me and Milosh alone.

'So, what do you think?' I ask. From what I've seen, he's only looked at himself once since he walked out of the changing room, and even then it was rushed.

'It's fine,' he states simply, moving a step closer to me. 'If this is what you want, then let's get it.'

'Okay. Do you want to wear this out of the shop?' I hold my breath when he tucks a few stray hairs behind my ear delicately, his hand lingering briefly.

'No, I'll be too hot. Let me go and change into something more weather appropriate.' I open my mouth to respond, but he beats me to it, dipping down to whisper into my ear. 'Don't worry, it'll still be Daphne Green approved.'

He walks off just as the sales assistant comes back with the black version of his outfit. 'Thank you. Could you add that to the yes pile, please, and wrap everything up?'

'Of course, madam,' she replies, walking off but stopping midway to the till and turning back. 'I just have to say, you and your partner make such a lovely couple! I wish someone looked at me the way he looks at you and I wish I could look at someone with the same amount of love that's in your eyes.'

'Oh . . . thank . . . thank you,' I manage to squeeze out with a strangled smile. 'That's very kind!'

The way he looks at me?

Love in my eyes?

I'm sorry, did I miss something?

We haven't even officially started this whole pretend-boyfriend thing yet, but I'm glad to know we're really selling it.

'Oh, no problem at all,' the sales associate rattles on. It's actually rather endearing. 'I just think, you're so pretty and he's so handsome. And he speaks to you so gently. It's like a beautiful fairy tale come to life!' she finishes, turning back round and continuing to the till.

Huh.

She bought it.

Me and Milosh.

Milosh and I.

Daphne and Mi— 'Way to sell it,' Milosh interrupts my thoughts, walking out of the dressing room. My eyes roam his body as I take in his outfit choice.

A black knitted polo with black chinos, paired with a

black belt with gold hardware and some black loafers.

It's still him, but with a touch more . . . me.

The perfect mix.

'What are you talking about?' I respond, once my mind actually registers what he just said.

'You're the stiffest person I've met.' He smirks, amusement dancing in his eyes.

'No, I am not,' comes my very reasonable answer.

'Daphne, she complimented us as a couple and you froze up. You need to loosen up.'

'Says you, Mr Be-downstairs-in-five and I-only-give-two-word-responses-because-I'm-Milosh.' I use my best Bulgarian accent to really drive the point home.

He frowns, though that stupid smirk stays on his face. 'I'm sorry, is that supposed to be me?'

'Not supposed to be, is,' I say as I start walking to the till. 'You know what, let's do a little test.' I turn back to face him. 'We'll see who can be the least stiff. You want a fake girlfriend, well then you're going to get the best fake girlfriend a man could ask for.'

He studies me for a moment before stepping forward and raising his hand to run two fingers along my jaw.

'Sure,' he murmurs into my ear. I'm enveloped in that clean, warm scent of his before he steps away all too quickly, continuing the walk over to the till.

'We're gonna take these clothes too, please,' I inform the sales assistant. She nods and smiles, handing me a pair of scissors to cut the tags off then holding up the card reader to me once I've done. I tap without bothering to look at the price, while Milosh takes the bags.

'Where to next?' Milosh asks, as we start walking out of the shop.

'Well, we still need to get you a tux, and a dress and some shoes for me. Let's start with the tux then we'll go from there,' I decide, leading him towards our next stop. 'Now, ideally I would've taken you to Savile Row, but the purple label will have to do instead. If we don't find anything there we'll go to Cucinelli, as we—'

'Daphne!' someone calls. I turn around and spot Isabella walking towards us, bags and boyfriend in hand.

'Bella, hi!' I smile, waving to her. We stop walking and wait for them to catch up. 'Cousin Isabella, same age, basically grew up together, along with my other cousin, Camilla,' I whisper to Milosh.

'I know who she is.'

I feel a nauseating pang of something akin to jealousy as he looks over at her.

Unwarranted and unhinged? Absolutely. But me and common sense are on the outs right now.

'How are you?' I ask once she reaches us, briefly looking

over to her boyfriend and smiling warmly. 'Hi, Eddie.'

'Hey, Daph.' He nods back.

'Daphne, oh my gosh, I haven't seen you in an age!' Isabella drawls.

'Is, you saw me at graduation a few weeks ago.' I laugh.

'Five weeks ago, Daphne. Five weeks. That's an age in my book,' she responds, even though her attention is now elsewhere. 'Aren't you gonna introduce me?' she says, eyeing Milosh up and down, as if Eddie is not standing right there.

'Oh goodness, yes, sorry. Milosh, this is my Cousin Isabella and her boyfriend Edward. Eddie, Isabella, this is Milosh, my bod—'

'Boyfriend,' he interrupts. I feel one of Milosh's hands lace around my waist as he drops the bags, using his other to shake Eddie's.

Oh, he's good at this.

I thread my fingers through his at my waist and bring my other hand up to rest on his chest.

'Yes, sorry. My boyfriend.' I laugh stiffly. 'I just can't get used to saying it!'

'Boyfriend? Daph, you never told me you were even interested in someone, let alone dating them.' Isabella frowns.

'I was going to tell you, but we wanted to keep it really

low key,' I explain, feeling awful for lying to my closest friend.

'Right . . . Sure.' She eyes me suspiciously before looking back over to Milosh and shrugging. 'Well, you definitely did good, Daph. You *definitely* did good.'

'You did good but I did better,' Milosh says, looking down at me. His eyes drop to my lips for a moment before I feel his hand move to my hip, gently squeezing.

'Oh, well, good for you both.' Isabella smirks. 'How did you even meet?'

'Monaco Grand Prix last year,' Milosh answers as I try to hide my shock. How did he know I was at the grand prix last year? 'We met when I was on a tour of the Greenway Motors cockpit.'

'Oh, so you're a Formula One man?' Isabella questions, looking more than impressed.

'Something like that,' he responds, his hand moving to rub soft circles on my lower back. My skin starts to heat under his touch and my breath involuntarily becomes shallow.

'Where are you guys off to now?' I ask, trying to keep it together.

'We were just about to head into Ralph Lauren to see if we can get a tux for Eddie because all of his are still in Switzerland,' she replies, rolling her eyes.

Eddie and Isabella met at school and have been that typical on-again-off-again couple for the past three years. If Eddie had it his way she'd already have a big fat engagement ring on her finger, but I've come to realize they both have very different ideas of how their relationship should be. Isabella gets bored quickly – hence the on-again-off-again – whereas Eddie's a committed relationship guy through and through.

'We were headed there too! Let's go together,' I suggest. I need a bit of space from Milosh, and if that means using my cousin as a human buffer so be it. I don't even bother looking back at him, because I know what his expression will be. Unimpressed and uninterested.

'Daph, I can't believe you kept this from me,' Isabella whispers as we walk into the store. 'I thought we told each other everything.'

Way to make a girl feel awful.

'I know, I'm sorry, it was just all so new and I wanted to stay in our little uninterrupted bubble a short while longer.'

Isabella sighs, squeezing my hand in that comforting way she did when we were kids. 'That's okay. As long as I'm the first to know I guess it doesn't matter.'

'Girls,' Eddie interrupts, looking through the tuxedos on display, 'do we need tails or not?'

'No tails,' Isabella and I say at the same time.

'All right,' Isabella says, dragging me off to the side, 'tell me everything!'

'There's nothing much to tell, Bella,' I say, very aware that Milosh can still hear us. 'I met him, we started talking, he asked me out and now here we are.'

'Okay, but tell me, what's he like? I kind of expected to see you with someone a little more . . .' She trails off, sneaking another look back at Milosh.

'Like Eddie?' I finish for her.

'Well . . . yeah, kind of.' We both look over to Eddie and Milosh, silently comparing them. They're around the same height, with Milosh being an inch or two taller, dressed pretty similarly, and are both white. That's where the similarities end. Where Milosh is obviously very muscular, Eddie is slimmer. Think the Flash and Captain America. Both strong but in vastly different ways. Eddie has a very sweet, kind, boy-next-door look to him, with fluffy blond hair and blue eyes, whereas Milosh looks like the guy your mother would warn you to stay away from. Dark hair and sharp features. He's one tattoo sleeve away from a biker-Bruce Wayne crossbreed.

'He looks like he's a heartbreak ready to happen, Daph.'

'I know how it looks, Bella, I really do, but he's not

like that. He's kind, protective and soft with me. That's all that really matters.'

'What do his parents do?' Meaning – does he come from money?

'They're in commercial real estate,' I lie.

'Well, all right then.' Bella looks sceptically at him for a moment before turning back to me. 'I'm happy for you. Just be careful, okay?'

'Of course.'

'All right,' Eddie interrupts as he and Milosh walk over to us, suits in hand. 'These are the ones we're starting off with. Are they good?' He holds the tuxedo up to show Isabella and Milosh does the same, holding his up to show me. He's picked out a traditional, single-breasted, black wool tuxedo with sharp lines, a crisp finish and silk lapels, whereas Eddie's tux is a double-breasted cream jacket and black trousers combo.

'Looks like a good choice,' I say to Milosh. 'Yours too, Eddie. Why don't you guys go and try them on and we'll look for some pocket squares?'

'I'm not wearing a pocket square, Miss Green,' Milosh states.

'Correction,' I breathe, turning to him and rising up onto my toes to whisper into his ear, my lips brushing his lobe. 'You'll wear whatever I want you to, *boyfriend*.'

'Is that so?' he responds, eyebrow rising ever so slightly as he turns to look at me, green irises burning right through me.

Is that so?

How three little words can sound so . . . charged . . . is beyond me. But nevertheless, here we are.

When I don't respond, Milosh dips down again, angling himself so now his lips are barely brushing my lobe.

Jeez, it's like a game of cat and mouse, but I don't know who is who at this point.

'I'll wear whatever you want me to, Miss Green, but not a pocket square. Okay?'

'Fine.' I breathe out. Why is he so hung up on a pocket square? To be honest, I really don't care, he can be hung up on whatever he wants to be as long as he whispers into my ear like that again.

'Good,' he says, smirking slightly before he takes his eyes off me and glances over to Eddie and Isabella who are staring at us with the same weird look on their faces. 'You ready?' Milosh asks Eddie and he nods, before walking with Milosh towards the changing rooms.

As they disappear I look back over to Isabella and can't help but chuckle when I see the current expression she's sporting.

'What?' I ask mid-laugh.

'Daphne, how did the two of you make a conversation about a pocket square so . . .' She walks over to the seating area opposite the changing room, still trying to find the right word. Honestly, so am I. 'Dirty?' she settles.

'What are you talking about?' I breathe out a laugh, hoping I sound nonchalant.

'Daph, the tension in the looks you two were sharing was one thing, but the whispering? The stares? Even me and Eddie were starting to get turned on.'

'I don't know what you mean, Bella.' I sigh, turning my face away to hide my smile. One thing about Milosh and I is that we can definitely put on a good show.

Because that's what this all is. An act. A show.

Right?

15

MILOSH

'Okay, this is the last one, promise.' Daphne smiles, walking into yet another store. I don't catch the name of this one as we step in but they clearly specialize in unnecessarily expensive, extravagant shoes. Daphne wanders over to a display, eyeing up a pair of heels that have a gladiator-like strap with butterflies attached to them, and a sparkly silver sole.

They look obnoxious.

'Aren't they stunning?' Daphne glows up at me. I'll be honest: I detest clothes shopping, but seeing her face light up every time she sees something she likes is like a reward.

'Excuse me.' Daphne picks up a gold, butterfly-less version of the shoe she just showed me and gently taps the sales assistant's arm as she's walking by. 'Do you have these in a size thirty-eight?'

The sales assistant stops for a moment, looking at Daphne as if she's trying to place a long-lost friend, before smiling at her and glancing down at the shoe in question. 'Sure! Let me go grab them for you.'

'Thank you!' Daphne smiles before taking a seat on a plush cream chair. I stay standing but move closer to her, ensuring her face is blocked from view to those outside the store.

The sales assistant comes back, box in hand, with an overly bright smile on her face. 'Let me know if you need anything else,' she says, as she hands the box to Daphne and moves away from us, but not out of sight.

'Okay, do you think these would go well with pink?' she asks, sticking her sparkle-clad foot out at me. She must have me mistaken for her yappy cousin.

'I have no clue.'

'Ugh! Boys,' chirps the irritatingly peppy sales assistant. 'They just don't get it, do they!'

'No, they do not.' Daphne giggles, melting away some of my irritation. I don't know what it is about her but even though I'm on high alert at every moment, what with the Daveeno threat still very real, when I'm around her she brings me back to the calm and peace I felt when I was a child. Not when I was in care or living with my aunt, but when my parents were alive. There's just something about the way she walks, talks, acts and smells that draws you in.

'What bag are you wearing with it?' asks the sales assistant, coming to sit down next to Daphne.

I tune them out as they talk endlessly about things that don't interest me, and take the time to remind myself of the emergency exits. I already know the layout of the mall from studying its blueprints when I got this job, somehow knowing I would end up being dragged here. But I've never been here in person and there's only so much you can get from floorplans and stills. I've been pretty vigilant since we arrived, looking out for potential threats, and all's been fine until we stepped in this store. I don't know what it is about this place in particular but it's set my body buzzing with anticipation.

I look around and spot four security cameras, three other members of staff and Little Miss Peppy. Something about her rubs me the wrong way.

She's just too . . . eager.

'Okay, it's settled. I'll take them both!' I turn to face Daphne, to see that she has a pair of the sparkly shoes in one hand and a pair of white red-bottoms in the other.

'Great, let's get you to the checkout!'

I walk closely behind Daphne, really playing up the whole boyfriend thing as I carry all the bags we've accumulated up to the counter with us. She leans against me as the girl wraps up the shoes, stroking her hand slowly up and down my arm without thinking, as if this is how we stand on a daily basis. The weight of her body mixed with her feminine, sweet scent begs me to close my eyes and savour this moment, but I have to concentrate.

This is all an act, not real life.

I just need to leave this store, get her home and create some distance between us.

She tips her head up, causing her chestnut eyes to appear bigger, and softens her voice, a dainty smile gracing her lips. 'Milo, are you sure you don't want to get another pair of shoes? You can never have too many.'

All I can do is shake my head stiffly, looking at anything but her, after the name *Milo* fell from her delicate lips. People have tried to shorten my name before and it always sounded forced. But, of course, as soon as Daphne Green does it, it becomes my new favourite sound.

'Would you like the receipt in the bag?' the girl jabbers, drawing me back to the present.

'Yes, please.' Daphne smiles brightly.

'I just have to say, I absolutely love your outfit! Where did you get it?' the sales associate asks, a weird look on her face, sending my brain into medium alert. She hasn't done anything to warrant a red alert yet, but her fidgety movements and darting eyes suggest she's not as innocent as she wants to seem.

'Oh, thank you!' Daphne all but gushes. 'It's from Zimmerman. I got it last year but I think they still have it in stock and the shoes are the Loro Piana summer charm slides!'

'Would you mind if I take a picture of it, just so I remember what I'm looking for when I'm searching online later?'

'Oh, um . . . ' She hesitates for a moment. 'Sure, okay.'

As the sales associate smiles and bends down to retrieve her phone from under the till, I notice the beginning of a tattoo just below her collarbone.

Is that . . . ?

Then it hits me. It hits me like a ton of bricks.

'You don't need a picture, all you need is the name,' I state, looking down at Daphne who's now sporting a confused expression. 'Do you remember what it's called, baby?' I continue the conversation, trying not to arouse suspicion as I look around discreetly at all the exits again, planning our route out.

'Um, yeah, it's the illustration buttoned mini,' she says slowly, still confused but following my lead anyway.

'There you go,' I tell the sales associate. 'Write that down and you won't need a picture.' Her face falls, morphing into a scowl for a split second before she pulls a strained smile into place.

'Thank you, that's super helpful. Have a great day.'

'That was odd, right?' Daphne asks as we move towards the door but I'm not paying attention to her, I'm watching the sales associate out of the corner of my eye. As soon as we checked out she left the till, even though there was a large queue behind us.

Now she has her phone to her ear and her back turned to us. I slow my steps, straining to see if I can hear anything.

'Yeah, I just saw her, I swear . . . yeah . . . pink floral dress and pink sandals . . . hair in a ponytail . . . I know, I know.' Then the girl starts giggling like a crazed teenager. 'But be careful, she's with her boyfriend . . . all black . . . yeah, it could be, I don't know.'

'Milosh?' Daphne's voice brings me back and I quickly devise a plan.

'Yep, sorry, got side-tracked,' I say, when the sales assistant turns around and spots us. 'Let's go.' I guide Daphne out of the store and start to devise a plan.

'Milosh, what was that?' Daphne says, increasing her speed to match mine.

'You know the guy who broke into your house the other night?'

'Yeah?'

'He has a friend. And she's the one who just tried to take a picture of you.'

'Wait, what?' Daphne looks at me in shock, momentarily slowing her pace before almost instantly picking it back up. I guide her down the escalator as I scan around for anyone who looks a little too interested in us.

'We need to change our clothes,' I state, noticing a group of kids gathered around the entrance to a store on the ground floor.

'Milosh, wait, how do you know that she and that guy are working together?'

'They both have the same tattoo with their organization's insignia.' We reach the bottom of the escalator just as I spot the sales associate with a burly guy on the floor above. 'I'll explain all of this later, but for now you need to trust me, okay?'

'Yeah, o-okay.'

I guide her through the group of kids and into the shop, grabbing a white shirt off the racks swiftly, looking for some pants. Daphne beats me to it and grabs a pair of grey slacks, pointing to a sign: *Women's Clothing, Bottom Floor.* I nod, slightly taken aback by how quickly she's adjusted to all of this, and bring her downstairs. I find a green top as she seizes some black joggers and looks up at me. 'What now?' I look around and spot changing cubicles on the other side of the room.

'Keep your head down and leave your bags here.' We walk over to the changing room and I grab two pairs of reading glasses and a tote bag as we head in. Luckily for us, it's unstaffed so we walk straight through and into a stall.

I close the curtain and turn to look at Daphne who's now visibly shaking.

'What languages do you know?' I ask, taking all the clothes off the hangers, trying to distract her.

'What?'

'Languages, do you speak any fluently?'

'Uh, French, BSL, Mandarin and Russian.'

'Okay, from here on out we're only to speak to each other in Russian. Don't use my real name, use a pet name or a fake name. I don't care, just not my real name. *Khorosho*?'

'Khorosho.'

I pass her the new clothes and start pulling off my shirt, speaking in Russian again: 'Get changed and put these on.' I pass her the glasses. 'Stuff your old clothes in the tote bag once you're done.'

As soon as I've handed her the items, I turn and face the wall to give her some privacy. I've been so busy figuring out the next move that I didn't even think about the fact that we'd have to get changed in such close proximity.

Together.

Just keep it professional.

Keep. It. Professional.

16

Now, I've watched Captain America and Superman and all those kinds of films, but I'm happy to report they have absolutely nothing on the man standing before me. When he takes his shirt off, I gaze down his front in the mirror, the current situation forgotten. His strong, toned abs mixed with his light tan gives him the look of a mythical god. Think Hercules.

My eyes trace up his arm and lead me to his broad shoulders, watching them gently move up and down as his breathing steadies. When he starts loosening his belt, I come to my senses and turn around, pulling on the joggers under my dress.

'Are you sure?' I hear faintly. I don't recognize the voice but I speed up, swiftly removing my dress and pulling the tight green top over my head. I turn back around and stuff the dress into the tote just as Milosh is shrugging on his shirt. He crams his old clothes on top of mine and takes out a pair of glasses I didn't even notice him getting. When he places them on his face, my chest constricts.

The man is a modern-day Clark Kent.

'Yes, I'm sure they went this way,' I hear the sales associate say, a little closer this time. I look up at Milosh as he pauses on a shirt button. He glances down at me, an unreadable emotion swimming in his eyes.

'Fine, you do a lap of the store and I'll check the changing rooms. Remember, we only need the girl. And don't hurt her, they want her alive,' says a deep male voice. I can feel my body start to shut down as heightening tremors take over. Within seconds, Milosh is only millimetres away from me. He pulls my hairband out of my hair gently, allowing it to drop from it's ponytail and cascade down my back.

'Do you trust me?' It takes me a moment to understand what he's saying until I remember the whole only-speaking-in-Russian thing thing.

'What?' I turn to look at the curtain as I hear the heavy steps of what feels like my end drawing closer.

'Do you trust me?' he whispers again, cupping my face and turning my body so that his shields mine, conflict brewing in his emerald eyes.

I search them before answering, 'Yes.'

'Good.'

He leans down, so close that our breathing intertwines and syncs. My senses heighten and all I can smell is him, all I can see is him and all I can hear is the roar in my ears as he brushes his lips hesitantly on mine. He pauses for a second, breaking the kiss to search my eyes. A small smile graces his lips before he pulls me in again, firmer this time, his hands moving to grip my waist and pull me closer until I'm flush against him.

I part my lips and an unexpected moan escapes my mouth, inviting him in.

And *my goodness* does he take that invitation.

He starts off with light, torturously unhurried glides, exploring my mouth, but as soon as I tug on his tongue, hungry for more, the atmosphere shifts around us, the kiss growing deeper, harder and more desperate.

Warmth fills my chest as I reach up and embed my hands in his hair, tugging slightly on the soft strands, a small groan falling out of his mouth as I do so. His hands begin to explore my body, one coming up to stroke my arm, the other descending lower, possessively tracing my gentle curves.

'Oh jeez, sorry man,' comes the same deep voice from before as I hear the curtain open and close again instantaneously. My hands leave Milosh's hair and come to cup his face, as his hands rest on my hips. Milosh continues to kiss me for a moment longer before slowly pulling back.

'Turns out, people hate PDA,' he whispers softly against my mouth, Russian forgotten. 'Good job, baby.'

We pull apart and he takes his thumb and runs it across my lips, his eyes darkening as he tracks the movement.

Something about the way he says *baby*, his sexy Bulgarian accent thick, makes me pull him in again, crashing my lips against his in desperation and haste, my hands exploring his chest this time. 'I can still hear him,' I lie into his mouth. I don't know if I'm ever going to kiss this man again so I might as well make it last.

He catches on quickly, bringing his hands up to my face, his gentle stroking of my cheek at odds with his commanding, dominating tongue. All too soon I slow it down and break away, instantly feeling a sense of emptiness.

Our breaths are heavy and staggered as we stare at each other, taking in what just happened now that the haze is lifting. 'We need to get out of here,' Milosh says, switching back to Russian, his eyes dark as they drink me in. I shift under his gaze as that same heat starts rushing back to my stomach. He pulls out his phone and fires off a text before pocketing it again. 'There are three emergency exits in this part of the mall, but we need to exit through the front of this store in order to get to any of them.' He switches back into bodyguard mode with ease, checking his phone again when it vibrates.

'Henry is gonna meet us outside the emergency exit and someone else will come to get your car later. Keep your head down, follow me and stay quiet. Only Russian and no real names.'

'Okay,' is all I can reply as my mind works a mile a minute to process what he's saying.

'Daphne, this is important. I need you to listen to me, okay?' He cups the side of my head, bringing my attention back to him. 'Look down, hold my hand and walk fast. No English and no names. Yes?'

'Yes . . . Yeah, okay.' I clear my throat and properly refocus. I would prefer to get out of this mall alive so now's definitely not the time to lose focus. He breaks the security tags off the clothes, before piecing them back together and placing them in the tote bag on the floor, so the alarm won't sound. 'Wait, what about our clothes and all the stuff I bought earlier?'

'We need to leave them here.'

'Oh, okay.' I'm not too sure why I'm sad. I know Daddy will buy them back for me but it just feels like a shame.

'We'll get everything back, okay?' Milosh's voice is

oddly comforting and I start to feel at ease, giving him a small nod. 'All right, let's go.' He looks back down at his phone. 'Henry's five minutes away.' He takes my hand in his and guides me through the store, exiting via the children's section, just to be safe. With both of us wearing glasses, our new outfits and my hair down, we're pretty hard to recognize. Apart from the fact that we're a pretty distinctive bulky white guy and dainty black girl combo. And the fact I've still got my very pink sandals on with my very dull, very stolen outfit doesn't help. Keeping up with Milosh's long strides is okay at first, but the faster he moves the more I have to work sustain his pace.

'Mi . . .' I stop, remembering what he told me about names. '*Rodnoj*,' I say instead, gaining Milosh's immediate attention. '*Slishkom bystro.*' I smile weakly as he slows down a little, still walking with purpose but at a more manageable speed. '*Spasibo.*' He turns to look at me and gives me a small lopsided smile, and I think it's the first time I've seen him properly smile. I've never used the nickname darling in Russian before, but if it results in smiles like that I'd happily do it over and over again. I need more. The way his lips tip up, light crinkles gathering around his eyes, makes me want to stretch up and kiss him again.

Whoa.

Nope.

154

Not doing that.

That kiss was an act. It wasn't real, it was just a diversion, but goodness was it one heck of a show. I shake off my thoughts and focus, but just as I do, someone bumps into me. If it weren't for Milosh grabbing me quickly I would have ended up on the floor.

'Sorry, miss,' the culprit says, but he's not looking at me. He's looking at my feet. My sandals, to be exact. Milosh and I seem to realize at the same time because, after a quick nod, we both start picking up speed again.

'He's following us,' Milosh says quietly, spotting the guy's reflection in a shop window.

'We need to lose him quickly,' he continues, pulling me through another shop and exiting out the other side, momentarily losing the man behind us. He hauls me into a small maintenance room at the side of the shop, leaving the light off. We stay completely silent for a moment, the only sound coming from the rise and fall of our chests as we catch our breath.

'The emergency exit is about thirty seconds away.' This close, I can feel his warm breath caressing my skin, bringing me back to the kiss that happened only moments past but somehow feels like a lifetime ago. So much has happened since we entered the mall, my brain is working overtime trying to place everything. 'We're gonna wait here a moment then we're gonna run. And I need you to really run, okay baby?'

'Mm hmm.'

He grabs my hand. 'Good girl.'

I have no time to process what just came out of his mouth because he immediately yanks open the door, the light outside almost blinding me with its brightness, and starts to run. Well, it's more like a jog for him, but I'm running – and that's not an easy feat in sandals. We reach the exit and emerge into a corridor, closing the door behind us. Milosh looks around and finds a discarded construction pipe on the floor, shoving it between the handles to secure the door.

Fire hazard? Yes.

Does he care? Not in the slightest, apparently.

He takes my hand again, at the same time pulling out his phone, before guiding me down the corridor that leads out onto the road. We pick up our pace again as we emerge onto the street, where Henry's car is now in view.

'Let's go,' Milosh says, opening the door to the back seat for me, before sliding in next to me.

'Daphne, sweetie, why is it that I can't leave you alone for a second without something happening?' Henry says from the front as he performs a quick U-turn, driving in the complete opposite direction to the house.

'Honestly, Henry, I don't know,' is all I can muster before I switch off as Milosh begins to explain what just happened. I can feel my adrenaline crashing as I close my eyes and try to steady my breathing. The combination of Milosh's deep, almost melodic voice and the soft hum of the engine lulls me to sleep before I can resist.

17

It always starts the same.

I'm running down the stairs to the basement, trying to avoid being caught up past my bedtime. I head into the pantry in the prep kitchen on a mission to find my favorite late-night snack, Manzanilla olives with crushed peppercorn and seasalt crisps.

I drag over a footstool, feeling unusually short, and reach up to retrieve the jar. Once I have it secured I make for the crisps but as I grab them with my left hand, the olives in my right, I am abruptly stopped by a loud thud echoing through the prep room.

Clasping the jar to my chest, I wait in anticipation for the owner of those footsteps to find me.

When a few moments pass, with my chest still heaving, I hear another thud, harder yet further away this time. Jumping off the stool I set the olives down on the counter and go to hide behind the door. I don't know how long I stay there, but once it sounds like the coast is clear I slowly open the door and make my way to the stairs. The renovation team was here earlier in the day, I think, maybe it was some of their tools that fell, causing the thuds?

Before I can reach the stairs I hear a soft muffled whimper coming from the soon-to-be swimming room. With the curiosity and confidence of the character that dies first in a horror movie, I move closer to the sound and stop when I see a bound man on his knees, blood dripping from his face and neck, his bare arms bruised and bleeding.

'Interesting how such a strong, proud man can end up in such precarious positions,' I hear a female voice say as she walks towards him. With the lighting so dim and her back turned to me I can't make out any of her features, but I notice something metal in her left hand, glinting in the moonlight seeping in from the lightwell in the hallway.

'Look at you,' she says, disdain dripping from her voice. She uses the metal object to tip up his chin as he continues to sniffle. 'You poor, disgusting, disgrace of a man.' She smashes the metal across his face, causing him to fall sideways.

A silent gasp pours out of my mouth.

It's a gun.

She has a gun.

A person has a gun in my basement and is torturing someone.

'Malcolm, we were supposed to do this together, you and me.' Her voice is shockingly sincere as she drops to her haunches. 'You weren't supposed to be the wild card. You were supposed to be the person I could depend on. But now, just because you're scared, you want to throw in the towel? Unfortunately for you, darling, that's not an option. I'm going to give you one last chance to tell me the truth. What did you find?'

From where I'm standing I can't see the expression on his face, but I hear the determination in his voice. 'I'm not going to tell you anything. Not any more. So, do your worst.'

'Malcolm,' the woman whines, 'please don't tell me this is all because of the child.'

A child? What child? And who in the world is Malcolm?

'No, it's not. I'm just choosing to do the right thing for once in my life.'

'That's admirable, it really is. But it's also rather disappointing, Malcolm, and frankly, rather embarrassing,' she says, mock pity soaking her voice. She gently runs her free hand over his bloody and now swollen face, before releasing a laboured sigh, striking him with the same hand she soothed him with. 'Well.' She perks up. 'I don't need

to remind you what happens to disappointments, do I?'
I can practically hear the smile in her voice. She stands
up and sets the gun down, out of Malcolm's reach, before
she retrieves a knife from her back pocket, twirling it
haphazardly in her hands.

Bending back down, she repositions Malcolm so he's
kneeling upright.

I shouldn't be here.

I shouldn't see this.

I turn to leave but stop when I hear a gasp. I look back,
only to find Malcolm staring right at me as the woman
plunges the knife into his chest. He drops lifelessly to the
floor, eyes still open.

All I can hear is white noise as I stumble over my feet
on my way up the stairs. I don't stop running until I'm up
the next flight of stairs and safely in my bed.

I've barely caught my breath when I hear footsteps
climbing the stairs. They come closer and closer and don't
stop until they're at my bedroom door.

I bury my head into the pillow, shaking violently as the
door opens and the footsteps enter the room.

'Daphne?'

My eyes burst open at the sound of a loud knock. I look
around and realize I'm lying on top of my bed, still wearing
the mismatched clothes from our eventful shopping trip.

My bedroom door creaks open and my father walks in tentatively, smiling gently when he sees that I'm awake.

'Hi, darling, I just came to check on you.' He comes to sit on the end of my bed, still hesitant.

'Hi, Daddy,' I whisper as I start to adjust.

It was just a nightmare. It wasn't real. Sitting up in my bed I look over to him. 'How did I get upstairs?'

'Well, Henry was driving around aimlessly after he came to get you and Milosh, just to make sure there was no one following you, and you ended up falling asleep in the car. Milosh carried you up and you've been asleep for about,' he breaks to look at his watch, 'six hours.'

Six hours? Milosh carried me upstairs?

I look at the clock beside me, shocked to see it reads 8:40 p.m. I think back to the car journey and I honestly can't remember a thing.

Huh.

Milosh carried me upstairs.

My mind involuntarily takes me back to the feel of his strong, warm arms wrapped around me when we kissed, noting that those same strong warm arms carried a very unconscious me out of the car, through the house, up the stairs and to my bed, all without waking me.

Forget about how cleverly he got us out of the shopping centre, that was the really impressive feat.

'Daphne, I'm so sorry.' Daddy sighs, bursting my thought bubble.

'What are you talking about?'

'I told you to go. I told you to go shopping, and now look. You nearly got attacked – kidnapped even. If anything happened to you, I wouldn't know what to do with myself—'

'But it didn't,' I interrupt, moving down my bed to place my hand over his. He looks at me in shock, probably because this is the first time I've got remotely close to him in weeks. 'Other than my favourite dress and a few new pieces still being at the mall, nothing happened, Daddy. Milosh got us out and away from there before anything could.'

'Yes, but it could've, Daph. That's the point. I wasn't thinking properly when I suggested you go. Milosh warned against it, but did I listen? No.'

'Stop trying to blame yourself,' I demand. 'Realistically, I was gonna go shopping whether you endorsed it or not, so it's really not your fault at all. And if you think about it, you're the one who hired Milosh. So technically you saved me with your forward thinking.' I shrug.

I watch him as he looks down at his hands, shaking his head.

'Daddy.' I pause, considering whether I really want to

ask this question. We've just got to an okay place, do I really want to cause another argument due to how cagey my father is whenever I ask him a question?

'Yes, darling?' he prompts when I don't continue.

Just rip off the Band-Aid, Daphne. 'Why is this happening?' I ask, looking at him cautiously for a response. When I don't get one, all my unfiltered thoughts start seeping out. 'I mean, it just doesn't make sense. These people break into the offices and labs of you and your co-workers, but to my knowledge only break into our house. Then they rifle through your study but end up trying to strangle me. Then I innocently go shopping, and someone tries to kidnap me. What do they want with me? I don't even know who they are.'

My father looks at me blankly for a moment, so blankly that I start to think he wasn't even listening, until life starts flooding back into his face. Holding so much emotional intensity it almost startles me.

He starts to shake his head slowly, once again refusing eye contact. 'Daphne, I—'

'Please,' I interrupt him, 'please just tell me the truth. And please don't get angry at me for asking these questions. I have the right to know what's going on, especially seeing as I seem to be the one who's been the most affected.'

'No, you're right, you deserve the truth.' After a short

exhale, as if to brace himself for the story he's about to tell, he begins. 'These people are after our money.'

'What do you mean?'

'At work, people had been getting these notes, rather threatening notes, demanding money or someone they love will get hurt, but none of us listened. When you're in a certain tax bracket you get used to the empty threats that always seem to come across your desk. But these threats were anything but empty. There's an organization called Davecno that has a weird Robin Hood complex where they want to steal from the rich but give only to themselves. These are the people who ransacked my work office and broke into our house. When I didn't give them what they wanted they chose to take things into their own hands and scare me into submission. But no more. I've been talking to the police and they've been building a case against them for a while now. We just have to sit tight and wait for the police to do their job, but in the meantime Henry and I have hired some more men to protect the house. I'm sorry, but as of right now you can't leave the house. You're able to go to the charity gala in a few weeks, because it will have heavy security anyway. But other than that, nothing. Just until this is resolved.'

'Okay, thank you for sharing that with me. I really do

'appreciate it.' He offers me a small smile before lifting himself off my bed, preparing to leave.

'Really, Daddy.' I get up off my bed and walk round it so I'm standing right in front of him. 'Thank you for your honesty.' I wrap my arms around his waist and we share our first hug in weeks.

I like that we're okay now.

I hate arguing with my father, but if he's actually embracing the whole honesty thing I know that we can work through all of this.

I let go of him and he walks towards the door in silence, pausing as his hand goes to turn the knob. 'Daphne, everything I do, have done and will do, is for you. I love you, darling, and no matter what happens that will never change.' He leaves swiftly without giving me a chance to respond, the door closing with a soft thud behind him.

I walk into my dressing room and pull open the drawer containing my mother's things. 'Gosh, I wish you were here,' I whisper as I reach down to retrieve her necklace. 'You'd know what to do.'

I drape the necklace around my neck, securing the clasp, before I go and pick out a swimming costume.

After today, and the news that my father just told me, I need to be anywhere but in my own head, and swimming has always seemed to help with that. You would think that

I'd hate swimming given what happened to my mother, but the first and probably best thing my father did after she drowned was force me into swimming lessons to strengthen my technique and ability.

I hated it at first, not understanding why I had to do it, but I truly believe if he hadn't done that I would've grown up with a fear of water.

But I love it. It's so freeing and relaxing and oddly helps me feel closer to my mother.

I know she wouldn't have wanted me to grow up fearing the thing she loved the most, so I choose to enjoy it. For her.

I pull on a white swimming costume, shrugging on my pink silk robe over the top to hide the necklace, and make my way to the basement. My father rarely uses the pool so I know he won't be there to see the locket.

'Hi, Daph,' Amelia says when I walk into the kitchen to pick up some blueberries and water to take downstairs with me. I look over to the end of the kitchen where Amelia and Henry are sat in the breakfast nook, eating their dinner. 'I didn't know you were awake. Would you like some dinner? I think Josh left you a plate.'

'I'm good for now, but thank you for offering,' I respond, retrieving the berries from the fridge and heading for a bowl.

'How are you feeling, sweetie?' Henry asks.

'I'm fine, Henry,' I say sincerely, turning around to give them my full attention. 'Thank you for coming to get us today. I really appreciate it.'

'Daph, part of my job is to ensure your safety. You were in danger, so I did my part. Milosh did all of the heavy lifting.'

Yeah, I can't disagree with him there. Without Milosh I definitely wouldn't have made it back home.

'Hey, random question,' Henry starts, a sly smile emerging on his lips. 'How did he get you out of that changing room? I know that you went in there to change your clothes but wasn't one of those guys hot on your heels? How did you get out? I wasn't fully listening in the car.'

'Oh.' I clear my throat, the memory of what happened in that changing room flooding back to me all at once. 'Um, well, w-we just distracted him and then left.'

I return my focus to the blueberries and start picking out the nice-looking ones to put into my bowl.

'And how did you distract him, again?' Amelia asks innocently enough, but I know if I look up right now I'll see an irksome smirk on her face, and another on Henry's.

'We just did.' I shrug, still keeping my eyes glued to the blueberries as if they're the most fascinating fruit in existence.

'Okay,' Henry probes, 'but paint us a picture, I want to feel as if I was there.'

No, you really do not.

'We pretended we were a couple to make the guy feel uncomfortable so he would leave without properly looking at our faces.' I blurt. They're going to hear the story anyway, so I might as well tell them now.

'Huh,' Henry says and I can practically hear the smile in his voice as I make my way over to the sink to give the blueberries a rinse. 'And how exactly did you pretend you were in a relationship, Daph?'

I finally look over to face them and I've never seen anyone more fascinated. They've both got the most ridiculous grins on their faces while still trying to feign innocence.

'We just did, okay?'

'Daph,' Amelia says, dragging out my name, 'did you kiss Milosh?'

I don't even know what to call what we did. Yes, technically it would be classed as kissing, but it felt like so much more.

It felt deeper, more meaningful and intimate.

Even though it was fake, it felt anything but.

When I don't reply, Amelia lets out a small, satisfied giggle. 'I'll take that back rub now, along with my thirty pounds.' I look over at them to see Henry shaking his head and reaching for his wallet while Amelia gloats.

'You two bet on me?'

'No, we bet on you and Milosh,' Amelia corrects.

'That's literally the same thing,' I deadpan. 'What was the bet?'

'Meels was certain that you two would get together within two months, whereas I said it would take three,' Henry explains.

'Milosh and I are not together, we just had to play a role to stay safe.' I sigh.

'Okay, well, let me ask you this,' Amelia says. 'Did you enjoy it?'

I look down at my berries, wishing I was anywhere else but here. 'It was an act. There was nothing to enjoy.'

Lie.

'Oh, come on, Daph. You really expect us to believe that?' Henry quips. 'He's a good-looking guy, and you're a good-looking girl. You two have more chemistry than me and Amelia, and I honestly didn't even think that was possible.'

'It's not,' I confirm. 'And we don't. We were simply trying to get out of a precarious situation, which just so happened to result in a small kiss. That's all. Nothing else to it. So, Meelie, you can give Henry his money back and end this bet because it's not going to happen.'

Who in the world am I trying to kid?

Them? Because that sure isn't working.

Me? That sure isn't working either.

I've had very limited kissing experience in my life but that one definitely topped them all. Whether it was under duress or not.

'You heard the woman, give me back my money,' Henry teases as I start to head out of the kitchen.

'Sorry, Hen, no can do,' Amelia answers, sliding the money into her back pocket before standing up with their finished dinner plates in hand.

'Well, if you're not gonna give it, I'm just gonna have to come over there and take it from you.' He stands up slowly and stalks over to her, giving her enough time to put the plates down before he picks her up, earning a squeal from her and a faster walking pace from me.

The situation between Milosh and me is clearly forgotten as soon as he gets his hands on her, but that's absolutely fine with me.

If they'd probed me about that kiss once more I might've blurted out how it really felt.

And we can't have that.

Honestly, I don't even know how I feel about it, only that I want to do it again.

18

MILOSH

I finish another lap of the pool and swim up to the edge, running back through the events of the day. Today was an absolute mess in all kinds of ways. That kiss being the messiest of all.

'Good job, baby.' Why the hell did I say that?

At the start of the trip, when we agreed on the whole fake relationship thing, she was stiffer than a board, but throughout the day she really relaxed into it, leading me to second-guess if any of it was real.

And then there was that kiss.

Her lips were softer than I ever could've imagined, and her taste? A delicate mix of mint and sugar. That little moan she let out when her hands were buried in my hair had me suppressing a growl of satisfaction, and left me aching for more. We both knew that guy had gone, but when she pulled me back into that kiss everything melted away, our whole situation forgotten. It was just me, her and our wandering hands.

I honestly don't know how I restrained myself. Everything about her beckons me. Her honeyed voice, her soft chestnut skin, her kind heart, her regal face with those plump lips, honestly, I could go on forever. I mean, don't even get me started on how her body felt beneath my touch.

She's one heck of an actress, too, because the way she was looking at me made me believe it was real, and had me ready to risk it all, job be damned. But I had to swiftly regain control to get us out of that situation safely. How anyone could want to hurt her is beyond me. But they did, and I had to get her out of there.

As I was taking Henry through what happened, leaving out a few minor details, she fell asleep. Her head rested gently on the window and her chest rose and fell steadily. She even sleeps with poise.

When I picked her up out of the car, she instantly curled into me, with one hand coming to rest on my chest. I felt such an overwhelming need to place a gentle kiss on her head, but when I looked over and saw Henry looking between us with a stupid smirk on his face, I decided against that.

Job. Her.

Employee. Me.

Blur the lines and you get a stupid decision waiting to happen.

I dunk my head under the water, holding my breath, trying to clear my head. I blurred the lines so viciously today, and now I truly don't know where we stand or how I feel. But what I do know is that my actions kept Daphne safe, so ultimately I'm not too fussed.

'Oh, Mr Petrov, I didn't know you were down here.' I hear muffled words from above me. I surface and look up to find Daphne standing there in her robe, her straight hair in a sleek ponytail, holding a bowl of blueberries.

She must have had another nightmare.

'I was just finishing up,' I say as I make my way out of the pool.

'Please don't leave on my account, the pool is big enough for both of us.'

'You had another nightmare?' I ask, changing the subject, walking towards her.

She looks at me, confused for a second, before glancing down to the bowl in her hands, a wave of understanding washing over her. 'Uh . . . Yes, yeah.'

'You wanna talk about it?'

Yeah, Milosh, great idea. Getting her to open up even more will definitely help with the already blurred lines.

Smart man. Really, I should give myself an award or something.

She shakes her head as I silently breathe out a relieved

sigh. 'Thank you, really.' She gives me that small, sweet smile, before dipping her head again. 'But, no, I just want to take my mind off of everything.' I don't miss how her eyes peruse my bare chest, my body heating as her eyes pass over me.

'Okay,' I say in response and walk past her to grab a towel. The Greens have a fully functional mini spa and gym down here with a sauna, steam room, heated pool and workout equipment, with amenities better than any gym I've ever been to.

A mini fridge is stocked with cool, damp washcloths that smell of essential oils. Next to it is a cupboard full of warm, fluffy white towels of varying sizes, with grazing snacks and a variety of beverage options laid out in the corner of the room.

It's all absolutely unnecessary, but I'm not complaining. Going from basic military-grade training facilities to this highlights just how different mine and Daphne's worlds truly are.

I hear her enter the pool behind me as I take out a towel from the cupboard. I walk back over to the chair where I left my belongings, using the towel to dry my damp hair, and look over to the pool where Daphne is doing laps.

She has a clean, concise technique, swimming with conviction and drive. She's wearing a white swimsuit, and the contrast of the stark white against her brown complexion is so strikingly beautiful. Although at this point I'm not sure there's a colour she couldn't pull off.

Sitting down, I grab my phone and scroll to check if Major Davis has messaged me back with any information about the two Daveeno members at the mall. As I begin to read through his response, the previously calm and consistent sounds of Daphne moving through the water turn rushed and sporadic. I shoot up from my seat on high alert as I see Daphne chaotically lurching around the pool, not swimming but not walking either. Kind of a weird mix of the two.

'Miss Green,' I say loudly so she can hear me over all of the splashing. 'Miss Green.' I try again, a little louder this time. 'Miss Green, what are you doing?' She looks up at me, her expression laced with panic.

'My necklace,' she splutters, splashing water everywhere. 'The necklace I had on fell off and I can't find it.'

'Get out of the pool,' I say calmly.

'What?'

'Get out of the pool so you can get a clearer view.' She stares at me a moment, considering if there's any validity to what I'm saying. Evidently she decides there is, as she walks to the edge of the pool and hoists herself out. I avert my eyes, because now, with no water as a barrier, every part of her perfect body is on display. I don't want her to feel uncomfortable – she clearly thought she was going to be down here alone – and I've never seen her in such little clothing, so I bring my eyes back to the pool, intently watching the water settle.

'What does your necklace look like?'

'It's gold, with a locket,' Daphne replies, coming to stand next to me. Somehow, even after being in the pool, I can still smell that sweet, innately feminine scent of hers.

'You should take it off next time.'

'What an astute observation, thank you, Mr Petrov,' Daphne bites out. I hold in a laugh because, yeah, I like her princessy put-together side, but when she has a bit of a fire to her, with that dry sarcasm . . . ?

That's when she gets dangerous.

I spot a gold chain glinting in the water and without a second thought I dive in to retrieve it. It takes a moment for my eyes to adjust but when they do I scoop up the necklace and make my way back to the surface, shocked to see that Daphne is also back in the pool.

'Is this it?' I ask, holding out the necklace as she swims closer to me, nodding in relief.

'It's never fallen off before when I've been in the pool. I mustn't have clasped it properly.'

'Turn around,' I direct. She hesitates, then does what I ask, leaving me looking at her now extremely curly ponytail.

'Pick up your hair for me,' I say softly, and she does, revealing her slim, delicate neck.

I thread my arms through hers in order to get the necklace into position. This close, I can see the delicate rise and fall of her chest and hear her shallow breaths as I fasten the clasp. I tug on it gently, making sure it's secure, and lower it back down carefully, my fingers brushing the base of her neck.

'There,' I say when I'm finished.

'Thank you,' she whispers, turning around to look up at me, her hands snaking around her neck to check on the clasp.

I spend a moment taking her in, revelling in the fact that I'm one of the few people that get to see her like this. Her once-tight, straight ponytail has loosened from the force of the water, giving way to a relaxed one that holds her now tight curls, with a few loose tendrils framing her face. The water droplets that accent her face lead my gaze down to her defined collarbones. But I don't allow my eyes to drop any further. Her face alone is all I can take right now.

'I like your hair,' I murmur before I can stop myself.

'Pardon?'

'I like your hair like this.'

She looks confused and taken aback for a second before replying, 'You like my hair messy and wet?'

'I like your hair curly,' I correct as I reach out and tuck a spiralling tendril behind her ear, feeling her gently shudder as I do. 'It looks pretty.' *You look pretty.*

Her warm mahogany eyes catch mine and her mouth parts ever so slightly.

'Can I ask you a question?' Her voice is tentative as her shy side peaks through again.

'Mm hmm.'

'You said you're Bulgarian. How do you speak Russian so well?'

'There was a little boy in my old children's home who could only speak Russian, so while I was teaching him English I subconsciously started learning Russian from him, which was pretty easy because Russian and Bulgarian are such similar languages.'

Daphne nods, a warm smile dancing on her lips. 'I like learning more about you,' she breathes, so quietly I want to lean in and make sure I heard her right.

I don't respond to her statement, instead opting to flip the focus back to her. 'How do you know so many languages?'

'Well, I learned French and Mandarin at school. My cousin, Camilla, is deaf so the majority of my family knows sign language, and I went to an international private school, so one of my best friends is Russian. She taught me all I know.' She shrugs as if speaking five languages isn't impressive at all.

'Thank you again for today.' She looks down at her hands.

'You know, for everything when we were shopping and for after . . . when I was asleep.'

'Miss Green, you don't have to thank me for doing my job.'

'I do when you keep going above and beyond for me,' she counters, chewing her lower lip. My eyes involuntarily drop there, tracking the movement.

'Really, Milo.' My eyes jump back to hers when I hear her say that nickname again. 'I really do appreciate it. I don't even want to know what would've happened if you weren't there.'

'But I was, so you don't need to wonder. You're safe and back home, Miss Green.'

'Yeah,' she breathes. 'I guess so.'

More than anything I want to bring her mouth to mine and kiss the worry away, but I remind myself to re-establish some boundaries.

Kissing her was a two-time thing, and it can't and won't happen again.

She's the job. Keep her safe and walk away.

My eyes return to her necklace and I can't help but reach down and lift the metal off her skin, rubbing it between my fingers.

'It's pretty,' I murmur, trying to figure out if I've seen her wearing it before. It looks vaguely familiar.

'Thank you,' Daphne snips, a little too sharp.

'Did your dad buy it for you?'

'Yeah, he did,' she answers quickly. I let it fall gently back onto her skin.

'Hmm,' I hum. She's being cagey, but I don't have time to explore why. The lack of sleep is finally starting to catch up with me. 'I'm gonna go get some rest,' I inform her as I start to back away. 'Are you gonna be okay down here?'

When she told me earlier that she's been jumpy since the break-in it made me realize that I hadn't thought about any of this from her perspective. Getting attacked in your own home, your place of comfort and safety, must be awful. I've been in multiple situations where I've had to sleep with one eye open, always on guard, but Daphne hasn't. This is completely new territory for her and even though there's more security around the house I'd completely understand if she still felt unsafe.

'Yes, I'll be fine,' Daphne answers. 'I'm only gonna do a few more laps then I'm coming upstairs.'

I nod, swimming to the edge of the pool, concluding that I'll keep an eye on her through the security cameras until she's back in her room.

'Milosh?' Daphne starts when I grab my towel and throw it around my shoulders. I turn around to face her, to hear the rest of her question, but she shakes her head and offers me a small smile instead.

'Goodnight, Mr Petrov.'

'Goodnight, Miss Green.'

19

Daphne

'Come on, Miss Green,' Milosh goads, trapping me with his arms either side of my face.

His eyes trail down my body as he smirks. 'You can do better than that.' I huff as I wrap my legs around his waist, pushing at his arm until it gives way, using that momentum to roll us, leaving him on his back with me now on top of him, legs either side.

I smile, imitating a blow to his head, lightly tapping instead of actually punching so I don't hurt him. 'That was good, right?'

'It was better,' Milosh agrees as I go to swing my leg off him, but before I do he captures my thigh in one hand and my hip in the other, locking me in place. 'But if that punch didn't work, they would be able to use their very free hands to hold you in place, and you do not want that.' I momentarily tune him out, trying to level my breathing.

With the feel of his hands burning into my body, I become all too aware of our current position.

I'm straddling him. I'm straddling Milosh Petrov, pinning him down with my body, while his hands dig into my flesh.

This is inappropriate. Yes, I've had romantic interests before, but I've never really made it past kissing and this position suggests a whole lot more than that. But with it being his firm, warm body underneath mine, it makes me feel a little safer. He's not going to take advantage of me or the situation we're in. Actually, I'm ninety-nine per cent sure he's completely unaware of our position. He's in training mode, and if there's one thing I've learned about Milosh, it's that he's a professional.

'You need to disable them in every way and as fast as possible,' he continues, loosening his grip on me, signalling me to get up.

See? Professional.

'Restrict their arms and legs to prevent their movement and give you time to run away. Let's try this again with a few different scenarios.' He walks over to the table of assorted weapons, picks up a rubber replica of a knife and tucks it into the waistband of his cargos.

'What I want you to do is jog up and down the length of the backyard. At some point I'm going to attack you and you're going to have to disarm me and run away. This time let's go with the pretence that once you have me where you want me and "knock me out", I pass out, giving you enough time to run away. We'll try different scenarios a number of times so you can get a better understanding of how to handle yourself in different situations.'

After we warmed up today, Milosh told me to put on some normal clothes so that I know what it's like to fight someone if I'm caught off guard, so I'm currently wearing a light pink flowy dress with my hair up in a curly ponytail and he's wearing his usual black T-shirt and cargos combination.

'Okay.' I nod. 'I'm ready.'

He nods in return and I take off in a light jog towards the end of the garden. Our back garden is vast, with trees lining the bottom overlooking a heavily wooded area, but a tall fence divides that section from our well-manicured lawn. It takes me a couple of minutes to actually reach the far end, but before I can turn to jog back up an arm clamps around me, locking me in and pulling my back close to the attacker's front.

Inhaling, I instantly feel at ease, recognizing Milosh by his clean, warm scent. I know he won't actually cause me any harm, but that doesn't stop him from securing his arm around my neck. I start to panic, thinking back to the last time I was in this position, but unfreeze when I remember it's only Milosh.

Before he clamps his arms around my neck, I bring my hands, palms facing outwards, to my throat, ensuring he can't cut off my oxygen supply.

I push to try to break free from his arm, but that proves useless because he's too strong. *Arms and legs.* I think back to what Milosh taught me about restricting movement, and swiftly wrap my leg around the bottom of his, pulling forward, causing him to lose balance for a second, resulting in a looser grip around my neck.

I break free and turn round to face him. Milosh has recovered quickly from the minor imbalance and now has the rubber knife in his hand.

'Good job, Daphne.' The mix of his praise and him using my first name gives me the encouragement I didn't realize I needed as he slowly approaches. 'Now, you need to get this knife off me, and defuse the situation.'

He strikes first, but I use my speed and co-ordination to dodge him, or so I think, until the knife pokes the side of my waist before flattening against just under my ribs. 'That would've been non-lethal, so continue, but slow your movements down because if this were real, you'd be hindered by the pain.'

I nod, adjusting my speed while still trying to evade

the knife. He aims for my side again but I move forward and capture his hand in my arm, twisting it until the knife drops. I kick the crevice at the back of his knee, which makes him buck, but not enough to fall. When I go to try again he beats me to it, swiping with his other leg, knocking me to the ground. I fall with a thud, looking up to see a flash of discomfort in his eyes when I wince in pain. I know he would've supported my fall if I hadn't asked him not to at the start of practice today.

If this was real, my attacker wouldn't care about my safety so I need to prepare for that, not be coddled.

Milosh picks the knife up from the ground and walks over to me. 'Whoever you're fighting will determine what happens next. A lot of men are stupid and they'll take their time walking over to you, taunting you as much as they can. Women are usually a lot smarter and will either throw the knife from a distance, or use their speed to quickly slit your throat. We'll go through all scenarios later, but for now let's play into the whole cocky guy thing.'

He sinks onto his haunches and runs the knife across my face. 'You do have a very pretty face, Daphne,' he murmurs, dragging the knife down my neck lightly. I reach out and grab his feet, jerking them forward, causing him to drop to the floor with a thud.

I shoot up and knock the knife out of his hands, kicking

it even further away. Before he can move, I straddle him again, locking him in, my knees pressed tightly against his obliques.

'My arms are still free, Miss Green. Do something about it.'

I push his arms up over his head and press them into the ground, pinning him by his wrists. My body is now completely flush to his, once again, only this time his mouth is just centimetres away from mine.

'Yeah . . .' he breathes, looking from my eyes to my mouth, his jaw clenching. 'Don't do that.'

Feeling bold, I lower my lips to graze his earlobe. 'You told me to do something about it, Mr Petrov, and I did just that.' I release my tight hold on his wrists and trace my fingers down his arms languidly, but I don't make it very far because he abruptly sits up, causing me to fall into his lap. His strong arm clasps my waist to steady me.

'Looks like we're gonna have to go over how to restrict the arms again,' he bites out as I roll off him and stand up, trying and failing to contain my laugh. He stands up and walks to retrieve the knife.

'I don't know what you're talking about.' I blink up innocently. 'I feel like I did a very good job.'

He turns around to look at me, his gaze darkening. 'Oh, you did a good job, Miss Green.' He closes the distance between us and lifts my chin up with one finger to look me dead in the eye.

I blink up again, flustered, as I feel my heart rate increase when he dips his mouth to my ear, his lip grazing the sensitive skin. 'You did a great job, in fact. But don't be so light with your fingers.' His hand starts travelling up the length of my arm with the lightest touch. 'That's too nice. Too cute. Too kind.' His touch starts to roughen, getting firmer, travelling back down my arm, stopping at my wrist as he places it behind my back with one hand. Firm and in control. 'I need you to be more certain. More demanding,' he murmurs. 'More rough.' My other hand flies to his chest for stability as he pushes me so we're once again flush against each other. He lifts his head away from my ear to bore those green irises into mine. 'Can you do that for me, Miss Green?'

All I can do is nod, as he smirks. 'Good.' He instantly drops my hands and moves away, walking back to the top of the garden where the table of weapons stands. 'Let's move on to the next scenario.'

I open the door to my dressing room, ready to get my things for a shower, only to be greeted by two women and a rack of pink, white and cream dresses that I do not recognize.

'You must be Daphne!' the blond girl on the right determines in a perky American accent.

'Yes . . . can I help you?'

'We're here for the dress fitting,' responds the beautiful Asian woman standing next to the dress rack. She's definitely American too, but her accent sounds a lot more refined.

'I'm sorry, what dress fitting?' I didn't organize a dress fitting.

'You weren't able to shop for a dress, so I brought the dresses to you.' I turn around at the sound of Milosh's voice behind me. He's leaning against the door frame looking irritatingly unperturbed.

'You organized this for me?' I walk towards him, the ladies in the back completely forgotten.

'Mm hmm,' is his simple response before he looks over to the two girls behind me. 'Daphne, this is Averie Lee and Hallie Valentine. Hallie was in the same children's home as me. She and Averie run a personal styling business in Connecticut, but they're over here visiting an international client so I asked if they could stop by.'

'Oh, wow.' I turn back to Averie and Hallie, a genuine smile blooming. 'That's amazing, thank you so much!'

'Of course,' Hallie replies. 'Anything for Milosh!' I look between them as a sour taste enters my mouth. Hallie is stunning, with long sandy-blond hair cascading down her back in messy but sexy waves. She's wearing a simple black tank top and some matching black slim-cut jeans but she somehow makes it look like the most fashionable outfit I've ever seen. Her tan, short red nails and minimal make-up help her look effortlessly sexy and cool, but still professional.

If I had to pick out a girl who would pair nicely with Milosh, it would be her. They would look *great* together.

Therefore, I'm not a fan. Especially with the way she's currently looking at him.

'You ready to get started, Daphne?' Averie chirps, dragging my attention back to the present.

'Um . . . yeah, sure.' I look back over to Milosh, who's already looking at me. 'Did you want to stay, so you can give me your opinions on the dresses?'

'You want me to stay?' He frowns and I suddenly feel I may have crossed an invisible line I didn't know was there, but, hey, it's a bit too late to backtrack now.

'Mm hmm,' I hum. 'Oh, and could you call Amelia in? I feel like she may want to see them too.'

'I'll go get her.'

'Thank you.' I give him a soft smile as I place my hand on his forearm, giving it a little squeeze before he nods curtly and heads out of the room, closing the door softly behind him. I turn back to Averie and Hallie only to find them grinning hugely.

'Oh, I soooo get it now.' Hallie smirks at me.

Letting out an extremely forced laugh I ask, 'What are you talking about?'

'You and Milosh! You're literally the cutest couple ever!'

Okay, see, now I'm confused. Is she being condescending? No, I don't think so, her tone was too genuine.

'We're not together,' I clarify, walking in front of the rack where they're standing.

'Yeah, sure you're not,' Averie says, rolling her eyes playfully, flicking her jet black hair out of her face. She has such an old Hollywood way about her with how she moves, talks and looks. She definitely comes from money, and she is absolutely stunning.

'I'm sorry, but what made you think we were together?' I ask, genuinely curious.

Averie and Hallie exchange the same knowing look that Amelia and Henry did last night when they asked about the kiss. 'What?' I breathe a laugh out, slightly apprehensive about what they may say.

'Daphne,' Hallie starts. 'Just the fact that Milosh was honest with you about how he met me tells me everything I need to know. He told you he was in care. He doesn't share that with anyone, least of all clients.'

'And,' Averie adds softly, 'have you seen the way that man looks at you? And vice versa? Daphne, I'm sorry that you're evidently the last one to know, but you guys clearly like each other.'

'I mean, I've known him since he was twelve, and I've never seen him look at a girl the way he was just looking at you. Not through many girls' lack of trying, though,' Hallie laughs. 'I was fourteen when he came to the home and it was so funny to see the younger girls tripping over themselves to get his attention. Then when he joined school it was even worse. Every girl in his grade and even the grade above wanted a shot with him, but he paid them no mind. When he got older and both of us moved out he stayed in contact with me, so I know he did entertain a few small flings, but nothing like this.'

'And what is "this" exactly?' I question.

'This.' Hallie gestures between the door and me. 'You, him, whatever you wanna call it. You may be his client, but the way he looks at you is anything but professional. The way you two talk to each other *alone* is absolutely laced with tension.' Hallie sighs wistfully.

'How about we get back on to the dresses?' Averie suggests, and I silently thank her with my eyes as we all look to the portable clothing rack.

There are around ten gowns on it. Some I've seen recently on the runway while others are completely new to me.

'These dresses are just my style. Goodness, you girls are good at your job!' I commend.

'Daphne, we didn't pick these out. Milosh did,' Hallie says with that same knowing look. 'We sent him, like, fifty options. All different colours and styles, but he was adamant that these ones were more you.'

I look back at the dresses through a new lens. They're all either light pink, white or cream, with classic feminine lines, and are soft, light and girly rather than overly sensual or seductive. That's my style completely.

'Milosh chose all of them individually?' I ask, my voice small as I feel the fabrics beneath my fingers.

'Mm hmm,' Averie replies. 'And judging by your fantastic closet, by the way, it looks like he got it pretty spot on.'

Huh. Would you look at that?

Me and Milosh.

Milosh and I.

Mr Petrov and Miss Green

Daphne and Milosh.

No matter how I spin it, I seem to come to the same conclusion.

We sound great together.

20

MILOSH

'This was really nice of you, Milosh,' Amelia says, as we walk into Daphne's room. I simply nod as I go to sit down on the sofa by the window, leaving Amelia perched on the end of Daphne's bed.

I shouldn't be here.

I honestly shouldn't have called Hallie to bring the dresses for her. This is all becoming too much too fast and I seem to be continually forgetting the fact that I'm nothing but an employee to Daphne, and she's nothing but a job to me.

Well, should be at least.

I've never been so unprofessional before. Granted, none of my jobs were to protect a soon-to-be eighteen-year-old, whose face is like a painting you never want to look away from. A painting that people would travel miles to see for just a moment.

But still.

All of this is inappropriate. What happened this morning

was understandable because we were training. We were bound to end up on top of each other at some point. But actively calling a friend to see if they're around to help out, arranging travel plans and accommodation for them and picking out dresses I think she would like was stepping way over the line.

I'm supposed to be protecting her from Daveeno, not playing boyfriend.

She's the job. Nothing more. Nothing less.

Keep her safe and walk away.

'So,' Amelia asks, pulling me out of my thoughts, 'how's the training going?'

'Good. Miss Green is making good progress.'

'Hmm,' Amelia hums, nodding her head. I keep my face impassive while she studies me. 'So what kinds of things are you teaching her?'

'Why?' I respond, instead of answering her question. She has this weird look on her face, and I really don't want to find out why, because I know the answer will definitely annoy me.

'Oh, you know, I'm just curious.' She shrugs. 'Sometimes I see you two outside in the morning, and wonder what you're up to.' She eyes me, feigning innocence.

'Take this morning, for example. I got up early and saw you guys outside . . . training.' She drags out that last word.

'I mean, as I was looking out the window, I really thought to myself, what in the world are those two doing? So . . . that's why I ask.' She's now smiling at me. The same smile she had when I walked past her with Daphne in my arms, after the mall incident.

It's irritating and annoying, and if she didn't mean so much to Daphne, and her husband wasn't a complete psychopath about her, I'd probably shoot that smile right off her face.

With a paintball gun, though. I'm not a monster.

I think back to earlier today, and I completely understand why she's talking like this. Daphne was on top of me, multiple times. The memory of one of them now replaying in my mind in a constant loop.

Her hands travelling down my arms, her light breath feathering over my ear as she whispered into it, the feel of her heart beating so close to mine, her lips mere centimetres away from my mouth.

So plump. So kissable. So ready.

If she wasn't a client, I don't know what I would've done.

Actually.

Scratch that.

I know *exactly* what I would've done.

I know what I would've done with my hands, with her lips . . . with her body.

But one of us had to come to their senses so I got up and

moved on before I did something I'd thoroughly enjoy, but ultimately regret.

'We were working through different scenarios where she had to overpower me, take me down and disarm me,' I explain to Amelia stiffly.

'Oh, she was disarming something, all right,' she mutters under her breath as the door to the dressing room opens revealing Hallie, Averie and Daphne.

'Okay, first dress,' Hallie sings, as she and Averie take a seat next to Amelia on the bed. Daphne walks out wearing a cream floor-length dress. It's tighter at the top with a low yet modest neckline and puffs out slightly at the waist.

'Oooooh, Daph,' Amelia coos, 'this is gorgeous! What kind of hairstyle are you thinking?'

'I'm thinking soft fifties-style curls, maybe?'

'Oooh, yeah!' Averie nods enthusiastically. 'With gold jewellery, for sure.'

'What jewellery were you planning?' Hallie directs her words to Daphne.

'Well, I have a couple of Graff pieces. Let me go and get them to show you.' She disappears into her dressing room again as Hallie sighs.

'One day I'm going to have my own Graff collection casually lying around in my walk-in closet.'

'Yeah,' Averie agrees, 'we both will.'

'Oh, shut up, Av.' Hallie rolls her eyes. 'Your brother's loaded, just ask for some for Christmas.'

Averie just laughs in response before turning her attention to me. 'So, Milosh.' Amelia and Hallie turn to look at me as well, both with that stupid smirk on their faces. 'What do you think of the dress you picked out for Daphne? Does it look the way you imagined?'

Just as Averie finishes her sentence, Daphne walks out, five jewellery cases in hand.

Good timing, baby.

'Okay, so I have a white-and-yellow diamond necklace and an emerald diamond necklace from their high jewellery collection, and a few smaller pieces from their regular line, but I think I want to wear the white diamond necklace to this event.' She opens up the box and I hear a collective gasp from the girls as they bend in to look.

'What was this making up for, again?' Amelia asks Daphne.

'When Daddy forgot my birthday and worked right through it,' Daphne answers, and I feel a spike of anger. How could her father of all people forget her birthday and just buy her a necklace thinking that's gonna make up for it? Daphne takes the necklace out of the box delicately, and walks over to me.

'Milosh, can you help me put this on, please?'

I nod and stand, completely ignoring the stares from

the other side of the room, and focus on the necklace. I'm careful to clasp it tightly and securely, knowing full well this single piece of jewellery is worth more than I've ever made in a year.

'Beautiful,' I murmur low enough that only she can hear me, allowing my fingers to graze down her back for a split second, before I step back. Daphne turns around to show the others.

Hallie gawks. 'Perfect. No notes.'

'I'd have to agree with her,' Amelia chimes in.

'Me too.' Averie smiles softly. 'And what's great about this necklace is that it will definitely go with all of the dresses Milosh picked out.'

At the mention of my name, all four women look back over to me as if they just remembered I'm still here. 'What do you think?' Daphne asks, her eyes big and pure.

'You look good,' is all can say, because if I told her how I really felt . . . Now *that* would be inappropriate and would probably lead to me clearing everyone out of her room, throwing her on the bed and . . .

Okay.

That's a bit much for right now.

Or probably ever. So I just stick to, 'You look good,' to stay safe.

'Okay! This was a good start. Let's try you in pink next!'

Hallie chirps as the three of them make their way back into her dressing room, leaving me and Amelia alone again.

'You know,' Amelia says, breaking the silence after a few minutes, 'when Henry and I met, the reason it took us so long to actually get together was because of the internal struggle we both felt about the fact that it would be inappropriate.'

'What are you talking about?'

'Milosh, your eyes say what your mouth can't. And right now your eyes are speaking a thousand words.'

'Mrs Harris, I'm just doing my job. That's it.'

'Is this the job that requires you to kiss her? The job that requires you to protect her from her father's bad moods? The job that requires her to straddle you, and you her, under the guise of training?' Amelia laughs. 'You know, Henry and I used to make up the most ridiculous reasons to see each other, be close to each other, touch each other. We denied our feelings for so long we almost lost our chance together.'

'What exactly are you implying, Mrs Harris?'

'That you like her,' she whispers, not missing a beat. 'You like her, and from the looks of it, that feeling is very much mutual.'

'Daphne is just a job, Mrs Harris. That's all.'

'Yeah.' She nods sarcastically. 'Because you'd fly Hallie and Averie out for just any job, right?'

Before Amelia has a chance to say anything more, the

door opens again and Daphne steps out wearing the same huge diamond necklace but this time in a strapless baby pink dress with a slit running from her lower thigh to the floor.

She looks beautiful. Graceful, elegant . . . and hot.

Before anyone can say anything, we hear a muffled shout from downstairs. I cross the room in an instant and pull the door open to see if I can hear any better.

'George!' an unrecognizable male voice calls.

'Teddy?' Daphne whispers, frowning as she hurries past me, calling the name again on her way down the stairs.

'Miss Green,' I shout after her, ready to walk out before turning around to face Hallie and Averie. 'You two stay here.' My tone leaves no room for argument so they both nod as Amelia comes to join me.

'Who the hell is Teddy?' I ask Amelia, jogging down the stairs after Daphne. But before she can answer, Daphne comes back into view with George at her side as they make their way over to a curly-haired guy standing at the front door. His face is half covered but as soon as he turns around I hear two gasps.

'Teddy?' George gasps.

'Oh my gosh, Teddy, what happened to you?' Daphne says, her voice laced with concern as she reaches up to gently move his face to see the extent of his injuries.

The guy has a busted lip and is sporting a mean black eye. He's completely soaked even though it's sunny outside.

'I'm sorry, George,' Teddy breathes heavily, dropping a small duffel onto the floor. 'I didn't know where else to go.'

21

MILOSH

'Hand off her thigh, Teddy,' Henry instructs coolly as I walk into the snug. I look around the room and spot Teddy and Daphne on the couch, sitting way too close together for my liking.

She's holding a washcloth in her hand and is almost face to face with him. Amelia and Henry are sat opposite on the other couch, with a scowl etched onto Henry's face as he watches them.

Teddy's hand is still lingering on Daphne's leg so I clear my throat, letting my presence be known, and it's almost comical how fast Mr Build-A-Bear shrinks back.

Almost being the operative word.

Everything about this guy irritates me.

From his curly blond hair to his polo shirt and sweater combo, he oozes charm. His glasses frame his face, despite the black eye, and really help him lean into the whole Prince Charming look that I'm sure works real well with Daphne's princess girly vibe.

Physically, he looks a lot like Eddie, Daphne's cousin's boyfriend. But the big difference is, Eddie seemed like a decent guy.

Teddy is simply a dick.

After Teddy showed up, George took him to get changed into some dry clothes, while Amelia went to get Henry. Daphne got changed back into her regular clothes and I helped Hallie and Averie pack up and leave. I know before they left they agreed on a dress for Daphne, but I don't know which one it was.

'Stop moving,' Daphne sighs, dabbing the washcloth to the side of Teddy's mouth, her other hand gently holding his jaw in place.

'Sorry, sorry,' Teddy chirps, smiling at her, then wincing in pain.

Good.

'So, Teddy,' I say, and all at once four heads turn to me. I lean against the wall, slipping my hands into my pockets as I look at him. 'How exactly do you know Daphne and her father?'

My eyes involuntarily wander to Daphne as she starts nervously biting her lip.

'Well,' Teddy starts, 'I've known the Greens since I was a child. Spent way too many Christmases here. Our parents are close friends.' He motions between him and Daphne, grinning. 'And I actually started working with George this year as an apprentice, of sorts.'

As if on cue, George walks through the door holding a hot drink.

'Here you go, Teddy.' I don't miss the subtle tremor in George's hands as he places it onto the coffee table and takes a seat next to Henry. 'All right, now we're all here, Teddy, take us through what happened.'

'Well, when I got back home after my workout everything was ruined. My apartment had been completely ransacked, with torn books, flipped tables, broken glass – you name it. I ran to my bedroom to check what else had been damaged but when I opened the door there were two huge men waiting for me. I tried to run but they were fast and caught up with me.' Teddy takes a dramatic pause. I look over to Daphne to see her brows are knitted together in concern and empathy. Amelia and George have similar expressions. Henry, however, is sitting there looking completely unimpressed as if this is the most mundane story he's ever heard.

'They started punching and beating me,' Teddy continues, 'and I honestly didn't know why. I thought this was a home invasion and they were after my stuff, so why didn't they just take it and go?' As Teddy is speaking a fresh scab on his lip bursts, causing blood to start dripping down his face. Daphne is quick to catch it with the washcloth, holding it firmly to his face while her other hand rests on his shoulder.

'Thank you, Daph.' He directs to her with a small smile against the washcloth before continuing. 'Anyway, they clearly knocked me out because I woke up bound to a chair with them throwing water over my head.' He clears his throat, evading any eye contact and looking down to the floor. 'They started questioning me about . . . you, George, and were asking about your old job. I didn't know any of the answers to their questions but they kept b-beating me until they eventually realized I wouldn't be of any help to them.'

He blinks viciously, as if trying not to cry. 'Th-they left, leaving me bound to my chair, so I tipped myself over to break it and I was able to untie myself. Since they were asking about you I thought it best to grab some clothes and come straight over, to give you a warning. I don't want anything to happen to you or Daphne.' He looks over to her and her eyes soften.

'That must've been really scary for you, I'm so sorry.'

'Thanks, Daph, but it's really not your fault,' he responds, dropping his hand to her knee.

'Keep your hands to yourself, Ted,' I warn simply.

206

He removes them instantly as Henry tries to stop himself from laughing.

'What did these men look like?' I ask, trying to get us back on topic. The quicker this is sorted, the sooner Build-A-Bear can leave.

'It was two white guys. They looked like they could pass as bodybuilders and they both had leather gloves on. Also, when they took off their jumpers I spotted matching tattoos on their necks.'

'What did these tattoos look like?' George asks.

'I couldn't see very well but I think it was a skull with a chess piece on top of it.'

'Is that the same tattoo that the guy who broke into the house had?' Daphne asks quietly, looking at me. I nod, while Teddy gawks.

'Someone broke into your house?'

'Yeah,' Daphne whispers.

'This house?' Teddy presses, looking only at Daphne.

'Yes, Teddy, they did, now move on,' Henry bites out.

George stands up, looking uneasy, and starts pacing the length of the room. 'This is all my fault.' He starts chewing his nails.

'I don't understand,' Daphne speaks up. 'You said they're after your money, but then why would they hurt Teddy to get to you? If they wanted money, why didn't they just ask Teddy or his parents? And why do they want to know about your old job? What old job? You've only ever worked at Greenway.'

'Daphne, please stop with the questions.' Agitation laces George's tone as he continues to pace.

'Hey.' I cut in quickly, shaking my head.

He looks at me for a moment before taking a deep breath. 'Sorry, Daphne, that was rude of me.'

'Sir, you need to tell your daughter the truth. Now.' At that, he stops pacing entirely.

Is it my place to decide this for him? No.

Should I have said that? Probably not.

Am I mad that I did? Absolutely without a doubt no.

From the start, I haven't been keen on lying to Daphne while everyone else knows what's going on. She's seventeen years old, not ten. But it's not my place to tell her the whole story.

Well. Not until now. This Daveeno case has affected her more than anyone and she still doesn't know why? That's absolutely ridiculous, if you ask me.

George glares icily, as if to scare me.

'What do you mean, the truth?' Daphne questions before looking over to her father, realization washing over her. 'The explanation you gave me in my room was a lie. Wasn't it?'

He says nothing.

'Wasn't it?' she asks again, her voice rising slightly.

'Yes,' George responds weakly.

She nods slowly, taking a few deep breaths before lifting her head high, a mix of anger and determination on her face. 'Okay,' she starts, 'someone is going to tell me the truth about what's been going on here, and they will tell me now. I'm done with being lied to.'

'Daphne, I lied to you to protect you,' George pleads.

'Well, a whole lot of good that's done,' she scoffs, rolling her eyes.

Jeez, she's sexy when she's angry.

'Daphne, that's not fair.'

'That's not fair?' she repeats in shock, her shoulders tensing. 'No, what's not fair is that Teddy's house got ransacked purely because he's associated with you. What's not fair is that I got choked and nearly kidnapped because of you. You have absolutely no right to tell me what's fair and what isn't. Now, someone, tell. Me. The. Truth.'

'There's an organization called Daveeno,' I start.

'Milosh, no—' George tries to interrupt, but I don't let him.

'They're a corrupt international intelligence organization that work with the worst of the worst, supplying them with weapons, intel and power. They're particularly well known for planting spies.'

'Spies?' Daphne gapes. 'As in Alex Rider?'

'Who the hell is Alex Rider?'

Daphne completely ignores me, and looks over to George, her mouth agape. 'Are you a spy? To be honest, that would answer so much.'

'No, Daph,' George responds. 'Well, not really.'

'Oh, great, here we go,' Daphne mutters.

'I used to work with MI6 as an independent contractor for antidote formulas. I really enjoyed it and it was a break from my mundane life. I was good at it, and I was helping people.' He glances over to Daphne. 'It's actually where I met your mother.' He smiles.

I watch Daphne as that news sinks in, her expression morphing from confusion to hurt. 'Mother used to work at MI6?'

'Yes.' He breathes out a laugh. 'She was the head of intelligence, actually.'

'I really don't know anything about you, do I?' she whispers in response. The pain evident in her voice crushes me.

'D-Daph, come on, it's not like that,' George says.

'No, it's fine, it's just eye-opening, is all,' she says quietly, offering a heartbreaking smile. All that fire in her eyes has been extinguished. 'Anyway, please continue.'

'Um, okay. Many years ago, I was working on an antidote for a toxin named serum 627. I mixed the wrong ingredients, and instead of making an antidote, I made the toxin worse. It was powerful and deadly and could snuff the life out of someone without leaving a trace. It also lowered their inhibitions during interrogation. I knew that if this got into the wrong hands the consequences would be terrible, and at the time MI6 had a problem with Daveeno double agents so I couldn't trust anyone. I created an antidote for the toxin, just in case, then destroyed any evidence that it was ever created. I kept a written copy of both locked away, and completely forgot about it.'

He kept a copy of the toxin and the antidote formula?

'Until recently. Somehow Daveeno found out about the toxin and want it for themselves. That's the reason they broke into my office and here, but they couldn't find it. They clearly thought that if they kidnapped you I would give it up, but Milosh got you out of the mall before they had a chance. And now with the increased security around the house, no one's getting in or out without us knowing.'

I look over to Daphne to check how she's taking all of this but I can't read her. Her face is blank. 'Why haven't you given it to them?' she asks.

'Because I don't have the formula any more. And even if I did, I couldn't. These people would probably sell it to the highest bidder and who knows what they would use it for. I don't even know how they found out that I made it.'

'Okay then, so what's your plan? Hide at home for the rest of your life?'

'No, that's actually where Milosh comes in.' I feel five pairs of eyes land on me as I keep my face passive. 'Milosh isn't actually a qualified close protection agent. Yes, all his accolades are real, but after his special ops mission he joined a task force that is focused on dismantling Daveeno. When my office at work got broken into, they reached out to me because they suspected it had something to do with Daveeno. I needed protection for you, Daphne, so they suggested that Milosh should come here and pose as your close protection agent, keeping you safe while also having eyes inside the house.'

Daphne simply nods, not looking at anything but the floor.

What are you thinking, Daphne?

I should be focusing on what George is saying but all I can think about is how I lied to her. I could've told her countless times why I was really here. The truth wasn't that far from what she believed, but still. How's she supposed to trust me, or trust anyone for that matter, if people are always lying to her – me included?

'The Major in charge of the task force has been kept up to date on the situation through Milosh,' George continues. 'Working with Interpol, the FBI and the NCA they've been building a case against Daveeno and are waiting for the final missing pieces before they can make a move on them. With my help, and all the information I possess, they think they can shut it down. We just have to be patient.'

The room goes silent when George finishes speaking. Daphne and Teddy were the only ones in the dark about all of this.

'Okay,' she replies plainly before turning to face Teddy. 'Teddy, you should stay here for now. You'll be much safer.'

'She's right, Teddy. Please do stay,' George seconds.

'Okay, thank you, I really appreciate it.' He smiles sincerely.

'I'm going to let the staff know we've got another person staying with us,' Amelia chimes in, standing up.

'All right,' George responds, walking to the door before looking over to Daphne. 'Daph, are you all right showing Teddy to one of the guest rooms?'

'Sure,' she responds, glancing over at Teddy. 'Where are your things?'

'Just outside.'

'Okay, let's go.'

He opens the door for Daphne and she slips out first, but as he passes me I grip his bicep, holding him in place.

'Careful, Ted. No touching,' I warn, my voice low and measured.

He swallows once, readjusting his glasses before nodding and walking out.

The door closes softly and I turn back to a smiling Henry. 'Glad to see there's another Teddy hater in the house. Welcome to the club, Petrov.'

'You don't like him?' I direct to Henry, a warm wave of satisfaction passing through me.

He shakes his head, leaning back into the couch. 'Nah, not since I saw him trying to take pictures of Amelia every time she bent down to grab something. I took his phone to delete the photos and he had hundreds of them, with a few of Daphne as well. In the pool. So I broke his phone then I broke his hand.'

'Good,' I bite out.

'Yeah.' He nods pensively. 'There's something off about that boy, I just don't know what.'

22

'So . . . Milosh,' Teddy says, as we make our way up the stairs.

'Yeah, what about him?'

'He's a little intense, don't you think? Not to mention he's absolutely terrifying with his whole military task force thing.'

'He's not *that* bad.' I try to laugh when Teddy rolls his eyes dramatically, but all I'm thinking about is what I've just learned.

I feel like I should be sadder than I am right now.

Milosh isn't a bodyguard. Okay, that's understandable. I'm not over the moon that I didn't know this but it doesn't really make much difference to how things are going or have gone. And he was the person in the snug to start to tell me the truth. He's been the one keeping me safe and I'm almost certain Daddy asked him not to say anything.

Daddy lied to me. Again.

Honestly, that's kind of to be expected. I'm slowly growing numb to him and his lies, and at least now I know the truth.

My mother worked for MI6 and so did my father.

My parents are basically Peggy Carter and Howard Stark.

'Yeah, he's not that bad. He likes me about as much as Henry does,' Teddy quips sarcastically. 'I'll never understand what I did to annoy that man.'

'Me neither. But you're absolutely right, he despises you. It's kind of funny, actually.'

'Oh, you would think that wouldn't you, Daph?' I simply nod and give him an innocent smile.

'I'm glad you're here, by the way.' I stop by the door to the guest room next to Milosh's. 'And I'm so sorry this happened to you.' I rub my hand along his forearm.

'Ah, that's all right,' he says, grabbing my hand and grinning. 'At least it gave me an excuse to see you again.'

'Is that so?' I laugh, dropping my hand and opening his door.

'So what exactly is going on with you and Milosh?'

'What do you mean?'

'Well, the way he looked at me when I touched you suggests you've slept together or something.'

I roll my eyes. 'We have not slept together, Teddy.'

'Well, then, what is it? Because I need to know if I should tread carefully.'

'We . . .' I trail off. I really don't know how to describe what's happening between me and Milosh any more. Technically, yes, he's simply my bodyguard. But saying that feels wrong. He feels like so much more but nothing at all, at the very same time. It's confusing and I hate it.

But I also kind of love it.

'Wait.' I pause. 'What do you mean, tread carefully?'

He enters the room, placing his duffel on the end of the bed and turning to look back at me knowingly. 'Ah, come on Daph.' He walks towards me, his steps slow. 'You mean to tell me you've forgotten what happened between us?'

Teddy was the first guy I ever did anything with. I was fifteen and he was eighteen and his family was spending Christmas with ours.

It was after dinner and we were sitting on the sofa watching a film while our parents were still in the dining room when he leaned in and kissed me.

'I've been obsessing over those lips for ever, and I wanted to know if they felt as good as they looked,' he had said to me.

'Well, d-do they?' I questioned, completely flustered. It wasn't like I'd never got any male attention before, it was that I didn't usually care for it. But that wasn't the case with Teddy. I'd known him all my life, and ever since I could remember our families had talked about how we'd grow up and get married. And I was never against it because to me Teddy was that hot older guy, of course I liked him. The fact he liked me back sent shivers racing down my spine.

'They do,' he whispered in response, moving closer to me. He kissed me again, and after a few minutes he lifted me onto his lap.

His hands started to explore my body but as soon as we heard the doorknob shake he practically threw me off him, proceeding to pretend like nothing had happened.

'How about a re-do, with a bit more *adult* content?' Now he slips his hands into mine and starts walking backwards, dragging us towards the bed.

'Teddy,' I sigh. 'No.'

'Ah, come on, Daph. Why not?' He pouts, sitting down on the bed and pulling me in between his open legs. 'I just want to take my mind off of what happened today.' He rubs his hands up and down the back of my thighs, adding in a whiney tone, 'Please,' when I don't respond.

Everything about this feels wrong.

His hands on my skin, our proximity, his whiney boyish nature. I feel uncomfortable and honestly wish Henry was here doing his helicopter parent thing right now, or Milosh was giving him one of those threatening looks. But they're not here so I have to get myself out of this one.

'How about we go on a run around the grounds after dinner?' I suggest, keeping my smile light and airy.

'A run?' he echoes sceptically.

'Yeah! A run will help you get your mind off everything and maybe we could do a little outdoor workout as well. I mean, who needs the gym downstairs when you have fresh air!' I jest.

He looks at me for a few seconds and I can see the idea whirling around in his head. 'Is it because of Milosh?' he asks.

'What?' How did we get on to Milosh?

'Are you and him together? Is that why you don't want us to happen?'

'Um . . .' I trail off.

Is it because of Milosh? I know a part of me wished it were his hands exploring my body instead of Teddy's but I don't think that's it. I'm fond of Teddy, I just don't feel anything romantically towards him any more. And it doesn't help that he's so pushy about this stuff. What would happen if I told him to stop, if I changed my mind. Would he listen?

'Wait, no. That's not it.' Teddy starts shaking his head

in disbelief. 'You're still a virgin, aren't you?'

'Yes,' I admit. It's not like it's a secret, but I feel icky talking about this with him.

'Oh, I get it.' Teddy smiles, simultaneously spinning me round and pulling me onto the bed, leaving me lying next to him. 'You're saving yourself for me, aren't you?'

'What?' I gape. But he doesn't respond because he's too busy studying the necklace that just fell out of my top.

'That's a pretty necklace,' he says quietly as if to soothe me, an unreadable emotion flicking across his face as he reaches down to touch it.

When I swiftly changed out of the gala dress earlier, returning the Graff necklace to its box, my neck felt bare. So I replaced it with my mother's necklace, tucking it down under my top to avoid any questions from my father. It had stayed there, successfully hidden, until now.

'Um . . .' I clear my throat, lifting myself off the bed to stand, tucking the necklace back under my top. 'Thank you.'

He simply nods and sits up on the bed, hands between his legs. He looks thoughtful for a moment so I turn to leave. I stop at the door when he says my name again. 'Daphne?' I turn around to face him, hand still on the knob. 'I think a workout would be great.' He smiles that boyish smile of his and I'm immediately at ease. This is the

Teddy I like. Fun, sweet and not pushy.

'Great! Dinner's at seven-thirty so we can work out after that.'

'Looking forward to it.'

As I close the door to his room, I see Amelia walking up the stairs. 'Hey, did you want to join me and Teddy for a workout after dinner?' She reaches me and we walk together towards her office at the end of the hall.

'Sure.' She smiles. 'Henry will absolutely hate it, and I haven't riled him up in ages so we're way overdue.' She laughs as she opens her office door and rounds the desk to sit down.

'He is really hot when he's angry,' I add.

'Daphne!' Amelia gasps. 'You're not allowed to say that.'

'Meelie, just because the man's known me since I was five doesn't mean I haven't got eyes. Your husband's hot.' I shrug. 'Deal with it.'

Henry has a roughness about him that just screams sexy, with his tall, strong build and his heavily tattooed arm. His fluffy brown hair is the only soft part about him. Well, minus his delightfully gentle counterpart.

'Mmm, you're not wrong,' Amelia agrees, starting her computer. 'But he's not the only good-looking guy in the house now, is he?' She looks up at me with the most unconvincing innocent expression. 'I mean, I personally believe when a guy constantly sticks up for you, gets a little protective when another guy starts touching you and, oh, I don't know, tells you the truth when no one else does . . .' She breathes a satisfied sigh. 'I don't know, I just think that's rather attractive.'

'Really?' I deadpan. 'How unexpected of you.'

'Daphne, when are you going to admit you find Milosh attractive?' she says, releasing an exasperated sigh.

'I never said he was unattractive.' I shrug.

'Well, that's good to know.' A low voice drawls from behind me. Ignoring Amelia's grin, I turn around to see Milosh standing by the door I left open.

'Mr Petrov.' I plaster on my most confident smile. 'Are you here to talk to Meelie?'

'No, I wanted to talk with you.'

'Huh,' Amelia quips. 'Who would've thought it?'

Releasing a heavy sigh, I motion for Milosh to turn back around so we can talk in the hall.

'How can I help you, Mr Petrov?' I ask as soon as I've closed the door.

'I wanted to check you were all right after everything you heard downstairs.' I look at him, studying his face.

'Yes.' I smile, starting the walk to my room. 'I'm fine, thank you.'

'You sure?' Something about the concern lacing his

tone makes me stop walking and lift up on my tiptoes to hug him. My arms snake around his neck while he stands there tense and rigid. I breathe a laugh as I drop my arms to find his and bring them to my back.

'Thank you for being the one to tell me the truth,' I whisper.

'You deserved to know.'

I smile into his chest as I feel his arms tightening around my waist, pulling me closer into him and his firm, warm body. Gosh he smells good.

With his strong arms wrapped around me and his hands pressed against my back, I feel oddly at ease, the closeness mixed with his all too familiar scent comforting.

It's strange: not half an hour ago I was listening to how my life has completely fallen apart, fear dominating my mind and worry climbing up my spine. But now, as I stand here, all I feel is peace.

Amid all the turmoil and uncertainty, Milosh has been the calm in the storm. Always knowing what to do, figuring out solutions for our problems and protecting me.

I know it's his job, but a tugging feeling in my heart tells me it could be something else.

Something . . . more.

'Milosh?' I whisper, starting to break the hug so I can look at him.

223

'Hmm?' His low voice rumbles as his gaze bores into mine.

'I—'

'Oh,' Teddy interrupts. He's standing awkwardly in the doorway to my father's bedroom. 'Sorry, I didn't know you two would be out here.'

'Teddy, what were you doing in my father's room?' I start to pull away from Milosh, but he holds me there, his hands firmly on my waist as he looks at Teddy with such cold calculation that Teddy starts shifting uncomfortably.

'Oh, well.' He starts laughing, looking anywhere but my face. 'I was looking to see . . . if he had a toilet brush.'

'There's a toilet brush in the bathroom in the guest room. Why were you looking for another one?'

His face starts heating. 'It's a bit embarrassing, I don't want to really get into it.'

'Answer her question, Teddy,' Milosh warns coolly. The cold steel of his tone is at odds with his gentle yet firm touch.

'W-well, I . . . ugh . . . made a bit of a mess.'

'A mess so large it causes you to slip and fall into another man's bathroom?' Milosh queries.

'Yes?' Teddy sounds like he's questioning himself.

'Oh, well, I'll call Charlotte to come and sort it out. Depending on the size of the problem she may need to call a plumber,' I respond. Milosh keeps his face impassive but I can hear him breathe out a laugh.

Teddy's face reaches a shade of red a ripe tomato would envy. 'No, no. Goodness, no. Th-that's all right.' He starts fiddling with his toilet brush-less hands. 'I'll sort it all out, no need to worry!' he calls out as he promptly walks into his room, shutting the door.

'That was odd, right?' I ask, turning back to look at Milosh, dropping out of his embrace.

'Yeah, it was.' Milosh studies me for a moment, slipping his hands into his pockets. 'Does your father keep anything valuable in his room?'

'I'm not sure.' I furrow my brow. 'Why? Do you think Teddy was after something?'

'Maybe.'

'Oh, I don't think so. Yes, Teddy has certain . . . eccentricities, but he's not one to steal.'

'Hmm,' Milosh hums, watching me silently. 'I know it's not my place to ask, but did you and Teddy ever . . .'

'Once,' I finish for him. 'We kissed once, a couple of years ago.'

His jaw ticks but he remains impassive, nodding curtly.

'Why do you ask?'

He shrugs. 'Curious.'

'Really?' He's curious about my romantic past?

'Apparently so,' he grumbles.

We stare at each other in silence, his eyes heating and his jaw clenched.

I drop my gaze to his mouth. 'I know he wants to do or be more, but I'm not interested.' I can feel my body temperature rising as I look up to meet his eyes. 'In him, at least,' I add in a whisper.

An unreadable expression passes over his face for a split second. 'Good to know.'

'It is?' I breathe.

'It is, Miss Green.'

23

I look at myself in the mirror, once again hiding the necklace.

I'm wearing the same baby-pink gym set with the matching tight jacket. If I keep the jacket on and zip it all the way up, the necklace will stay hidden. I walk out of my room only to be met with Amelia walking up the stairs.

'You and Teddy start, I've just got a few things to do then I'll change my clothes and meet you outside. How was dinner?'

It's an hour after we've eaten, the sun has long set and the temperature has started to drop. With Daddy having his meal in his study, I was left to eat dinner with Milosh, Henry and Teddy.

That went about as well as when I told my father I wanted to study Midwifery at university instead of

Business or Chemistry. Awkward, painful and draining.

Amelia was working and couldn't join us to break the tension, so it fell to me alone to keep the peace and power the conversation.

'Oh, dinner went great.' My voice drips with sarcasm. 'Henry and Milosh really took to Teddy, and by the end of dinner they were holding hands and singing "Kumbaya".'

'Wow, who knew all the boys would get along so well?' Amelia jokes, starting back towards her office.

I give a fake smile as I descend the stairs. 'Not me!'

I walk into the kitchen and spot my father with his head in the fridge, rummaging for something. 'You just ate dinner, how are you still hungry?' I ask, then go to sit down in the breakfast nook to push my trainers on.

'I'm trying this new thing,' Daddy responds, looking up and smiling gently when he hears my voice. 'It's called stress eating.'

I finish tying my laces up before I look over to him again. 'Yeah, I wouldn't recommend that.'

He laughs before fully taking me in. 'You going to work out?'

'Yeah. Me, Teddy and Amelia are going to run a few laps in the garden and maybe fit in a little strength training. You want to join? It might help you take your mind off things for a little while,' I suggest.

'No,' he lightly chuckles. 'I've got a lot of work to catch up on, but you have fun and run a lap for me.'

'So what should we start with?' Teddy asks, straightening his glasses as he walks out of the garden door. I turn to look at him and laugh. I feel like Milosh probably did when I walked out to our first training session in my fur coat.

Teddy clearly didn't bring any workout clothes with him as he's clad in a navy cable-knit jumper, a pair of tartan pyjama bottoms and cream loafers. 'Interesting outfit choice,' I quip.

'This was all I had.' Teddy shrugs, grinning.

'I would go and ask Milosh to lend you some clothes, but I don't think they'd fit.'

Where Teddy is slender and toned, Milosh is broad and muscular.

Where I'd place Teddy at 5'11", Milosh is at least 6'3".

Milosh looks like if you sat on his lap it would be firm and strong and secure, whereas Teddy, bless him, looks like if you sat on his lap he'd ask you to get up every now and again to give his legs a break.

Teddy is still strong and lean, don't get me wrong, but against Milosh, or even Henry, he wouldn't stand a chance. However, what he lacks in muscle, he makes up for in looks.

Teddy is the definition of a pretty boy. With his curly blond hair and his blue eyes protected by his glasses, he's the poster boy for *'Take me home to meet the parents. I'll bring flowers and white wine.'* And for the last nearly eighteen years that's what I've gravitated towards.

But then there's Milosh. With his dark hair, sharp features and overwhelmingly striking face, he can command a room simply with his presence, his quiet dominance oozing out of every pore.

'Even if his clothes did fit me,' Teddy says, abruptly pulling me from my thoughts, 'I think I'd be the last person he'd help out. I'm pretty certain if I was trapped in a burning building, he'd leave me there.'

'Oh . . . that's not true.' *Bold-faced lie.*

'Yeah, sure,' Teddy says sarcastically. 'Anyway, shall we start with a warm-up jog to the bottom of the garden?'

'Sure.'

'Do you have any secret entrances or exits in your garden?' Teddy asks as we begin.

'What do you mean?'

'Well, you know, I wanna make sure this house is properly protected and there's no way for anyone to get in or out.' He starts looking around the garden for any doors or broken fencing.

'Oh well, in that case, you're completely safe. There is

an exit through –' I point to the far end of the garden – 'there, but it's locked and gated, and during the day there's a security guard positioned there. Daddy even said he hired someone to keep watch there at night too. He starts tomorrow, I believe.'

'So he's not there now?'

'No, but don't worry, you're completely safe.' I smile.

'Ah . . . yeah, good. That's good, thank you.'

We reach the bottom of the garden and stop. 'Why don't we do our workout down here today?' Teddy asks, looking around.

'Okay, sure. Let's stretch first.' We start with our arms, stretching one across the front of our chest and holding it there for a second before switching to the other. We continue making our way through arm and back stretches before moving on to a standing forward bend. As I lean down, my necklace falls, dangling in front of my face for a second before I tuck it back into my jacket, rezipping it fully.

'So that necklace that you're wearing, where did you get it?' Teddy asks innocently enough but I instantly tense up. It's not the question, it's more the necklace itself. I don't know why but I always seem to get a little cagey about it when someone asks.

'My mother used to wear it,' I answer. Teddy knew

my mother; he was twelve when she died and his family practically moved in for a month to help bring life back into the house.

'Oh, that's why I remember it,' he recounts slowly. 'Elizabeth used to wear it all the time.' I flinch involuntarily when I hear my mother's name. I can't remember the last time I heard that name aloud and a rush of sadness dawns as an assortment of memories crash back into my mind.

'Yeah,' I respond, my voice small and remote as I slowly begin to roll up out of the stretch. Teddy takes one look at me and walks over, embracing me in a warm hug.

'Sorry Daph, that was a bit thoughtless of me,' he mumbles into my hair. He rubs my back but his hands settle near my neck. He starts rubbing it and I feel his fingers skimming the back of my necklace.

I jerk back and his face heats as his hands fall. 'What are you doing?'

'I was just checking if the clasp was secure.' He looks at my chest. 'It is.'

Before I get a chance to respond we hear footsteps coming from the top of the garden.

'Amelia!' Teddy cries, way too enthusiastically. 'You're here. I didn't realize you were joining our little late-night workout.'

Amelia laughs lightly as she pulls her hair up into a

ponytail. 'Yeah, I thought I might as well, now that all my work is done.'

'Great!' Teddy exclaims. I study him for a moment, trying to figure out what's going on with him. Beads of sweat are forming along his forehead even though we've barely started the workout. He's also acting a little jumpy. Plus the random groping of my neck. Gentle alarm bells are ringing. Something's wrong . . . but what?

'Hey, Amelia. I just noticed none of us have any water out here. Would you mind grabbing us a few bottles, please? I want to go over one of the stretches me and Daphne just did one more time.'

'Sure,' Amelia responds, heading back towards the house.

'I'll come with you,' I say, before she leaves. Teddy's being weird and I'd rather have other people around than be alone with him right now.

'No, I need you to demonstrate the stretch, if that's all right?' Teddy objects.

'Okay, well, Daph, you stay here. I'll be back in a moment,' Amelia finalizes as she walks off. I stare after her for a moment before looking back to Teddy.

'What was the stretch you wanted me to demonstrate?' I ask, but he's not paying any attention to me. He's still watching Amelia. As soon as she vanishes into the kitchen he turns to look at me, panic in his eyes.

'I'm sorry, Daphne, but I need that necklace.'

'What?'

He inches closer, his eyes focused on my chest where the pendant sits. 'I need that necklace, Daphne. And I'm going to take it one way or another so please just give it to me.'

'Teddy, what are you talking about? If this is some kind of weird prank, please stop, because you're starting to scare me.' I back away from him, but he takes one step closer.

'I'm so sorry, Daphne. I truly am.'

'For what? Teddy, what is goin—' I don't have a chance to finish my sentence before he grabs the front of my jacket, yanking me into him.

'Teddy, stop,' I gasp, my breath shortening. The impact of the pull causes the necklace to pop out and as soon as Teddy sees it he grabs it, trying to rip it from my neck.

The clasp holds, but the pain of the jerk sears into my skin.

He doesn't let go of the necklace, his breathing getting heavier and more staggered. I try to pull his hand off but his grip is too strong. So, I do the next best thing.

I kick him in the groin.

He yelps in agony, doubling over and loosening his grip on the necklace. I pull away and stamp on his foot for good measure, causing him to stumble back.

'I just need the necklace, Daphne. Give it to me.' His voice is dark, firm and desperate. But his body is shaking.

He's scared.

I stumble back, ready to ask him what he's doing, but before I can speak Amelia jogs up to us, bottles in hand.

'Teddy, are you okay?' Amelia asks, concerned.

Before I can even tell her to run, Teddy stands up tall, simultaneously retrieving something from the waistband of his trousers. It's too late for me to stop him as he raises the butt of a gun to Amelia's head, striking her hard.

'Amelia!' I cry, as she topples to the floor.

Lifeless.

I run over but stop abruptly when Teddy points the gun at me.

Our erratic breathing intertwines as I face the barrel of a gun.

A real gun.

A real gun is being pointed at me. By Teddy.

His hands shake as his breathing picks up. His whole face covered in sweat now.

'Take off the necklace, Daphne,' he says.

'Teddy, please put down the gun.' *What did Milosh teach me? What did Milosh teach me? How can I disarm him?*

'I can't do that, Daphne,' he starts, his face racked with fear. 'I didn't want to do this, but you wouldn't give it up.'

Is he . . . crying?

He silently starts to sob, pointing the gun at my face with his shaking hands.

He's never done this before.

He's inexperienced.

He's not even holding the gun correctly.

If I took a few steps forward I could disarm him, but I've only ever done that with Milosh and a fake gun. I really don't think now is a good time to play Black Widow but I don't have a choice.

Amelia is on the ground, unconscious, and we're all alone. No one is coming to rescue us. This is what Milosh has been training me for.

'Teddy, listen to me,' I say as softly as I can, taking a small step towards him. 'I don't know what's going on, but let me help you.' I take another step but stop when he tightens his grip around the gun. I hold my hands up.

'Stay back, Daphne. I will shoot you.'

'I know, I kn–know,' I respond, halting.

'You don't believe me, do you?'

'What?' I ask, terrified. I don't want to die. Least of all at the hands of *Teddy.*

'This is a real gun.'

'I know, Teddy.'

But apparently my words aren't enough. He fires a

warning shot that nicks my upper arm. The adrenaline of the situation delaying any pain.

All I need is one more step and I can disarm him.

'Teddy, please stop. I'll give you the necklace, okay? I'm going to walk towards you and hand it to you.'

He nods once, still holding the gun to my face as I take one more step.

Moving fast, like Milosh taught me, I reach up to the gun before Teddy can react, pushing it away from my face. I clutch it, twisting until the trigger is out of his reach, and lift up. Because of the height difference it's hard to pull away, so instead of the gun ending up in my hands it drops to the ground. I reach for it but before I have time to grab it I feel a shoe connecting with my stomach, dropping me to the ground.

Then I feel it again.

And again.

Teddy kicks me repeatedly until I can't move.

I can't talk.

I can't scream.

The pain is searing.

But then it stops.

I start coughing uncontrollably, my battered body spasming. It takes a moment for me to register that someone is calling my name.

'Daphne,' a deep voice calls. 'Daphne, get up!' It calls again. Louder this time.

I roll over and find Milosh hammering a punch into Teddy's jaw before kneeing him in the gut. Teddy doubles over, giving Milosh leverage to place him in a headlock. One arm wrapping around his neck and the other behind it, restricting his air.

'Daphne, baby, look at me,' Milosh practically shouts. I look over at him, finding his eyes so full of power and darkness it shocks me for a moment. 'Daphne, I need you to run inside and get Henry.'

'But the gun!' I gasp out.

'Forget about the gun, go and get Henry and your dad.'

'Bu—'

'Now, Daphne.'

I get up, stumbling when I'm aggressively reminded of the pain in my stomach, but managing to break into a run.

'Henry, Daddy!' I scream as I run back to the house.

'Henry! Daddy, please!'

Henry and my father rush into the kitchen at the same time, panic-stricken. 'Daph, what's wrong? What was that noise?' Henry asks, bracing me when I almost run into him.

I cry out when his hands clasp my arm where Teddy nicked me with a bullet, bringing their attention to my sleeve which is soaked in blood.

'Daphne, your arm, what happened?' my father says, eyes widening in horror.

'Milosh . . . Teddy . . . Amelia . . .' I try to catch my breath and speak clearly, but fail. 'Teddy attacked me and Amelia, Milosh got me away but he—'

'Stay here,' Henry demands, cutting me off once he's heard enough. He and my father run past me into the garden.

'He has a gun,' I shout after them, just before I hear a boom.

The gun.

The gun went off.

'No,' I whisper to myself, imagining the worst. Terror saturates my body, enveloping my pain. Not caring about the consequences, I run back out to the garden to check what happened.

I can see a fallen body at the far end, but I don't know whose it is.

Daddy continues running, but Henry stops as soon as he reaches Amelia. He picks her up and carries her back towards the house, his eyes black with rage.

'Daphne, go back inside,' he instructs. '*Now*, Daphne,' he continues when I don't move.

'But I have to check Milosh is okay,' I plead, walking towards them.

'He's fine. Now go back inside.'

His tone leaves no room for argument.

We speed-walk through the kitchen and into the snug. Henry places Amelia down on one of the large sofas, planting a light kiss on her head before moving her stray hairs off her face to assess the growing bump. He gives her a full-body once-over before turning to me.

'Are you okay?' he asks, worry emanating off him. My lip trembles as the adrenaline wears off and I start to process what just happened. Pain sears through my upper arm and my stomach all at once.

Teddy attacked me.

Teddy, the boy I've known my whole life, just threatened me with a gun and shot at me.

'No,' I whisper as the first tear falls. Henry glances back to Amelia before walking over to me to analyze my injuries. He helps me take off my workout jacket and top so I'm just in my sports bra and leggings, his eyes darkening as he assesses my arm, stomach and neck.

'Stay here, I'm gonna go get Josh.' His voice is lethally calm so I don't dare do anything other than exactly what he told me as he walks out of the room.

Josh had been a doctor for ten years until one day he realized he simply didn't fancy it any more. So he quit and went to culinary school, proceeding to work in multiple

Michelin-starred restaurants for a number of years, where he happened to meet his now-wife Bethany, all before they both came to work here as our private chefs.

When I hear the door reopen I look over expecting to see Henry returning with Josh, but I'm shocked when my eyes meet a sea of green. Milosh closes the door gently and walks over to me, his jaw tightening as he takes in my injuries.

Fresh tears prickle my eyes, the memory of what just happened coming back in flashes.

'Don't cry,' Milosh commands. 'He doesn't deserve your tears.' His hand comes up to cup my cheek wiping them away.

'What happened when the gun went off?' I ask between shaky breaths.

'I shot him in the foot,' Milosh explains calmly.

'I didn't know if something had happened to you,' I whisper.

'I'm okay, baby, don't cry over me.' His voice is gentle and soothing as he continues to wipe the tears from my eyes.

'Where is he now?' I ask.

'I knocked him out and he's currently tied up in your father's study. We're just waiting for him to wake up.'

'Okay.'

'Where exactly are you hurting?'

'My arm, stomach and my neck, where he pulled on my necklace. But Henry went to get Josh, so he'll sort me out.'

He nods in response then points to the necklace that still lies on my chest. 'Is that what he was after?'

I nod.

On the outside, Milosh looks calm and collected. There's not even a scratch on him, but something dark and slightly unhinged is swimming in his eyes.

The door to the snug opens again, but with Milosh towering in front of me I can't see who it is.

'I'm gonna go and take care of Teddy; get some answers for you,' he drawls, his voice low and intimate. 'You gonna be okay?'

I nod, offering him a small smile. 'Could you take the necklace to my father for me?'

He nods, languidly removing his hand from my cheek. 'Turn around.'

I comply, my lips parting in a silent inhale as I feel his warm hands on the back of my neck. My skin erupts in goosebumps at his touch. He's gentle with his movements, trying not to agitate the darkening bruise. I'm certain he can hear the erratic beats of my heart.

'There,' he murmurs as I feel the necklace lift from my skin.

'Thank you.' I turn back to face him, his eyes potent as they bore into mine. He nods once and turns to leave, before I stop him. 'Milosh?' I breathe, grabbing his hand to stop him. We both look down at where our fingertips connect for a moment before we lock eyes again.

'Yeah?'

'Don't go easy on him.'

He smiles slyly. 'Whatever you say, Miss Green.'

He lingers for a moment, his eyes coasting down to my mouth then lazily back up, holding my burning gaze for a moment, before someone over by the door clears their throat. I drop my hands to my side as Milosh breathes out a chuckle.

'See you soon, Miss Green,' he says, before turning and leaving, ignoring Henry's stare on the way out.

'Totally platonic, my arse,' is all Henry is able to mutter before Amelia stirs behind me.

Henry rushes over to the sofa, dropping to his haunches.

'Hi, gorgeous,' Henry whispers down at her, smiling to mask his worry. Amelia startles when she fully comes round, but as soon as she sees Henry's face she reaches up and wraps her arms around him, melting into him and whispering something inaudible from where I'm standing. Henry whispers back and starts rubbing circles on her back in an intimate, familiar way.

I love their love. Their love gives me hope. Their love makes me long for the day someone will look at me the way Henry looks at Amelia.

I want to care about somebody that much. I want somebody to love me, to care for me, to protect me. To leave everybody behind for me, not caring about the consequences as long as I'm okay.

It's the stuff of fiction. But if Henry found Amelia, who's to say I can't find my Henry?

Milosh could be your Henry. A small voice in my head chimes.

Huh. Maybe I need to add possible brain malfunction onto my list of injuries.

'Does your head hurt?' Henry asks when they break apart.

'A little, but it's okay,' she says as she starts searching the room. Her eyes land on me and she sighs with relief. 'Daphne, are you okay?'

'I'm okay, Meelie.' I make my way over to her as Henry moves aside so I have room to hug her.

'Oh my gosh, Daph, your arm,' she gasps, cupping her mouth with her hand. 'And your neck,' she adds. Her eyes widen when she sees my stomach. 'What did he do to you?' she whispers.

'Josh is just gathering his things to take a look at her

now,' Henry interjects. 'You too, Meels.'

'Good.' Amelia nods. She swings her legs around and places her feet on the floor, ready to get up, but as soon as she lifts her upper body she starts swaying, losing her balance. Henry rushes in to steady her, his brows knitting together in concern.

'You okay?'

'I got up too fast, that's all, Hen,' she answers softly, stroking his jaw. Her gaze flicks over to me again when I stand back up, clutching my stomach. 'How did you manage to get away from Teddy?'

'Milosh,' I admit. 'I'm glad he came outside when he did, otherwise . . . I don't know what would've happened.'

'Yeah,' Henry agrees. 'Milosh is probably the best hire your dad ever made. And he cares about you, Daph.' He steps back a little so he can look me in my eyes. 'He really cares about you. Almost to the level I care about Amelia.'

'No one cares about anyone as much as you care about Amelia, Henry,' I say with a small smile.

'Before Milosh, I would've agreed with you,' Henry admits, 'but now I'm not so sure.'

Thankfully, I don't have to respond to that because Josh chooses the perfect time to walk in with his medical bag and Bethany in tow. As soon as they see me, their faces drop and they let out horrified gasps.

'Oh Daphne, what has he done to you?' Josh says, before he spots Amelia looking a little worse for wear. 'No, not you too, Amelia?'

She grimaces and nods as they close the door behind them and cross to the sofa.

'Daphne, you look like you need more immediate attention so I'll start with you,' Josh states. 'Bethany, could you please sit with Amelia? Henry's going to need to go and help with the questioning, and she looks like she needs some support.'

Bethany makes her way over to Meelie as Henry stands up.

'Henry, what's going to happen with Teddy?' I ask.

'Ah.' Henry smiles. And it's the most unnerving expression I think I've ever seen cross his face. 'Well, now that you two are with Josh and Bethany, I'm gonna go have a little *chat* with him, if that's all right with you girls?'

Amelia gives him a slightly creepy smile. 'I suggest you make him wish he'd never been born.'

'Will do, gorgeous.' Henry's eyes heat up for a moment as he stares at Amelia, before cooling as he looks over to me. 'And you, Daph? Are you all right with me having a little chat with him?'

If Henry has his way, Teddy will be leaving the house in a body bag.

'Do what you need to do,' I respond. I feel completely numb. I don't know why Teddy did this, and honestly, I don't care. He held a gun to my face.

But what if he was being threatened? That little voice in my head queries, and it's a valid point. This is completely out of character for Teddy so there must be a reason – not that Milosh, Henry or Daddy are going to want to hear it – but there has to be. He wouldn't do something as drastic as this unless he was being blackmailed or something. However, blackmail or not, he still shot and attacked me.

He *shot* at me. That's not okay.

I look back over to Henry. 'Just don't kill him,' I add, rolling my eyes. 'Although I'm pretty sure Milosh may have beaten you to it.'

Henry laughs. Like, really guffaws. 'Yeah. I think you're right.' He places a chaste kiss on Amelia's lips before making for the door. 'I'll be lucky if there's any Teddy left.' He opens the door still laughing to himself. 'This is gonna be fun.'

24

MILOSH

Teddy lets out another howl of pain as I slam my fist into his jaw for the tenth time.

Since tying him to an old wooden chair in George's study, I've broken his nose, his wrists and all his fingers. He's passed out twice already from the pain but now he's come around again, I'm working on rearranging his jaw.

I'll leave his knees for Henry.

I'm considerate like that.

'Please, stop,' Teddy sobs, spluttering blood onto the hardwood floor.

'You chose to hurt Daphne,' I state, my voice void of emotion. 'Now I choose to hurt you.'

'I didn't want to!' he wails.

'Hey, Ted,' I cut in. 'You're embarrassing yourself. Stop it.'

I know I need to keep him conscious until we question him but his face is just so punchable I strike him again. After hearing that delightful crunch I gain some much needed restraint and step back, letting him catch his breath just as Henry walks in.

'You got started without me I see.' He smiles when he notes the state of Mr Build-A-Bear. Teddy's face pales several shades when he looks up with his one unswollen eye to see the look on Henry's face.

'Henr—'

'No.' Henry stops Teddy abruptly, walking over to him and bending down until they're eye to eye. 'There are certain people that you just don't wanna piss off, Teddy. Yet you've managed to piss off all of them. It's actually quite impressive, really.' Teddy's stopped crying now, but when the cold unnerving smile passes over Henry's face again, Teddy's lip starts quivering, prompting an automatic eye-roll from me.

'Now, lucky for you, Milosh has self-control and has shown you grace.' Henry stands up, treading on Teddy's shot foot. Even though it's been wrapped so he doesn't bleed out, he shrieks at the increased pain and it's music to my ears.

'But Milosh works for the military,' Henry continues, 'so he has to show some level of restraint. I, on the other hand, don't.' Henry snarls, that cocky accent thickening. 'Now normally, if someone touches my wife, they lose their hands. But you? You didn't do that.' His voice is eerily calm.

'You hurt her. You knocked *my wife* unconscious. Then

you shot Daphne. But not only did you shoot Daphne, you beat her up. That girl now has marks and bruises all over her body because of *you*. My wife may have a concussion because of *you*. You know what that means, Teddy?' He walks away, coming to stand next to me.

'Not only have you got to deal with Mr In-denial-about-his-feelings over here.' *Dick*. 'You also have to deal with me. And you hurt my wife.' He chuckles, shaking his head. 'You're as thick as they come, Teddy. Really just remarkably stupid.'

'I didn't have a choice,' Teddy grits out.

'That's where you're wrong, Ted,' I say. 'You've always got a choice.'

The door opens and George storms in. 'Oh, good, he's awake.' When I went to check on Daphne, George went to search Teddy's things to see if there was anything to lead us to the truth, but from the look on his face he's clearly been unsuccessful.

Apparently, all Teddy needed was a gun, audacity and stupidity to get him through the day.

'You ready to start?' I ask. I just want to get this questioning over so I can go check on Daphne again. The thought of her sitting there in pain from all those injuries brings a new wave of rage crashing over me.

'Teddy, tell us the truth. Why did you do this?' George asks. His tone is measured and neutral, but his eyes tell a different story. Where me and Henry feel anger, George feels hurt. A boy he considered a son just attacked his only child with no explanation.

'M-most of my story was true, George,' he stutters. 'I came home and my house was ransacked. There were two men who knocked me out then woke me up with ice water.' He stops to cough, wheezing in pain before continuing. 'The only difference was they instructed me to complete a task . . . by giving me a riddle . . . and a gun.' He's still sniffling, snot and blood running down his face. He looks like the mess that he is.

'They told me that I needed to complete the r-riddle and give them the item it mentioned within two days.'

'Or what?' Henry queries.

He hesitates for a moment. 'Or they'd send an anonymous tip to the police, telling them about the under-the-table deals my parents made with several judges to keep my name clear.'

'Keep your name clear of what?' George asks.

'Drunk driving, assault, battery. I-I don't know, there were a lot of incidents.'

'I see.' Anguish swims in George's eyes as he walks slowly to his desk to sit down.

'What was the riddle, Ted?' I ask, to get us back on track.

'They told me to find what's close to her heart. I didn't

know what that meant so I thought I'd come here and look around George's stuff once everyone had gone to sleep. But when Daphne was lying down on my bed her necklace fell out and landed right on top of her heart, making me think that could be it.'

'Wait,' I interject, my blood running cold. 'What was Daphne doing lying on your bed?'

'W-w-well,' Teddy stutters, 'we were talking and I suggested we had a repeat of something we did a few years ago.'

'And what was it that you did a few years ago, Ted? That would require her to be on your bed?' I grit out, slowly but very surely losing any restraint I have.

'We kissed,' he says quietly. 'On a sofa,' he adds quickly. 'Nothing happened a few years ago other than that, it was just this time that I suggested we . . .' he trails off.

'We what?' Henry probes.

'We m-move on to something a little more adult,' he practically whispers.

George closes his eyes and takes a few deep breaths. 'Did you force yourself on my daughter, Theodore?'

'No! No, of course not, George. I may have . . . prompted her. But I never pushed.'

'See, now why don't I believe you, Ted?' I push off the wall I'm leaning against and stalk over to him. 'I'm only gonna ask you this once more.' I drop to my haunches. 'How did she end up on your bed?' I can hear my Balkan accent thicken as I try to remain as calm as possible.

'I flipped her onto the bed, but nothing happened, I promise.'

'Your promises mean very little to me, Teddy,' I state.

His breathing picks up and he looks a second away from losing the last shred of his composure.

'Calm down, I'm not gonna kill you,' I state coolly. 'I'm just gonna take you through a death-like event.'

Teddy's eyes widen in horror, while Henry laughs behind me.

'A what?'

'Here, let me show you.'

'Please, don't. I don't think my body can take it any more.' The expression in his unswollen eye is panicked and he's shaking.

'That seems like a *you* problem, Ted.' I retrieve the knife from my back pocket and stab it into his thigh. I purposely miss any arteries and blood vessels because he needs to finish answering the questions, but it does bring a flood of satisfaction when he cries out in pain. I leave the knife in his leg and stand, walking away.

'And who was all that for, again?' Henry chirps at me, his eyes bright with glee.

'I have zero problem stabbing that smirk off your face,' I warn him.

'Right, right, right, right,' Henry nods before muttering, 'because that answered my question.'

'All right, let's get back to tonight,' George says as he stands up and comes round his desk. 'You saw a necklace on Daphne's neck?'

'Yes,' Teddy says between whimpers. 'It triggered the riddle in my head but I went to check your room as well to make sure there wasn't a clue in there. When I couldn't find anything and Daphne told me the necklace used to be Elizabeth's, I knew that had to be it.'

'Elizabeth's necklace?' George questions. 'Daphne was wearing Elizabeth's necklace?'

'Yeah, she was. I recognized it when I was checking her injuries,' Henry confirms.

That explains why I recognized that necklace in the pool. Every picture I got shown of Daphne's mother before I came here had her wearing that necklace. It's the same in the few remaining photos of her that are dotted around the house.

'She told me she lost it.'

'Well, she lied. I'm guessing she learned that from you,' I respond, taking the necklace out of my pocket and handing it to him. He stares at it for a moment, unmoving, but as if someone pressed *Play*, all at once he comes to life again, grabbing the necklace from my outstretched hand.

'So what exactly was your plan, Teddy?' Henry asks. 'You thought you'd rip off the necklace and go on your merry way?'

'I thought if I could get it off her neck I could jump the back fence and bring it back to my apartment where they told me to leave it.' He moves ever so slightly but with the knife still in his thigh he lets out a grunt of pain, his lip quivering. 'I promise you, I didn't want to hurt Daphne, but she just wouldn't give the necklace up.'

'Oh, so now you're telling me this is Daphne's fault?' George snaps.

'No! N-no. It's completely mine, it's jus—' He doesn't get to complete that sentence because Henry rips the knife out of his thigh, dropping it to the floor.

'We're done with questioning him, yeah?' He looks to me and George, and once George shrugs and I nod, he smiles sadistically.

'Good.' He starts pummelling Teddy. Blow after blow. Until Teddy passes out a third time from the pain.

'That's enough for now.' Henry sighs, backing away. 'What are we gonna do with him?'

I whip my phone out and shoot off a quick text to Davis. 'Major Davis is gonna want to question him, so some people are going to come and take him, then I don't know what will happen to him. Most likely he'll get cleaned up, face the consequences of those charges he admitted to and go to jail. On top of conspiring, he'll be in there for a while.'

'So I can't kill him?' Henry gapes.

'No.'

'Well, that's wildly irritating.' He looks back at Teddy and throws one last punch. 'That'll just have to do, I guess.'

'Do you know anything about this riddle?' I ask George, refocusing.

'Yes,' he whispers, looking at me. 'It was taken from the book that was stolen from my office.'

'Your journal?'

'Malcolm, my old lab assistant at MI6, was the only one who knew what I'd made. He told me not to tell anyone about it, and to destroy all evidence. I couldn't bring myself to get rid of all of my hard work, though, so I hid the formula for the toxin along with the antidote – yes, I pretty much had the formula memorized, but it was good to have a backup, just in case. He told me not to tell him where I hid it, but to hide the location in a riddle so it couldn't be easily deciphered.'

'And where did you put the formula?'

He looks at me wearily, then over to Teddy who's so far passed out, I contemplate checking his pulse.

'In my late wife's necklace. She never used to take it off,

so when she was sleeping I removed the pictures of Daphne and her and wrote the toxin formula down on one side and the antidote on the other before putting them back. It was stupid, but it worked. No one would ever look behind the pictures or even suspect she had the formulas, not even her.'

'So Daph's been walking around with the toxin and antidote formulas around her neck for years?' Henry questions.

'Yes.' George nods. 'She wasn't to know, but yes.' He caresses the necklace for a moment before walking towards the door.

'George, that's evidence,' I say. 'I need to hand it in.'

'No.'

'George, the longer that stays in your possession, the longer you put Daphne and yourself in danger.' Right now this deal with the task force is mutually beneficial: he gets protection for his daughter and the task force gets access to his house. But George can request I leave at any time. It would be ridiculously stupid but sometimes George isn't the most critical thinker. I can't take the necklace by force, but I know George won't give it to me either.

'No, it won't be safe with your team,' he decides, opening the study door.

'Where are you going?'

'To hide it.' He turns to look at me. 'To hide it somewhere no one will ever find it.'

25

I walk out of the snug and round the corner.

After Josh treated my injuries the best he could I stayed in the snug so I wouldn't have to be alone with my thoughts, but it got a little too much when Josh and Bethany kept asking questions.

Why did Teddy do this?

Do you think he's working with that group?

Weren't you and him supposed to . . . you know . . . ?

Why didn't you just give him the necklace?

These were all valid questions, I just didn't have it in me to answer them, so when Meelie conveniently felt dizzy again and they rushed over to tend to her, I took the chance to escape.

I turn the corner only to come face to face with my father.

'Are you okay—'

'I'm so sor—'

We blurt at the same time.

'Are you okay?' Daddy asks again.

I nod. 'Josh patched me up, so I'm okay.'

'I'm not talking about physically, Daph. I'm talking about everything else. You and Teddy were close. This mustn't be easy for you.'

'It's not,' I admit. 'But right now, I don't think my brain is letting me fully process anything so maybe check back with me in the morning.' I let out a small laugh, but it comes out flat. I want to know what they found out when they questioned Teddy, but my brain already feels overworked and overtired and asking about Teddy would only add to the noise I so desperately want to quiet in my head.

I'm drained and numb, and honestly I just want to sleep.

'All right, well, I should go. I need to put this somewhere safe, I guess.' He holds out the locket.

'Daddy, I'm so sorry I lied about losing it.'

'I can completely understand why you did.' He shrugs. 'I haven't been a very good role model or father to you recently, Daphne. What with the lies and secrecy and so forth. But I want to change that. And I mean it this time. I want us to have open and honest conversations, about everything and anything.'

'I'd like that too.'

'Well, all right then.' My father smiles. 'It's settled. Goodnight, darling.'

'Night, Daddy.'

I watch him as he retreats up the stairs and wait until I hear the faint sound of his bedroom door close until I move again. My movements are slow and stiff, and I have to stop every couple of seconds when a new throb of pain rakes through my body.

I begin to make my way up the stairs but stop halfway, sitting down on one of the steps to gather myself. I drop my head between my knees and try to even out my breathing.

I'm not sure how much time passes, but after a while I hear someone coming up the stairs, stopping when they get to me. I know it's Milosh purely from his footsteps but I get confirmation when he sits down next to me, his clean scent filling my nostrils. We sit in comfortable silence for a couple of minutes, only hearing the gentle tick-tock of the clock in the entrance hall.

Lifting my head from my knees I place it on his shoulder. 'How did you know to come outside?'

'I heard a gunshot from my room and when I looked outside my window I saw a little dot of pink. I didn't know what you were doing, I didn't even know Teddy was with you, I just knew you were there so I went to check.'

Tick, tock, tick, tock.

'Well, thank you,' I say, my voice barely above a whisper. 'For saving my life. Again.'

'I wasn't all that fond of Build-A-Bear anyway, so really it was a win-win.'

I breathe out a laugh, and I think it's my first genuine one of the night. 'Build-A-Bear?'

'I think it has a nice ring to it. Sure beats *Teddy* anyway.'

'You're not wrong about that.'

Tick, tock, tick, tock.

'I can't believe I got Amelia hurt.'

'What are you talking about?'

'If I'd just told Daddy I had the necklace and given it to him, all of this could've been avoided.'

'Hey, look at me,' Milosh says, his voice stern. I lift my head off his shoulder and turn my face to his. 'This is not your fault at all.'

'Yes, it is,' I stress. 'The only person to blame for all of this is me. The first night you came here my father asked if I'd seen the necklace, and I said no. If I'd stopped being a hypocrite for a second and just told the truth, Amelia wouldn't be sitting in the snug with a mild concussion and I wouldn't have got shot and beaten up.'

'You wanted to keep that necklace to feel closer to your mother. You weren't to know what was actually inside.'

'Actually inside?' I frown. 'What are you talking about?'

His jaw tightens. 'The toxin and the antidote formulas your father made are written on the back of the pictures inside the pendant.'

My jaw drops. 'You know what? Of course they are. Why am I surprised?'

I don't even get into the fact that the writing is probably illegible from the amount of times I've worn the necklace in the water, or the fact that I've been unknowingly carrying those formulas around with me for years. Today's been a long day.

I just need to sleep.

Milosh's phone vibrates in his pocket but when he pulls it out, all I notice is the state of his knuckles. 'Milosh, your hands,' I gasp. He glances down at them and shrugs.

'It was worth it.'

His knuckles are bloody and rough. I can't tell if it's his blood or Teddy's so I pick up one hand for further inspection. 'This needs to be cleaned up,' I decide. I start to rise from the step but a sharp, painful throb has me clutching my stomach and Milosh's hand snaking around my back to steady me.

'Need some help?' His low voice drawls.

'What was your first clue?'

He chuckles, shaking his head. 'Up you get, smart-mouth.'

I try to ignore the tingle I feel when he calls me that, and how my heart vibrates when I hear his sexy chuckle, but I can't. I've realized it's getting harder and harder for me to ignore all the little things Milosh says or does that make me laugh, smile or get flustered.

But again, it's too late to think about that now. I'll let that be tomorrow's problem.

His hands are firm around my waist and pull me up slowly until I'm standing upright. He walks at my pace up the rest of the stairs and to my room, opening the door with ease while still keeping me secure. Once we get into my room his hands start to loosen but I grab them, holding them in place.

'Just because I'm hurting doesn't mean I can't clean you up.' My stomach pain has lessened since we made it up the stairs, so I'm good to walk now, just at a slower pace.

'Daphne, you're in pain. I can sort out my own hands, it's okay.'

'No, it's not. You saved my life, the least I can do is patch you up. Come on.'

We walk into my bathroom and stop by the sink. I start to bend down but Milosh stops me.

'Tell me what you need and I'll get it for you.' He gently spins me around then lifts me up onto the counter. 'You stay here.'

I direct him to a spare flannel and a small first-aid kit in the cupboard and he finds them with ease before coming to stand in between my legs and passing them to me.

'Th-thank you,' is all I manage to get out when he rests his hands on my knees.

'Where do you want me?' he asks in an innocent tone, but his eyes betray him. They're laser-focused on me, heat building in them with each passing second.

'I . . . um, w-well . . .'

'Use your words, Miss Green.' The undeniable tension crackles in the air around us as he inches his hands up ever so slightly, softly squeezing my lower thigh. 'Where do you want me?'

Our eyes meet and my breathing dips. As if in slow motion, his tongue darts out slowly, wetting his lower lip, while his eyes stay glued to mine.

So . . . so . . . sexy.

Somehow I snap out of my daze, clearing my throat and lifting up the first-aid kit.

'Could you get out some antiseptic, gauze and a light bandage, please?' He takes the kit, our fingers brushing together briefly before I let go, pick up the flannel and lean over to turn on the tap, wetting it with warm water.

Once I've wrung it out, I lean back and notice Milosh has lined up everything that I asked for next to me.

'Hands.'

He brings them up for me to analyze again. I gently place the left one back down on my thigh, choosing to start carefully wiping the right one first. I'm meticulous, taking my time to be soft yet thorough. After I finish with the flannel, I set it down and add antiseptic to the area before blowing on his hand.

'Sorry, I know that's got to sting,' I empathize. When I don't hear a response from him, I look up to find Milosh studying me with a small smile. 'What?'

He shrugs. 'You're cute when you're concentrating.'

Not quite knowing how to respond to that, I decide it's my turn to ignore him so I lean over to the sink again and re-dampen the flannel before starting on his other hand.

'There,' I murmur once I've finished, lifting his hands to my lips and placing a feather-light kiss on each of them. 'All better.'

He pulls his eyes slowly away from mine, looking down at his hands, a gentle, lopsided smile on his face. 'Thank you, Miss Green.'

'You're welcome, Mr Petrov.'

He throws the flannel into the dirty laundry basket behind the door and cleans up the surfaces, putting the first-aid kit away. Then he lifts me off the counter and onto my feet, restoring our usual height difference.

'Well, I should go to bed,' I say, breaking the silence.

'Hmm,' he hums. 'Do you need me to get someone to help you with changing into your pyjamas?' A light coat of concern sheets his face as he glances to my bandaged shoulder.

I shake my head. 'No, I'll be fine if I take my time, but thank you anyway.'

He holds my gaze a moment longer before nodding and turning to the door, stopping to turn back when he's partway through it.

'Goodnight, Miss Green.'

'Goodnight, Mr Petrov.'

He closes the bathroom door behind him and I wait until I hear my main door close before I let out a breath I didn't even know I was holding.

I walk into my dressing room and start to remove my clothes.

You're cute when you're concentrating. Did he mean cute as in 'Aww, look at that baby' or cute as in Gabriella Montez dainty and sweet? The way he was looking at me didn't suggest the former, or am I just reading into it?

I groan, trying to get out of my own head but I can't. Not when I can hear his deep voice with its Bulgarian-American accent playing on a constant loop in my head.

Milosh has managed to seep into my mind and I don't

know how to get him out. To be honest, I don't think I want to. But if this is how I'm feeling now, what will happen if he finds his way into my heart?

26

MILOSH

'Are you sure you don't want us to stay?' Amelia asks Daphne for the seventeenth time.

'No. I don't. It's your anniversary week, you should be anywhere but here,' she answers before bringing another forkful of breakfast to her mouth.

'See,' Henry chirps, looking at Amelia who is sitting right next to him. 'She'll be fine, Meels, and Milosh will be here if anything happens, even though nothing will.'

It's been a week since the Teddy incident and everything's been pretty quiet.

Amelia's concussion has subsided and Daphne's walking at her normal speed now with her stomach healing. Her neck scar is barely visible and her arm, that was getting rewrapped regularly by Josh, and has now progressed to the large Band-Aid stage. We haven't done any training sessions since Teddy, to allow her to rest, and with her being either in her room or the snug I haven't had much reason to talk to her so have kept pretty much to myself, until now.

With Amelia and Henry set to leave for their two-week-long anniversary trip to Italy, Amelia asked if she, Henry, Daphne and I could all have breakfast together before they go.

'And she's going to the gala tonight,' Henry continues, 'so she won't even need us.'

'Actually,' Daphne cuts in, 'I don't think I'm gonna go tonight.'

We all stop and collectively look at her while she casually sips her orange juice.

'What do you mean you're not going?' Amelia gawks, and to be honest I can understand her reaction. Daphne has been going on about this gala for weeks, probably months, now, so for her to suddenly not want to go causes alarm bells to ring in my ears.

'I mean, I'm not going.' She shrugs. 'It just doesn't feel right any more.'

'Daph, you have to go,' Amelia almost pleads. 'You've got the outfit, you've got the date,' she points to me, 'and there's going to be plenty of security, literally nothing bad could happen. And you'll be able to see your friends and your cousins who you haven't seen in a while.'

'I know, I know, I've just lost the desire to go. That's all.'

'Are you feeling okay? Is it your stomach?' Henry asks

sincerely, his face crumpled with worry as he turns to Amelia. 'Maybe we should stay home.'

'No, no,' Daphne rushes out. 'It's nothing like that, I feel fine. Please don't stay here on my account.'

'I don't know,' Amelia says, 'you do look a little grey.'

'What?' Daphne almost shrieks. 'No, I do not.' She turns to look at me. 'Do I look grey to you?'

'Oh, don't ask Milosh, that's cheating.' Amelia rolls her eyes. 'That's like me asking Henry if I look ugly.'

Daphne completely ignores her as she stares at me, waiting for an answer.

'You look fine.'

Almost instantly, Henry starts laughing, whereas Amelia looks like she wants to chop my head off.

'Right, well, if you're not grey, I see no reason for you not to go tonight,' Amelia counters.

Daphne groans then turns to look at me. 'What do you think?'

'I think you should go,' I respond, my voice low.

Am I saying she should go just so I get to see her in whatever dress she picked out? No.

Am I saying she should go because I'll be able to spend some time with her? Absolutely not.

Am I saying she should go on the off-chance we have to do that fake girlfriend-boyfriend thing and I get to kiss her and touch her the way I did when we went shopping? That's absolutely ridiculous, of course not.

But am I aware that those things may happen if she does go? Definitely.

She studies me for a moment, completely ignoring Amelia and Henry's mockery.

'I think you should go,' Henry imitates me.

'No, he's more gruff, like this – *I think you should go*,' Amelia tries.

'What do you mean he's more gruff? I'm as gruff as they come.'

'Hen, he sounds like he has ties to the Mafia, you sound like someone from *Kingsman* or *The Gentlemen*.'

'Right? So how is that not gruff?'

'It's sexy, not gruff. His is sexy *and* gruff.'

'What are you even talking about right now? I'm literally the definition of sexy and gruff.'

'Of course you are, sweetie,' Amelia soothes, stroking her small hand up and down his arm. The size difference is almost comical. 'Of course you are.'

They continue bickering, but I tune them out as soon as Daphne says, 'Okay, I'll go.' She says it quietly so only I can hear her, and, man, if that doesn't make me feel special.

'Good,' I respond, trying to damp down a smirk when she gets shy and flustered under my gaze, reaching for her orange juice like it's a lifeline.

After a sip, she places it down and begins to lift out of her seat. 'Meet me in my room in half an hour,' she whispers into my ear, so close her lips brush the skin. She walks out of the dining room without so much as a goodbye, and I have to gather myself before I stand so I tune back into Henry and Amelia's conversation.

'I'm literally the cutest, most princessy person you've ever met.'

'No, Daphne's cute and princessy, you're like that sexy lady-in-waiting, if that's a thing.'

'Ugh, I don't want to be a lady-in-waiting.'

'Well, tough luck, gorgeous, that's who you are. Actually, no, you're more of a hot librarian.'

'What?' Amelia gapes.

'Yeah, I definitely see that.' Henry sits back in his chair, his eyes coasting over Amelia and his voice dropping low. 'You're all professional and hot . . . and sexy, and hot and—'

Okay, yeah, that's my cue to leave. Jeez, they really do need a vacation.

I pull my chair up and stand, and only then do they break off their increasingly uncomfortable conversation. I mean, I get it, they're two very attractive people. With Amelia's tanned skin, light brown hair and hazel eyes matched with Henry's large build, tattoo sleeve and symmetrical features, they're a very good-looking couple. But just because they match well does not mean I need the ins and outs of their marriage.

'Where did Daphne go?' Henry asks, looking around the room as if she's just gonna sprout up out of thin air.

'She left.'

'That was really informative, thank you, Milosh.'

I shrug and walk out before he can say anything else, and go to my room to get my swim shorts. Daphne said to meet her in her room in half an hour so that gives me enough time to get in a few laps.

'Come in,' I hear Daphne call out from behind her bedroom door. I enter her room and am greeted with a freshly showered Daphne, clad in what I've recently learned is called a loungewear set.

Her hair is straight again and it cascades delicately down her back. And her face is completely bare. She fiddles with her hands as I shut the door then close the distance between us, meeting her in the middle of her room.

'Okay, so, now that I know we're definitely going to the gala tonight we need to go through a few things.' She perches on the end of her bed so I go to sit on her reading chair. 'Number one, you're gonna need to play my boyfriend again, if that's okay with you. Isabella will be there and that girl can't keep her mouth shut, so it would be weird if we don't act like a couple.'

'Okay.'

'Okay, yes?' She looks at me sceptically.

'Okay yes, Miss Green. Continue.'

'All right.' She eyes me weirdly before continuing. 'Number two, if we're gonna do the whole relationship thing we need to make some boundaries around touching.'

'That sounds wise.'

'Okay, well, let's stick to handholding and simple, cute touches but no kissing unless absolutely necessary. Cheek or forehead kisses are fine, though. Is that all right with you?'

My jaw ticks, but I just nod in response.

'Okay, and last thing. If you're my boyfriend, chances are you'll know how to dance. Do you know how to dance, Mr Petrov?'

'Why would anyone see me dancing?'

'It's a gala. There will be dancing. Very boilerplate stuff, like waltzing.'

'Oh.' I pause. In my twenty years of living I've never once needed ballroom dancing as a skill. I can dismantle a bomb, I know the pressure points in the body that cause the most pain and I can speak five languages. I actively sat out of any dances at the military balls because there was no one I wanted to dance with. But none of this helps me now. 'No. I don't know how to dance.'

In response to my answer, this girl's face lights up like I've never seen. You'd think I just solved world hunger from the way she's glowing at me.

'Great! I get to teach you.'

Oh, boy.

She gets off her bed and walks to her bedside table, picking up her phone and connecting it to her speakers. A familiar slow song starts and Daphne walks towards me holding her hand out for me to take.

'This song is what got me into ballroom when I was younger. It literally takes you through the steps of a waltz.' She smiles as I rise and take her hand. It's soft in mine as she stops me, moving to stand in front but still keeping our hands linked.

'I think I've heard it before,' I say.

'Really? Well, it's called "Can I Have This Dance", from *High School Musical*.'

'Hallie used to play this song all the time at the children's home,' I explain.

'Ah, well then, she has good taste.' She smiles. 'Okay, so this arm is going to come and rest just here.' She pulls my hand onto her upper back, keeping my elbow out. 'And this hand stays in mine. Now, normally the man is supposed to lead but I'll have to teach you the steps first before we do that.'

'Okay.' That cute concentration face appears as she takes me through the basic steps and tests my rhythm and pace. I try to focus on the movements but all I can think about is how close she is and how good she smells. It takes me back to last week when she was cleaning and bandaging my hands. She was so cute and caring, it made my heart ache.

Is that what it's like to have someone fuss over you?

If so, then sign me up because I want her to fuss over me every day of the week.

We practise dancing for two hours before we call it quits. She looked pretty impressed with herself, and me, so I think I'll be all right tonight.

It's seven o'clock when I hear Daphne's honeyed voice invite me into her room once again.

As soon as I open the door, I'm taken aback.

'Beautiful,' I murmur, closing the door behind me.

Her hair looks different now as it flows down her back in vintage-looking curls, and her face is lightly dusted with make-up. Her neck is bare as she holds her necklace box in her hands, and then there's her dress.

The dress she picked out is a silky light pink – almost white – colour, going in at the waist and fanning out only slightly when it reaches mid-thigh and then tracks all the way to the floor. The top of the dress is off the shoulder, covering her Band-Aid and perfectly sculpting her upper body.

'It's Alexander McQueen.' She glows up at me.

'Mmm,' I rumble. 'That's nice, but I wasn't talking about the dress.' I couldn't care less who made it. All I care about is how she looks in it. And she looks like art.

Like regal, graceful, elegant art. Almost too striking to touch.

Almost.

All she needs is a tiara and you could easily convince me she's royalty.

'Oh.' She's flustered, looking down at her feet. 'Thank you.' She looks back up at me and frowns slightly. 'Why's your bow tie undone?'

'I was hoping you could help me with that,' I drawl, closing the distance between us and coming to stand in front of her.

She nods, placing her necklace box on her bed before reaching up to attend to my tie for me, her delicate fingers working with the precision of a sniper. I know exactly how to tie a bow tie from all the military balls I've been to but I just wanted to see that concentration face again, and I always seemed to get them wonky when I did my own.

'There.' She smiles. 'Now, stand back, I want to look at

you properly.' I take two steps back and await her verdict.

'Where did you get this from? It fits you perfectly.' Her eyes peruse my body languidly, her gaze travelling from the black leather dress shoes to the custom tuxedo and then up to my hair.

'When Hallie and Averie came over they also brought me a suit they had made by a designer friend of theirs. I couldn't tell you the name of the designer, all I know is that they told me to send over my measurements, so I did.'

'Wow,' Daphne breathes, feeling the material between her fingers and taking a closer look at the cut. 'You're gonna need to send me their numbers so I can find out who it's by.'

'Sure.' My body tenses when her hands graze my neck as she assesses the lapels of the jacket and again when she analyzes the buttons. Stepping in closer to get a better look.

'Gosh, you smell good,' she mutters, so low I almost don't hear it. I ignore the words because I don't think she meant to say them out loud, and wait until she takes a step back to finally release a breath. We're still standing close, just not pressed together any more.

'Well, Mr Petrov, I think you look rather lovely.'

'Is that so?'

'Mm hmm. Very much boyfriend material.'

I look at her for a moment and remember the lack of

jewellery on her neck. 'Would you like me to help you put your necklace on?'

She nods, picking the box back up and handing it to me, turning around as I carefully take the absurdly expensive diamond necklace out, casting the case back onto the bed.

'Pick up your hair for me,' I request, draping the jewellery around her neck once she does so. 'Done.' She turns around and drops her hair.

'You look beautiful, Miss Green.'

'Thank you, Mr Petrov.'

I notice a stray hair so I tuck it behind her ear for her, holding her gaze while I do so.

A knock at her door forces us apart as George enters.

'Oh, Milosh, I didn't realize you were in here.' He frowns briefly before recovering and focusing on Daphne.

'Daphne, darling, I just wanted to . . . I have a little . . . well, this is for you,' he says eventually, making his way into the room, thrusting a pink box wrapped in a gold bow into her hands. 'It's an early birthday present.'

'Oh.' Daphne looks at him with a mixture of surprise and glee, and it's the sweetest expression I've ever seen on her face. 'Thank you, Daddy.' She opens it delicately, removing the bow carefully before peeling off the wrapping paper.

'It's only small, and there are more gifts to come,' George

prefaces, looking apprehensive. 'This is just something I thought you might like for tonight.'

Daphne lifts the box lid to reveal a bottle.

'Oh, it's perfume, thank you!'

'It's actually your mother's old fragrance. I know it got discontinued many years ago, but I got this one made especially for you.'

Her lips part as she takes in what he says. She lifts the perfume fully up out of the box and sprays it on one of the throw blankets at the end of her bed, lifting it to her nose once it's settled.

'It smells exactly like her,' she whispers, her eyes glossing over. 'Thank you, Daddy, thank you so much.' She hands me the perfume and makes her way over to George as he wraps her in a hug.

'That's all right, darling. I thought you might want to wear it tonight, unless you already have perfume on.'

'I've already put mine on for the night, but as of tomorrow I'll be wearing this!' She beams as she pulls away from him. She takes the perfume from my hand and walks into her dressing room leaving me and George in the main room.

'Well, good, I'm glad,' he calls out, rocking back on his heels awkwardly. 'I also wanted to let you know I've got a bit of work to do tonight so I will be coming, I'll just get there a bit later than you. Ideally, I'll be there around ten-ish.'

The door knocks again and this time Amelia and Henry enter.

'We're leaving now, but we just wanted to say goodbye,' Henry announces, glancing around the room. 'Where's Daphne?'

As if on cue, she floats out of her dressing room looking like the princess she is.

'Wow, Daph, you look gorgeous!' Amelia gushes.

'She's right as always, sweetie, you look beautiful,' Henry adds.

'Thank you!' Daphne responds, practically glowing.

'All right, well, we do need to get going now, so you guys have fun,' Henry says, looking between me and Daphne, George clearly forgotten in this equation.

'Hey, Daph, could you just go stand next to Milosh? I wanna see how you two look together.'

I sigh in agitation, because I know exactly where this is going.

'Wow!' Henry quips. 'Don't you two just look like the perfect couple.' George goes to stand next to Henry and Amelia and starts nodding his head.

'Wow, you're right, I can really see it.'

'All right, that's enough.' I glance over to Daphne. 'Are you ready to go?'

'I just need to grab my bag,' she says, making her way

back into the dressing room. I watch her as she walks away, only to find three pairs of eyes looking at me when I turn back.

'Ah, jeez,' George groans, 'it's like Henry and Amelia all over again.'

Henry starts laughing, Amelia looks horrified and I roll my eyes, all in time for Daphne to walk out, bag in hand, completely oblivious to it all.

'What?' Daphne asks impatiently.

'Nothing. Literally, nothing at all,' I deadpan. 'You ready?'

'Mm hmm.'

'All right, let's go.'

'You guys take my car,' says George. 'I'll take the driver so I can work in the back.'

'Okay, bye Daddy.' She places a kiss on his cheek before saying her goodbyes to Amelia and Henry and walks out in front of me.

'Hey.' Henry stops me by the door, his expression serious. 'Keep her safe, all right?'

'Of course.'

This girl means a lot to him. But I've come to realize she means even more to me. And there's nothing I wouldn't do to protect her.

27

The annual Greenway Group charity gala is always a stunning event. This year there are chandeliers hanging from the venue's high, decorated ceilings, candlelit tables and a live jazz band playing 'The Way You Look Tonight' by Frank Sinatra. Everyone's dressed impeccably, from the servers to the guests, and all I can smell is a mix of niche fragrances all battling it out in an imaginary projection contest.

Milosh guides me to the seating chart, his hand against the small of my back, thumb rubbing languid strokes against the fabric of my dress. I lean into his touch as I lazily search for our names, not really putting much effort in so I can prolong this as much as possible.

We drove here mostly in silence, with light jazz music filling the space. Tension crackled high in the air in anticipation of what we were about to let ourselves do, and it took every ounce of self-control not to touch him or play with his hair. But now we're here I can play with it as much as I want.

As soon as Milosh handed the car keys to the valet his hands found mine and they haven't left my body since. Not that I'm complaining.

'Daphne!'

When I hear Isabella's all-too-familiar voice I turn around and plaster a smile on my face. It's not that I'm not happy to see her; I am. It's just that she interrupted a perfect moment that I don't know if I'll ever get back.

'Bella, hi!' I give her a quick hug and kiss on the cheek when she comes to join me and Milosh.

'I've already checked what table you are: table seven, next to me and Eddie at table eight.' Her eyes find Milosh and her smile turns a little too seductive for my liking. 'Hi, Milosh, good to see you again.'

'Yep,' is all he says as he slips his hands into his pockets.

Isabella gives me a look that suggests she wants to talk to me alone, so after an internal huff I turn to Milosh. 'Would you mind getting me a drink, please? Non-alcoholic?'

He looks between me and Bella before nodding. 'Sure.'

He walks off and leaves us staring after him.

'Daph, he looks good,' is the first thing she says to me.

'As in, really good. As in, if I could, I'd drop Eddie for him in a heartbeat.'

'Isabella, you love Eddie.'

'Yeah, I do, so that should tell you all you need to know about how good your boyfriend looks.'

I watch him as he orders a drink for me at the bar while a petite brunette tries to talk to him.

'Ew.' Me and Isabella grimace in unison when she starts grossly caressing his arm then moves on to his chest before he stops her. He captures her arm and holds it firmly before saying something inaudible to her, then practically flicks her hand away.

'Ugh, he's even loyal, too,' Isabella groans. 'Is there anything he can't do?'

'Not really, no.' The funny thing is, that's not even a lie. I think back to earlier in my room when I was teaching him a basic waltz and how quickly it came to him. He almost immediately knew how to lead me in the dance, purely by instinct, and was able to pick up steps with no difficulty whatsoever.

'How's it going with you two?' Bella turns to look at me.

'It's going good.' I smile. 'Really good.'

'Are you doing anything with him for your birthday?'

'I don't know. I mean, I don't have anything planned

but he might,' I lie. I haven't told Milosh it's my birthday in a few days, purely because it doesn't matter and he's had a lot more pressing issues to deal with. And it's not like we're actually dating so there's no need for him to know.

'Oh, he's definitely gonna surprise you, in one way or another.' She looks back at him with a knowing smile.

'Where are the tables?' I ask, in desperate need of a new topic.

Originally when I told Milosh we were going to need to fake date tonight, I was pretty excited. I get to live out the relatively new fantasy of us actually being together without any consequences or awkward conversations. But now that we're here, all it's done is make me realize how lonely my life actually is. Yes, I'm always surrounded by people but I still have that hole in my heart. That ache for something more.

I will for ever be grateful for my father, my friends and my house staff that have turned into somewhat of a second family to me, but I want more. I want non-platonic affection. I want someone to call my boyfriend and it actually be real. I want birthday surprises and little 'just because' gifts. I want the opportunity to learn someone's love language, and show them how much they mean to me through it.

Faking has its perks, but that's all it is at the end of the day. Fake.

I watch as Milosh gets handed our drinks and makes his way back to us, his eyes solely focused on me. When he watches me like that it warms my heart. It makes me believe he may actually feel something too. In the short time I've been at the gala, I've come to realize that I don't just want *someone* to call a boyfriend, I want it to be Milosh.

'Oh, they're on the other side of the hall,' Bella announces half-heartedly as she recognizes someone across the room.

'You go talk to them,' I suggest. 'Milosh and I will find our table and talk to you more later.'

'Okay, great,' she says, completely disregarding me, walking away. I laugh after her, but my laughter dies as a large warm presence enters my personal space.

'She's just a joy,' Milosh says, handing me a champagne flute. 'It's the non-alcoholic one.'

'Thank you,' I reply softly. 'And she's not that bad, she's just a little oblivious to social cues sometimes.'

'She has the attention span of a gnat.'

I just about choke on my drink when an uncharacteristically heavy cackle fights to leave my mouth.

'Mr Petrov, there are some things we just don't say out loud.' I'm still fighting the remnants of a laugh as he looks at me with that bored expression on his face. 'No matter how true they may be.'

'Hmm,' he hums, completely disregarding everything I just said. 'Shall we go and sit down?'

'Sure.'

We begin to walk towards our table but are stopped before we get there.

'Daphne?' I hear a male voice calling from behind me.

I turn around to see my Cousin Camilla and her fiancé waving, walking over to us.

'Hi!' I say and sign, after I pass my drink to Milosh. 'Milosh, this is my Cousin Camilla and her fiancé Oscar Huang. Oscar and Camilla this is my boyfriend, Milosh.'

A boyfriend, Daph? Bella told me you had one but I didn't expect him to look like this, Camilla signs, eyebrows raised. She gives Milosh a once-over. *To be fair, I get it, he's gorgeous.*

I mean, look at the arms, I had no choice, I sign back, but don't repeat that part out loud. She laughs and turns her attention fully onto Milosh, waving a hello.

'Hi,' Milosh says to Camilla and Oscar, taking Oscar's outstretched hand for a brisk shake. 'I'm sorry, I don't know sign language but it's nice to meet you.'

'Honestly, neither did I until I met Cam,' Oscar replies verbally and in sign. 'But she's really good at lip reading, so just enunciate your words and you're good for now.'

To that, Camilla nods her head, smiling before looking back over to Milosh.

So, Milosh, tell me, what exactly are your intentions towards my cousin? Oscar starts translating as she signs.

He looks to me for a moment, his jaw ticking and his eyes moving from my mouth to my eyes before he turns back to Camilla and shrugs. 'To love her the way she deserves to be loved.'

Well, that was a statement and a half.

28

MILOSH

'So, Daphne,' a stuffy-looking older woman drawls. 'What are your plans now that you've finished school?' My arm is slung around Daphne's chair and as soon as the woman finishes her question I can feel Daphne tense in her seat as she plasters a polite smile on her face.

'I'm going to study Midwifery, starting in October.'

'Oh, how . . . noble.' The woman has the audacity to look disgusted. 'And what does your father think about this? Surely he thought you should take Business, no?'

I lift my arm slightly off the back of Daphne's chair and lightly touch the back of her shoulder, moving my hand in small lazy strokes. I don't think she realizes she leans back slightly, sinking into my touch as she braces herself to explain her choices to this random woman.

I want to jump in and tell her to mind her business but I decide against that. This is Daphne's world, has been for all of her life, so she's more than able to handle people like this.

'He knows I'm not all that interested in business and thinks midwifery is a great fit for me, but, hey, I'm very young so I have plenty of time if I change my mind!' She keeps her tone light and sweet, but I know she's itching to make a sarcastic remark.

'You don't think it's a little . . .' the older woman trails off, probably looking for some politically correct words. 'Beneath you?' she finishes.

Daphne's eyes narrow slightly. 'How exactly is healthcare beneath me?'

'Well, for starters your father is George Green,' the woman says, like the statement is self-explanatory.

I know the Greens have money but I don't think I grasped quite how much until I came here. Isabella, Camilla and Daphne are the only Greens in attendance at the moment and it seems everybody wants a piece of them. But not to actually talk to them and get to know them, more to talk *at* them about their parents. Daphne hasn't gone one conversation without someone asking where her father is or how he and the business are doing.

'I think midwifery is cool,' chirps a handsome black guy who looks to be about my age, as he takes his seat between Daphne and the older woman, not before pressing a kiss to Daphne's cheek. 'Been a long time, Daph.' He smiles as he places his drink down, holding out his hand to me. 'Hi, I'm Jake.'

'Milosh.'

As soon as Jake sits down I can feel Daphne relax, and I know I should be happy about that but I'm not. Why does she feel better now he's showed up? Who the hell even is he?

'Jacob, hello!' The older lady beams. 'How are you, dear?'

'Well, I was great until I heard you disrespecting healthcare professionals,' he says, apparently not caring how he sounds or who hears him.

'Oh, well . . .' The older woman gets flustered, turning a deep shade of red. 'I wasn't disrespecting them, I was just pointing out that Daphne is a Green. She shouldn't be concerning herself with things like that. I mean, surely you understand?'

'I hear what you're saying,' Jake replies diplomatically, 'but I think you're wrong. Just because Daphne comes from a certain family doesn't mean she has to follow what they do. I just so happen to be following in my father's footsteps because I like it. Not because I have to.' He turns to Daphne. 'Do whatever makes you happy, Daph. The rest will sort itself out.'

She smiles at him and looks relatively pleased when the older woman excuses herself to 'freshen up'.

'Thank you,' Daphne breathes when she's gone. 'If I had to explain to one more person why I'm choosing midwifery over working with my father I would've been charged for murder.'

Jake laughs lightly. 'Don't worry, I get it.'

They continue to converse but I tune out.

I've only recently accepted that I have feelings for Daphne, and since then I've been whirling the idea around in my head seeing how it could work. But ever since I handed the keys to the valet this evening, that idea has been on pause. After seeing and hearing from Daphne about the kinds of money these people possess, it put everything into perspective. She fits into this world like a glove, as she rightfully should, accustomed to this kind of lifestyle. A lifestyle I can't provide.

Yes, I know we're young, but I wasn't lying when I told Camilla I want to love her the way she deserves to be loved. She deserves to be showered with gifts, live in a big house and have everything her heart desires. But on a military salary I can't do that.

Really, she belongs with someone like Jake. Handsome, smart, affluent. They even look perfect sitting next to each other. It's easy to imagine them married with kids, a big house and a great life. But I don't have to accept that.

I don't have to be one of those guys who complain about their situation and don't do anything about it. I can build a life for me and Daphne. A life she deserves, if she's willing.

I'll do whatever I need to do to make it work.

Then there's the fact she's not just anybody, she's literally a job.

I've always remained professional, but from the moment I walked into the Greens' house and sat next to her, I knew that was gonna be a problem. What will happen once I've finished the task force project? Will I be able to see her? The only reason I'm in this country is for a job, but as soon as it's finished I move back to the States.

I hate thinking about this, but it needs to be done. I can't run into a real relationship with her with no plan. But right now is not the time to have deep meaningful conversations with myself, so with an effort of will I tune back into the conversation between Jake and Daphne. I can think about all of this later.

'You look beautiful, by the way,' Jake states, his eyes respectfully skimming over her. 'Milosh, you're one lucky man and I think I'm gonna need your game card because you're the first one to lock her down.'

'Oh, please,' Daphne scoffs. 'You had your chance, you just blew it.'

'That's why I asked Milosh for his game card. He definitely did not blow it.'

All right. That's enough of Jake for today.

'I think it's time for a dance,' I state as I rise to my feet, holding out my hand to Daphne. The meal has long been served and eaten, and now people are either floating from table to table, catching up, or dancing to the slow song that the band is playing.

Daphne looks a little startled at my abruptness, but that quickly fades and she takes my hand, excusing herself to Jake.

She wraps her fingers around my forearm and we make our way into the crowd of couples wrapped up in each other.

'Explain something to me,' I say as I spin her into me, the jazz band transitioning into 'That Old Feeling' by Frank Sinatra. She drops her head to rest on my chest as we move together. Slow and rhythmic. 'Why do you want to be a midwife?'

She doesn't answer for a moment, letting the music float around us. 'I want to help people, women especially.' She melts further into me and just like that all my concerns about the future disappear as I hold her firmly against me, one hand on her back and the other wrapped around hers. 'Birth is such a scary yet wonderful thing, and I want to be the person that helps families through it. I want every woman and baby that leaves my care to have a positive birth story. As calm and peaceful as possible, surrounded by a loving team.'

'Well, I have no doubt you'll be a fantastic midwife,' I murmur into her hair. 'You're the most caring, loving person

I've met, and I know you'll give these mothers the best care they could possibly receive.' She lifts her head off my chest, her mesmerizing chocolate eyes boring into mine.

'You really think so?'

I let go of her hand and tuck a stray hair behind her ear, my fingers lingering on her neck for a split second before I look back into her eyes and nod. 'I do.'

Bringing my hand back to hers we continue dancing, our bodies moving together in perfect harmony as I take the lead.

'Milosh?'

'Hmm?'

She tips her head up and I bring mine down so she can speak into my ear. 'I really like pretending to be your girlfriend.'

The corners of my lips tip up slightly upon hearing her confession. I dip my head so now I'm the one with my mouth to her ear. 'I like being your boyfriend too.'

I purposefully leave out the word 'pretend' to see how she reacts. She pulls away slightly, searching my eyes intently. Her gaze drops to my lips before she reaches up and places her hand on the nape of my neck, pulling me in slowly. Just as she tips her head up, her lips preparing to meet mine, a throat clears behind her.

I look up and she turns around, and we see a black man who resembles George staring at us. 'Uncle Leo, hi!' Daphne breathes, removing her hand from my neck and creating some distance.

'Hi, Daph, sorry to interrupt.' He makes a point of looking between us before continuing, 'but, where is your father? I wanted to introduce him to someone but I couldn't find him anywhere.'

'Oh,' Daphne says, taking my hand and making her way off the dance floor and to our table. 'He said he would be here by ten because he had some work to do.'

'You didn't come with him?'

'No, he told me and Milosh to go by ourselves and he'd join later.'

Leo looks at his watch before frowning. 'It's nearly eleven forty-five.'

'Let me call him to see where he is,' Daphne suggests, reaching over into her seat to fish for her phone.

'So you're the boyfriend?' Leo directs the words at me.

'Yes, sir.'

'I thought she was with that Teddy kid.'

My jaw ticks. 'No, sir.'

He watches me for another moment. 'Well, all right then, as long as you make her happy.' He turns to Daphne. 'Daph, have you got through to him yet?'

She walks up to us shaking her head. 'No, not yet. Sorry, Uncle Leo.'

'That's fine.' He gives her a kiss on the head. 'Let me know when you do.' He walks off, leaving me and Daphne alone again, but the tension that was there before Leo arrived has vanished, replaced with worry.

'What's wrong?'

'I tried calling my father four times and he hasn't picked up. He normally picks up straight away.' I pull my phone out and notice there's a missed call from Josh, the Greens' cook. Pressing *call back* I bring the phone to my ear but after a long ring it goes to voicemail. I try George twice and it goes to voicemail both times. I muster the calmest expression I can and look back to Daphne.

'Get your bag and say goodbye to your cousins.'

'Do you think something's happened?'

'I don't know, but we're gonna find out.'

29

My blood runs cold when we turn into the driveway of the house and see the door standing open, with no sign of the security guards.

Milosh turns the engine off and looks at me. 'I don't know why no one's out here or why the door's open but I need to go check it out. I don't want you to sit here by yourself so you're gonna come with me. Don't leave my side, okay? I can't have anything happen to you.'

'Okay,' is all I manage to squeeze out. I'm scared. So scared of whatever is lurking behind that door, figuratively and literally.

He rounds the car and opens my door, grabbing my hand as soon as I get out. This time there's no romantic undertones. Flirty Milosh has been replaced by work Milosh.

Slightly scary, rough and commanding work Milosh.

We walk into the house, going in and out of every room with speed and finding them all empty and completely trashed.

In the snug, all the sofas have been torn apart, the carpets raised and all the artwork ripped off the walls. In the kitchen, all the food cupboards are open and non-perishable items lie strewn all over the tiles. A few plates are broken and one of the taps is running. In Daddy's study it's hard to make out the floor through all the ripped books and artwork. His computer is completely smashed and his paperwork is everywhere.

My lip quivers as we pass through the eerily silent house that no longer feels like a home. But then we get to my room.

When Milosh opens my door, I gasp.

Everything's ruined, from my mattress to my bathroom mirrors. Whoever did this left no stone unturned. We walk into my dressing room to find most of my clothes on the floor, crumpled and dirty with footprints embedded in them.

'I know this is hard to look at but I need you to focus right now.' Milosh tugs on my arm, bringing my attention to him. 'I need you to lock your bedroom door behind me and pack a bag of non-ruined clothes. I'm gonna quickly go and check the rest of the house and pack a bag myself.

I'll be back in five minutes and I'll knock four times. If you don't hear a knock after six minutes I want you to call the police and stay in here until they arrive. Can you do all of that?'

'Yes,' I choke out. My sadness now replaced with anger as I take in what they've done.

'I'm working on downloading the security feed but that'll take a while. So we don't know who did this, where everyone is or why this happened. Right now we're fully blind so we need to get out and leave as quickly as possible.'

He places a chaste kiss on my cheek then leaves. I follow his instructions, locking the door behind him and packing a bag. I tip out a week's worth of knickers and socks from their drawers and add them in, along with a few bras. I find a clean pink gym set, three dresses still on their hangers, a pair of linen trousers with the matching shirt and a pair of loafers. I go to zip up my bag, but my eyes coast over to the dresser where I keep my make-up and perfume. I grab my make-up bag and the first perfume I can find and stuff them into the duffel, then move into the bathroom. I gather the bare essential toiletries and place them into my bag as well, just in time to hear four strong knocks at the door. I unlock it, luggage in hand, and once Milosh sees the duffel he takes it and grabs me, moving us down the stairs and out of the house with haste.

The wind howls around us as we climb into the car and he throws the bags in the back as he waits for the gates to open.

'We need to ditch this vehicle as soon as possible, so I'm just warning you now, I will be stealing a car. It's not ideal but it needs to be done.'

'That's fine.' Stealing a car is the least of my worries right now.

'When I went to the top floor there was no one there,' Milosh continues. 'My guess is they took your father and all the staff. Why, I'm not too sure, but by the looks of it they didn't go willingly.'

'How do you know it wasn't willing?'

'There were bloodstains on the floor of Charlotte's bedroom and in your father's study.'

I feel numb.

I feel sick.

I feel too many emotions yet nothing at all at the same time.

Daddy's gone.

So are Josh, Bethany, Charlotte and the rest of the staff.

All of my family.

'We need to tell Amelia and Henry.'

'Yes, but not now.'

'What do you mean?'

'Right now they're safe and in their own little bubble. No one knows exactly where they're going in Italy because Henry wanted it to be a surprise for Amelia so no one can track them. They're safe where they are.'

Henry and Amelia are safe.

Daddy's gonna be okay.

This is all gonna be okay.

We stop at a red light and I haul the door open, vomiting onto the road. Once I'm done, I close it and pull out a tissue from the glove compartment. Milosh rubs my back as I tip my head over my knees.

'Where are we going now?' I cough out after a few minutes.

'I've contacted your pilot so we're gonna meet him and fly to Provence. I know you and your father have a small cottage there so that's where we'll stay until I can figure out our next move.'

I nod and straighten up, rolling down the window so I can get a bit of fresh air. I've never been more grateful for Greenway Aviation in my life.

'I need you to write down these numbers on this piece of paper for me.' He hands me his phone, a piece of scrap paper and a pen. 'I know this must be really difficult for you but you're doing really well with all of this.'

I glance over at him for a moment but he's watching

the road. 'Thank you,' I say before focusing back on the number transfer.

'Done.' I say, putting the lid on the pen and handing the phone back to Milosh.

'Good job, Miss Green. Could I borrow your phone a minute, please?' I hand him my phone, unlocking it, but he clearly didn't need it unlocked because he locks it straight back, rolls down his window and throws it out of the window, along with his own.

'Why did you just do that?' I ask.

'It's easy for people to track you from your phone. We already have to publish a flight plan, and I don't really wanna make it any easier for anyone to find us. The numbers I got you to write down are all we need.'

On a quiet road, Milosh pulls over in front of a family car.

'Stay here.'

He gets out of the car and I feel a second surge of nausea. I tip my head down between my thighs again and close my eyes, trying to focus on my breathing as it dawns on me he's actually stealing a car. In the grand scheme of things it's not that bad, but the thought of an innocent family waking up in the morning only to find their vehicle missing makes me feel so wretched it's almost unbearable.

The rear car door opens and closes, which I assume

is Milosh getting our bags out, and then my side swings open.

'Let's go.'

I get out and jump into the front of the new car. The two children's car seats in the back give me a renewed pang of guilt.

'How did you unlock it without sounding the alarm?'

'The children's home was in a pretty rough area so I picked up a few things when I was there. I never stole a car myself, but the older boys taught me how.'

'I'm so sorry you had the childhood you did.'

He shrugs. 'It came in handy tonight.'

We make it to the private air strip twenty minutes later, the darkness of the night and the chill in the air in perfect harmony with my mood. Milosh pulls out the two duffels from the boot and gets out, coming around my side to open the door. He pulls off his Tuxedo jacket and wraps it around me, picking back up the duffels in one swift motion, carrying them in one hand and grasping my shaking hand in the other.

His jacket practically swallows me whole and his scent envelops me, offering me a smidge of comfort as we walk towards the stairs to the plane.

'Good evening, Mr Petrov and Miss Green,' the air steward greets us. Milosh nods in response but all I have in me is a weak smile as I pass her.

Once we're in the air, I unclip my seatbelt and head to the bathroom at the back of the plane. I lock the door and open a packet containing a disposable toothbrush and a small tube of toothpaste before quickly brushing my teeth.

I look up at myself in the mirror and laugh without humour.

I look great. I look like my world has not just fallen apart and instead I'm taking an impromptu trip with my boyfriend, after attending an event like something out of a James Bond film.

I finish up in the bathroom and walk out, to where Milosh is watching something on a phone.

'Whose phone is that?' I ask as I go to sit in the seat opposite his.

'The flight attendant's. I emailed myself the CCTV footage from your house so I logged into my email from her phone to check it.'

'Has it loaded?'

He nods.

'Can I see?'

'I don't know if that's a good idea.'

'Please, Milosh, my brain can't possibly make up any worse scenarios.'

He studies me for a moment, unease resting in his eyes,

before he nods and hands me the phone. He's emailed himself multiple videos of different angles of the house. I click on the first one and it shows a grainy picture of the driveway, the gates opening and five black SUVs driving up. One of the security guys at the front of the house walks up to the first car, speaking to the passengers for a moment before a pair of hands reaches out and twists his neck, causing him to collapse to the ground.

I let out a gasp, covering my mouth, and watch as the other security man pulls out his radio but doesn't make it far because three big men dressed head to toe in black step out of the car and rip it from his hand. The video stops so I slide on to the next clip. This one is short and shows about six of these men walking into the house and pairing off to search different rooms.

I move on to the next clip of the kitchen where Josh and Bethany are cleaning up after dinner. Josh is by the sink and Bethany is standing next to him, packing the dishwasher. Her head rises and she drops the plate in her hand. The crash gets Josh's attention and he turns around only to be greeted with a gun pointed at him. My heart breaks when they both hold their hands up in surrender and follow whatever instructions they're given, walking out of the kitchen.

There are no cameras in the bedrooms, the bathrooms

or my father's study so I can't see what happened there, but there is another clip showing the first-floor hallway as the masked men go in and out of the rooms.

I turn the phone off and pass it back to Milosh, saying nothing. I look at my hands, not quite knowing what to do with myself.

'What do you think they wanted?'

'I think they wanted to scare George into giving them the formula. The camera cut out after that last clip so I don't know how many people were in the house, but I do know that they won't hurt him until they get what they want. As far as they can tell, George is the only one who knows where it is so killing him wouldn't be beneficial.'

I stay quiet, taking in what I just heard.

He's alive.

He has to be alive.

And they didn't harm anyone on camera so there's a good chance they're alive too.

There were bloodstains on the floor of Charlotte's bedroom and in your father's study. Milosh's voice echoes back to me.

They may be injured but they're okay.

They have to be.

I will my tears not to fall but they don't listen. So I cry.

I cry for my father.

I cry for my house.

I cry for my family.

'Come here,' Milosh says, so I stand and he pulls me into his lap. He stays silent and lets me sob into his chest, rubbing my back methodically. 'It's gonna be okay, we'll find them.'

We have to.

30

It's 3 a.m. when the taxi drops us off at the cottage. I take the spare key out of a small alcove to the side of the window and open the door. The hallway is dark, cold and uninviting as we enter and an unexpected wave of nostalgia washes over me when Milosh flicks on the lights. I haven't been here in years.

My father bought this cottage as a Christmas present for my mother when I was six. She kept telling him that we needed a small, cosy getaway, far from all the noise and people because, unlike me and my father, my mother didn't grow up with money. When she married him, a house full of staff took some getting used to. So my father bought this small two-bed cottage in the middle of the French countryside, with wooden beams lining the ceilings and a fireplace gracing the bedrooms and the living room. My mother loved it and didn't let anyone use it but us. For three years, we spent every possible holiday here, even a couple of weekends, and my mother had a strict no-work-phone rule so that she and my father were just present in the moment.

'I'm just gonna do a quick sweep of the house,' Milosh says, opening the living-room door and dropping our bags in there. I walk into the kitchen, turning the lights on and looking in our cupboards to see what we have. It's been around five years since my father and I visited so it's not a shock when I open an empty fridge and empty cupboards, save for a packet of pasta. I reach for it and check the use-by date. Yep. Went off two years ago.

'The house is clear,' Milosh states as he walks into the kitchen looking around. 'I'll go and get some food in the morning.'

I nod and close all the cupboards again, shivering slightly when I feel a gust of cold air.

'I lit the fire in the living room and what I assumed was your room, so it should warm up in a bit.' His eyes are soft when they meet mine. I wrap myself tighter in Milosh's jacket before making my way upstairs. My bedroom is the first door, so thankfully I don't have to walk past my parents', but when I go inside, I'm hit with a pang of longing.

Longing for a different time.

Longing for different circumstances.

The room is decorated the way you'd think an eight-year-old would want. The walls are coated in a sparkly pink paint and the bed is covered with Disney princess pillows. To one side of it sits a bookcase with all my favourite childhood books, and on the other side sits my Barbie collection. The last time I visited I wasn't able to sleep in here and I slept in my father's room while he took the sofa, but I can't think of anything worse than spending the night in my father's room so I make my way back downstairs.

When I walk into the living room, Milosh is on his haunches flicking through all our old DVDs with a small smile on his face.

'Find anything you like?'

He looks up at me, holding *A Cinderella Story, Another Cinderella Story* and *Cloudy with a Chance of Meatballs*. 'I'm guessing all of these movies were picked by you?'

I laugh lightly as I drop to the sofa, a yawn escaping me. 'You would think, but no. *Ratatouille* and *Cloudy with a Chance* were Daddy, and the Cinderella franchise was my mother. But everything else? Yeah, that was all me.'

The cottage is so remote, you can't get very good wi-fi. When we used to come here we only had a DVD player, some board games and books to work with, so we amassed quite a collection.

Not wanting to talk about the sleeping arrangements, I opt for a light topic. 'You wanna watch a film?'

'Sure,' Milosh responds, standing up to his full height. 'What movie?'

'I don't mind, you choose.'

The fire crackles away in the background as he flicks through the options, finally settling on one. After slipping the disc into the DVD player he comes to sit next to me. Our thighs brush together, sending my own crackle of fire up my leg.

I close my eyes for a moment and bring my hand to my neck, trying to massage the knot out of it, when I hear the familiar overture of *Aladdin* filling the air.

'Good choice.' I glance over at him, but am shocked to find his eyes already on me, or, more accurately, my neck as I try to work away the tension.

'You want some help?' Milosh asks, his eyes darkening.

Do I want him massaging my neck?

'Yes, please.'

Huh. Turns out I do.

'Turn around.'

I move so that I'm sitting sideways on the sofa and drop my hand, watching the film out of the corner of my eye.

I feel the seat dip as Milosh comes closer and I suck in a breath when he gently pulls my hair to the side. The air is charged with anticipation as tension rakes through my body.

His touch starts out gentle at first but gets firmer when he finds the knot and goes in on it. I let out an involuntary whimper as his warm hands knead my flesh and my breathing drops. *Aladdin* plays in the background but I can't hear it anymore. Not over the roaring in my ears.

'There,' Milosh says, voice gruff. 'Does that feel better?'

I turn around to face him, moving my hand back to my neck, testing it out.

'Much better, thank you.'

He watches my fingers. 'Good.'

I let my hand drag down the length of my neck, before dropping it in my lap. Milosh tracks the movement intently.

I watch him as his eyes coast back up my body, settling on my parted lips.

I know it's not the right time to do this but he's a welcome distraction so I lean over and kiss him.

It's tentative and unsure at first but as I move my hand to cup his face, drawing him closer, it starts to deepen. His hand finds my waist and squeezes, causing the kiss to pick up some speed.

'Daphne, we shouldn't.' He breathes heavily against my lips, pulling away so he can see me.

'Then stop looking at me like that.'

A groan erupts from deep in his chest. 'You know I can't do that.'

'Well then, we seem to be at an impasse,' I whisper, biting down on my bottom lip. 'But don't worry, Mr Petrov, I think I know how to fix that.' My mouth crashes back onto his as his fingers make their way through my hair, tugging gently to move my head into a better position. He breaks the kiss, one hand starting its way down my neck, while the other rests on my lower back.

'You smell so good,' he rasps against my throat.

I don't respond. I'm in a breathless haze, the air heavy and thick around us. He lifts me on top of him, bunching up the dress slightly so I'm more comfortable, and I shed the jacket, letting it drop haphazardly to the floor.

I pull his mouth back onto mine, nibbling lightly on his bottom lip, smiling against his mouth when he lets out a groan.

'You're gonna make me go crazy, Daphne Green.' His voice is warm and his Balkan accent heavy.

Butterflies take flight in my stomach.

I embed my hands in his soft hair, playing with it. 'That's the plan, Mr Petrov.'

He chuckles deeply as he brings his mouth back down,

lazily stroking his tongue along mine, his hands cupping my jaw.

I pull back, looking him dead in the eye. 'Stop being so sweet with me, Milosh.'

'No problem,' he growls.

All at once he brings one hand up and yanks on my hair, while the other grips my hip. Hard.

He pulls me by the hair to where he wants me and dominates my mouth. At first, I controlled the kiss but now he sets the pace.

His tongue is aggressive and greedy, taking up space in my mouth, while his hand moves from my hair down my spine, past my hip, to my thigh, branding me.

It's too much and not enough at the same time.

I need more.

I need him.

'Milo,' I whimper. Tracing his strong arms with my hands.

He groans into my ear, his other hand tightening around my hip. 'Say that again.'

'What, your name?'

He hums in response. 'I love when you say it.'

'Which one?' I whisper, moving my hands to rest on his chest. 'Milo, Milosh or Mr Petrov?'

'All of the above.'

317

I smile as I bring my mouth to his neck, kissing and nibbling lazily. 'We should probably stop and get some sleep.'

'Yeah,' he agrees.

His hands run down the length of my thighs and my breathing shallows. I buck against him, instinctively, beginning to roll my hips but he stops me, hands firm on my thigh.

'No, like you said, not now. I want to do this right.'

'What do you mean?' I breathe against his neck.

'Daphne . . .' He pauses, moving his neck back and tipping my face to look at his. 'I wanna make this work. You and me. For real. Long term.'

'Really?' I whisper, a smile fighting its way to the surface.

'Yeah.' He searches my eyes. 'Is that something you'd want?'

I roll my eyes. 'You cannot seriously be asking me that question.'

'Of course I can. We come from two separate worlds, Daphne, and I don't know how I'm going to be able to provide for you. Yes, I know we're young, but I want a future with you so I will do everything in my power to be the man you need me to be.'

'You would do that? For me?'

'I've come to realize that I would do anything for you, Daphne Green.' He cups my face and places a tender kiss on my lips. 'Anything.'

31

'Daphne?' I feel a soft kiss on my forehead as I slowly open my eyes.

'Daphne, wake up, baby.' I smile as Milosh comes into view.

'I'm gonna go get us some food and a couple of burner phones. Do you need anything else?' I shake my head, still slightly out of it, as he nods, putting his shoes on. He's changed out of his tux and is in his usual black T-shirt and cargos combo. He looks freshly showered.

'I won't be gone long, and I'm gonna take the key with me, all right?'

'Okay.'

He lingers a moment longer before kissing me on the forehead again and disappearing out of the door.

I sit up and reacclimate myself. Yesterday, so much happened that I have to take a moment to run through the events.

You're gonna make me go crazy, Daphne Green. I smile when I think back through everything Milosh said and did on this sofa, but then I process why we're here.

Gala.

Trashed house.

Kidnap.

Escape.

France.

After our conversation, I climbed off Milosh and we finished watching the movie. I ended up falling asleep on his shoulder, but some time between then and now he must've got up and laid me down on the sofa to go and have a shower.

I'm glad Milosh stopped us when he did. I wasn't in the right frame of mind to go any further. I always knew I wanted to save myself for someone special, potentially even until marriage, but that ideal was nowhere to be found last night. I was ready to give it all to him.

On my childhood holiday sofa.

Yeah . . . Not the best look.

I want it to be special and preferably not straight after finding out my life's been upended.

I don't know how I'm going to be able to provide for you. Yes, I know we're young, but I want a future with you so I will do everything in my power to be the man you need me to be.

I smile as I think back to what he said last night. My father has always had money so that was never a problem in my parents' relationship, and I never really thought about how it could affect mine.

I grew up in a circle where everyone has money, so financial strain never really crossed my mind. I think that's why I'm so okay with becoming a midwife. I'll always have my trust fund to fall back on and I always assumed I'd marry someone like Teddy, who would one day inherit his family's company.

But when Milosh brought up his concerns yesterday it shed new light on the topic. Am I okay to swap out the life I'm used to? Absolutely not. And I don't think there's anything wrong with that, but I also don't want a life without Milosh and he works for the US military.

But there's something to be said about his determination and drive.

He has discipline and resolve and a big old soft spot for me. That's how I know this can work. He doesn't want to stay where he is, he's willing to work for a better life.

For me. For us.

And he's generous.

Generous with his words, generous through his actions, and one day I have no doubt he will be generous with his wallet too.

I'd take a generous man over an affluent man any day.

Money doesn't equal generosity.

But a man who's generous now always will be, no matter how much money he makes.

I'll do anything in my power to be the man you need me to be.

I wholeheartedly believe that.

I get up and walk to my duffel, taking out all the toiletries I need and one of the dresses I packed last night. I rummage through to find some underwear but stop when I realize what perfume I've brought with me.

Taking it out of the bag I bring the perfume my father gifted me yesterday to my nose. I'm still a little confused about how he got it to smell so similar to hers, when the one I got recreated ages ago didn't even come close.

Smelling that scent while standing in my mother's favourite place brings memories rushing back.

Her sitting on the sofa as I sat on the floor while she braided my hair. Me, her and Daddy playing board game after board game and them always letting me win. Us on the very same sofa where I nearly got defiled last night, watching Christmas movies with a bowl of popcorn, snowman cookies and a cup of hot chocolate with mini marshmallows in it.

Her scent makes me feel like she's a part of my life again, in a weird, comforting way.

Scooping up my things, I walk into the shower and place my toiletries next to Milosh's, smiling when I notice how domestic our shower gels look standing beside each other.

I'm in and out of the shower in ten minutes and as I begin to lather moisturizer over my body, I hear the door shut downstairs. 'That was quick,' I mumble to myself, finishing up and slipping my dress on.

'Milosh?' I call, making my way downstairs, last night's outfit folded in my hand. 'You didn't buy any bacon by any chance? I've got such a craving for it.' I walk into the living room placing my dress neatly on the floor next to my bag, but I don't hear a response.

Wariness pricks at my skin, heightening every second the silence continues. I pick up the fireplace poker and walk gingerly to the door, opening it slowly and making my way into the dark hallway, cautiously peeking into the kitchen.

My blood runs cold.

There's a man.

A man that isn't Milosh.

There's a man that isn't Milosh, and he's standing in my kitchen looking out of the window.

My mind whirls, full of questions I don't have time to think about.

I need a plan.

I need a plan and I need it now, because I've only got so long before this man turns around.

Right now, he's facing away from me and he doesn't know I'm onto him so I've got an advantage. I think back to all the situations Milosh went through with me until the perfect one pops into my mind.

I just need to get to a pan so I can Rapunzel him and knock him out.

Taking a deep, silent breath I steady myself then run into the kitchen full speed and strike him in the back of his knees with the poker.

He howls in agony as I whack him again, hitting the front of his knees this time. I keep hitting until I hear a satisfying crunch. He's on the floor now, rolling around and gripping his legs.

Still holding the poker, I rummage through the drawers and cabinets looking for a metal pan with my back turned to him.

I haven't been in this kitchen for so long that I've forgotten where everything is. I finally find what I'm looking for and go to pull it out but a hand clamps around my stomach pulling me away before I can do so. Although my bruises are practically healed they still throb when he pulls hard on them. I'm slightly winded as my back thuds against his chest.

'I do like a challenge,' the icky guy mutters, his bad breath fanning past my nose.

I jab my elbow hard into his ribs before stabbing the poker into his trainer-clad foot earning a childlike scream out of him and a chance to get away.

Dropping the poker, I run to the drawer while he hobbles around clutching his foot, and retrieve the pan.

Moving with speed, I aim for his temple and strike him with acute precision.

He hits the floor with a dull thud, unconscious. But you can never be too sure so I batter him again. And again. Picking the poker back up I aim at his knees again, hitting until I hear a more convincing crack. Clearly the first one wasn't good enough if he was able to walk. I look around for something to tie him up with, but can't find anything in the kitchen so I move to the living room. Spotting the curtain ties I pull them off and run back into the kitchen, binding his feet together first, then his hands.

'What was it you were saying about a challenge?' I ask innocently, patting him down. I find a wallet and take it out, then I look for a tattoo. He's wearing a black polo shirt and when I pull it down to check his collarbone I spot it.

What kind of employment website does Daveeno use to always get the scummiest-looking dullards?

'What a sad little man.'

32

MILOSH

I open the door, bag of groceries in hand, and am greeted by a Rapunzel-looking Daphne.

'Whoa.' She swings the pan in her hand and I duck just in time for it to miss as realization dawns on her.

'Oh my gosh, Milo! I'm so sorry, did I hit you?'

'No, you just missed. Why do you have a pan in your hand?' But I don't need her to reply because as I walk into the kitchen I get my answer.

'What the hell happened?' I turn around and she has the most bored, unimpressed look on her face.

'He got in while I was in the shower so I couldn't hear him. When I came downstairs I realized he was here and attacked him. He tried to hurt me but didn't do much damage.'

'Are you okay?'

'I'm fine, I was just waiting for you so we could question him together.'

I drop the bag of groceries on the counter and walk over

to the intruder, who's lying on the floor, bound and bloody, one side of his face swelling up.

'You did this?' I turn back to look at Daphne, who starts nodding with a satisfied smile on her face. I breathe out a laugh, shaking my head. 'Well done, baby, good job.'

'Thank you!'

'Did you check him for ID?'

'Yeah, as soon as I tied him up.' She walks out of the room, returning only seconds later with a wallet in her hand. 'His name is Ryan Moore. Oh, and . . .' She walks past me, over to Ryan, and pulls down his polo neck.

I spot the all-too-familiar Daveeno tattoo and nod. I pull out one of the chairs by the dining table and haul him up onto it, fixing the curtain ties so they bind him to the chair too, leaving him nowhere to go when he wakes up.

I stand up and turn to face Daphne who still has the pan in her hand. 'Is that what you used on him?'

'This and the poker, yeah.' Her eyes dip sensually as she walks over to me. 'Turns out those training sessions really paid off. You're a good teacher, Mr Petrov.'

'No, baby, this was all you.' Using my pointer finger and thumb I take her chin and lift her face to mine, pressing a lingering kiss to her mouth. 'And apparently violence suits you, because you look beautiful today, by the way.'

Her lips tip up. 'Thank you, Milo . . . I think.'

'Hmm.' I run my thumb over her bottom lip, revelling in the moment a second longer before I focus on the task at hand. 'Since you beat him up, you wanna question him?'

'Sure. You're still going to be here, though?'

'Of course.'

I hesitantly pull away from her and go and fish out a bowl.

After I find one, I fill it with cold water, add some ice cubes, carry it over to Ryan, and tip it over his head.

'Wake up, asshole,' I say coldly, my tone dry.

He splutters awake almost instantly and starts fighting the restraints. When he realizes he's not going anywhere he calms down a little and I take a chair and sit down.

Pulling out my knife, I play with it lazily as I look back to Daphne.

'Go for it, Miss Green.'

She smiles at Ryan, slowly making her way over. 'Hi, Ryan. I would introduce myself but I have a feeling you already know who I am so let's just cut to the chase, yes?'

She gives him a moment to respond, but when he doesn't, she continues.

'Why are you here, Mr Moore? What do you want?'

'I want you, Daphne.' He smirks.

'Wrong answer.' She treads on his foot and he yelps out in pain. 'Now, let's try again, shall we? How did you know we were here?'

'Made an educated guess,' he spits.

Daphne's jaw clenches as her nostrils flare slightly before she looks over to me. 'Pass me your knife, please.'

'Baby.'

'Give me the knife, Milosh.'

I think that might just be the sexiest thing that's ever come out of her mouth.

I hand her the knife without a second thought and sit back, highly turned on by this side of her.

'Ryan, darling, I'm going to ask you some questions and you're going to answer them. Failure to do so will result in me injuring you further. If you then continue to withhold the answers, I'll have to get my boyfriend involved. And I assure you, Mr Moore . . . you *really* don't want that.'

I know I should be focused right now but when she called me her boyfriend a warm rush flooded through my body.

This is the first time she's called me that without it being fake and I can't help but smile. Ryan just happens to look over at me at this exact moment and his face turns an ugly greenish grey.

It dawns on me that he thinks I'm smiling at the possibility of hurting him and not because the sweetest girl just named me her boyfriend, so I probably look like an absolute psychopath to him.

Good.

'How did you get into the house?' Daphne probes.

'With a key.'

'Where did you get the key?'

'At your other house.'

She stills. 'Were you one of the men that ransacked my house?'

He gives her a creepy smile. 'Yeah, that little cleaner of yours got a nasty tongue on her. But don't worry, I shut her up in my own way.'

Daphne looks horrified before wiping the smirk off his face with a hefty punch to the jaw.

'Ow, ow, ow!' She shakes her hand. 'I've never done that without a boxing glove on before.'

'You okay?' I check.

'Hmm, aside from the pain it felt quite good actually.'

So, so sexy.

'That hurt, you b—'

'I suggest you do not finish that sentence, Ryan,' I bite out.

She turns back to look at him. 'What did you want from this house?'

He stays quiet for a moment so Daphne takes my knife and starts lightly tracing the tip down his leg. He still keeps quiet so she increases the pressure until she sees beads of blood collecting. 'What did you want?' she repeats. Again he stays quiet, so she takes a rougher approach.

Moving to his arm, she runs the knife along it from shoulder to finger, slicing. Not so deep he'd bleed out, but deep enough to leave a scar.

Ryan howls. Literally howls, like a wolf. It's actually quite disturbing.

'What did you want?' she repeats, raising her voice slightly.

'The necklace,' he spits. 'I came to get the necklace.'

'What are you talking about? I don't have a necklace.'

'The necklace with the locket. We know it has the formula inside but we don't know where it is. We tore your house completely apart and still couldn't find it so we concluded that you must have it.'

'You tore my house apart for the necklace?'

'Yeah, now can you please stop hurting me?'

'No.' She looks at me, then back to Ryan. 'Why did they take all the staff and my father?'

'As collateral. You were the missing piece of the puzzle but we knew we couldn't get to you because of your guard dog over here.' He tips his head in my direction.

'What do you mean, I was the missing piece?'

'Your dad cares about your staff, but not as much as he cares about you. Even when we threatened to hurt them he wouldn't give up the location of the necklace, but if we had you and threatened to hurt you, he would.'

'So did you come here looking for me or the necklace?'

'Either or. Ideally, I'd get the necklace off you then leave but if you didn't have it I'd take you instead and we'd threaten your dad by hurting you.'

'But I don't have the necklace, I don't even know where it is.'

'Well, that's too bad, because George isn't telling us the formula and if management does not have the formula in three days they're gonna kill him and all your other house friends.'

Daphne rears back, dropping the knife to the table.

'Where are they all being held?' I jump in, trying to take some pressure off her.

'I don't know the current location. They were just about to move them when I was leaving.'

'Who's on the management board?'

'I'm not one of the people who know their identity.'

'If you got Daphne or the necklace, where would you bring them once you got back?'

'Her house. There's gonna be a team waiting for me in a few days to take her or the necklace.'

I don't have any more questions and Daphne looks like she's a second away from throwing up, so I rise to my feet, sweeping the pan from the counter, and walk towards Ryan.

'Thank you for your honesty.' I strike the pan against the less swollen side of his face, and within seconds he's out cold.

Turning around, I face Daphne. 'Your father is alive, so I need you to take this conversation as a win.'

'How can I take it as a win when they'll kill him in two days if they don't get the necklace?'

'Do you remember what the necklace looks like?'

'Of course.'

'If I could get a guy to draw it, do you think you'd be able to explain it to him well?'

'Yeah . . . ?'

'Okay, great, then I have a plan. I'm gonna call Major Davis who's in charge of this task force and explain the situation to him. He'll get a team to come take care of him.' I point to Ryan. 'They bypass the cops so you won't need to do any unnecessary questioning. I just need to give them a report of what happened.'

'But we're in France?'

'I was in America when I got called in for this. We work with Interpol.'

'Oh, okay.'

'When someone comes to take him I'll ask for a sketch artist as well and you'll describe the necklace to them.

My major will have a replica made and in a few days will send someone to your house to hand over the 'necklace'. They'll trail the men and follow them to wherever all the hostages are, make an assessment on how to proceed, and we'll go from there.'

Daphne looks at me blankly as she processes my plan, before nodding a second later.

'Okay, that's a good idea.'

'Yeah?'

'Yeah, my father will be fine. Everyone will be fine and this will all be over soon.' She gives me a small smile. 'This is a good idea. It's gonna work.'

She continues to repeat those words under her breath as she walks over to the sink and starts scrubbing her hands. I come up behind her and wrap my arms around her waist.

'Everyone will be fine and this will all be over soon,' I echo, trying to provide reassurance. She melts into me.

'That was really hot, by the way,' I drawl against her neck. 'You with that knife?'

'Milosh!' She twists the tap closed and turns to look at me, eyes wide. 'I feel like you're trying to make me into a psychopath.'

'Well, that depends.' I lean in closer. 'Is it working?'

'A little bit, yeah.'

'Oh, yeah?'

She breathes out a stifled laugh and nods twice.

My eyes drop to her parted mouth and I cup a hand around her jaw and brush my thumb across her bottom lip. 'Good,' I reply softly.

'You know, I think I'm beginning to like boyfriend Milo.'

'Good, because he's here to stay.'

I step away and pull the burner phone I just bought out of my pocket, the number I need to call already memorized. But before I reach the doorway I turn back, one last thought needing to be spoken. 'Let's watch *Tangled* tonight.'

33

The sun shines bright in my eyes as I stir awake, feeling Milosh's chest rising and falling below me. Yesterday, just as Milosh said, two men showed up at the cottage. One was a sketch artist and one was from Interpol, here to take Ryan away for further questioning. The sketch artist was remarkably talented and managed to draw the necklace so that it looked almost exactly as I described it, so I'm feeling pretty good about the plan. Milosh explained to me that after they find the location where my family is being kept, a specialist firearms command unit will breach.

When Milosh spoke with his major he set up a safe house for us to stay in until this is over. Davis also told us that he'd send a car to take us, the sketch artist and the Interpol team up to the safe house. After the team left we packed up our things and took the car, driving back to England where the safe house is.

We got here late last night and crashed on the sofa, sticking in one of the DVDs we took from the cottage before promptly falling asleep. All we need to do now is sit and wait for everything to come together and hopefully I'll see everyone again soon.

Now, I sit up off of Milosh and start massaging the crook of my neck. After a few minutes, I hear Milosh start to stir.

'Good morning.' I smile, looking back at him.

He flashes a sweet unguarded smile in return before speaking, his voice deep from sleep. 'Good morning, Miss Green.' He sits up and stretches his neck, and I can practically see the tension in his delts.

Leaning back, I bring my hands around his shoulders and start kneading into them. I work on the knots until they melt away, then move on to his back, languidly trailing my fingers up and down.

'Feel better?' I ask after five minutes.

'Feels amazing, baby, even though I should've been the one doing that to you, given it's your birthday and all.'

I pause. 'How did you know it's my birthday?'

'It's my job to know everything about you, Miss Green.' He rises and walks over to his duffel, fishing something out.

'Here.' He pushes a small box into my hand and comes to sit back down.

'You got me a gift?'

'It's only small,' he states gruffly.

My heart blooms when I carefully open the box to reveal a light pink fob watch.

'For when you start wearing scrubs,' he explains.

I bite down on my lower lip and fight the tears that are threatening to invade my face. There's no way he could've bought this yesterday; which means he must have got it before we even officialized everything, before we even spoke about my career choices at the gala, and purposefully packed it in his bag when we were rushing out of the house amidst all the stress and worry.

'I think . . . I think I'll be able to get good use out of this.' I wrap my arms around his neck and he wraps his arms around my waist.

'Thank you,' I whisper into his neck, the first tear falling silently. 'Thank you so much, Milo. This means more to me than you could ever imagine.'

'I'm glad. Happy birthday, Daphne.'

We stay like this for a moment as I start silently sobbing. When Milosh realizes what's happening he pulls away to look at me, worry lining his face.

'Hey, what's wrong?' His thumb comes to my cheek, drying my tears.

'Nothing, I just . . . I think this is gonna work out. You and me.'

He smiles fully and it's absolutely devastating. 'I think so too.'

My tongue juts out to lick my bottom lip and his gaze darkens as he follows the movement. 'You want me to make you some bacon and pancakes?'

'Yes, please,' I answer. 'I'll have a quick shower while you do it.'

'Okay.'

Neither of us moves.

Milosh's eyes are still lingering on my lips with a hungry gaze. A gaze that I don't think even bacon and pancakes could fix.

'Are you going to kiss me, Mr Petrov, or are you going to stare at me all day?'

'Such a little smart-mouth.' He chuckles, crashing his lips down to mine. One of his hands comes to the nape of my neck, angling my head, while the other bears down on my hip. His tongue is punishing as it dominates my mouth, so much so I have to grab his shoulders for stability.

'Yes, but I'm your smart-mouth,' I whisper against his lips, my breathing slightly laboured.

He pulls back a fraction. 'I guess you are.'

My hands trail along the breadth of his shoulders as I

drop my mouth to his jaw and start placing kisses along it.

'So, I was wondering . . .' He pauses for a moment when I nip at his earlobe, his heady sigh filling the room.

'Hmm?'

'I was . . . wondering if you could teach me some sign language?'

I pause on his neck. 'You want me to do what?' I raise my head to meet his gaze.

'I want you to teach me sign language.' His hand relaxes on my hip as his thumb traces lazy circles on it. 'It was beautiful watching you sign at the gala, but it also made me realize there's a whole group of people I'm unable to communicate with, one of them being someone who means a lot to you, so I wanna learn. Well, that and the fact that talking without speaking is pretty cool.'

I stare at him for a moment, at a complete loss for words. 'You want to learn sign language to be able to speak to my cousin better?'

'If it's important to you, it's important to me.'

'Well, all right then.' I smile. 'Let's start with the alphabet. Once you learn this, if you ever get stuck on a word you can just spell it out.'

For the next hour I teach him the alphabet and the basic words, pancakes completely forgotten until my stomach starts to grumble.

'Let me make you some breakfast,' Milosh suggests.

'Okay, I'll go have a shower, then after I can start teaching you the days of the week.'

He places a sweet kiss on my cheek and walks out of the room.

I grab all my shower bits out of my bag, along with another clean dress and some underwear, and head up to the bathroom, smiling to myself. He bought me a watch for my scrubs and asked to learn sign language so he can talk to my cousin better. He's crossing off all the love languages faster than I thought possible.

My shower is quick, and as I moisturize I can smell a delicious waft of bacon which spurs me to get ready faster so I can eat. I untie my hair, letting it cascade down my back and pick up my perfume with haste to give myself a few spritzes.

I pause when I hear a light clinking noise. Lifting the bottle up again, I turn it upside down and squint to see if anything moves. The liquid is quite dark and the bottle has a slight tinge to it, but I can just about make out a floating object.

Walking to the window I hold it up to the light, and sure enough my mother's necklace is inside my new perfume bottle.

Of course it is.

Because that's a fantastic place to hide something.

I think about how the Daveeno boys completely trashed my room and how many times they must've unknowingly walked past the thing they tore my whole house apart to find.

And now I have it.

I have the very thing people are willing to kill over.

I feel sick.

But also slightly powerful.

I know something they don't.

I slip my clothes on and hurry downstairs, bottle in hand.

'Yeah, I'll keep you updated . . . All right . . . mm hmm . . . bye.'

I walk into the kitchen just as Milosh drops his phone from his ear, turning when he hears footsteps.

'That was Henry. I updated him on everything from after the gala to now. Him and Amelia are gonna stay in Italy because that's the safest place for them right now, but as soon as this is over they'll fly back.'

'Okay, but they're all right, yes? No one has come looking for them?'

He shakes his head. 'No, they're okay.' His eyes drop to my hand. 'Why are you holding that?'

'Oh.' How did I manage to forget about such a big

thing in the space of two minutes?

I walk up to him and hold the perfume up to the light.

'Do you see that?'

'What?'

'Look inside the perfume.' I lift my hand a little higher and tip it slowly.

'Is that . . . ?'

'Yeah.'

'Huh.'

'Well, what do we do?'

'Nothing for now. Put it back in your bag and forget about it. They're gonna have the replica ready and on its way to your house by the end of today, so we wait and see what happens. After the raid is complete and everyone who's a threat is in custody, we'll tell Major Davis. But for now, we wait.'

He takes the bottle from my hands and holds it at eye level, moving it around to see the locket. 'How did George get it in there?' he mumbles to himself.

I scoff. 'My father has a weird ability to exceed the laws of physics, apparently.'

He hands it back to me. 'Well. Good job, George, I guess.'

34

It's later in the day when I wake on the sofa with a gasp, clutching my chest and sitting bolt upright. I reacquaint myself with my surroundings.

The distinct smell of spaghetti bolognese wafts in from the kitchen as I brush my hair out of my face.

After breakfast me and Milosh spent our time studying BSL and watching a film. It was when I was wrapped up in Milosh's warm arms as we watched *The Avengers* that I drifted off. I don't know how long I've been asleep for but judging by the blazing sun coming from the window and the smell of cooking I would say it's maybe 2 p.m.

Leaning down and putting my head between my knees, I start trying to calm my breathing. Somehow during my short nap I had another nightmare.

The same one but a lot more vivid.

I need blueberries.

I need blueberries and a glass of water, right now.

Getting up, I make my way into the kitchen only to be greeted by a sexy, cooking Milosh. I don't know where the man learned to cook but I'm glad he did, because I certainly can't. I burn water.

'Oh, you're awake,' Milosh says, coming to kiss the top of my head. 'How did you sleep?'

I open the fridge and start my search for blueberries. 'I had another nightmare.'

Milosh groans. 'I don't think there are any blueberries in the fridge.'

'Oh, that's okay.'

No, it's not.

No, it really is not.

I don't know what's happening to me, but I start panicking.

Panicking over stupid blueberries.

I close the fridge and sit down on one of the dining table chairs as my lungs start to constrict.

In and out.

Just breathe in and out.

I don't know when blueberries began to provide an odd sense of comfort after my nightmares. Maybe it's because they're what my mother used to give me when I was sad, and I associate them with her. I don't know. But what

I do know is that I've never not had blueberries after a nightmare and it's starting to stress me out.

'Hey, hey, Daphne, it's okay. I'll go get some. I'll go get some right now.' Milosh is crouching in front of me, hands braced on my knees, stroking them gently. He looks at his watch. 'I'll go to the store now.'

'Are you sure?'

'Yes, Daphne, it's fine. I'll go right now. I just need you to breathe for me.'

Now I know the blueberries are coming, my breathing starts to level. So I nod at him and he stands, turning off the stove, and walks into the living room swiftly, before coming back to the kitchen.

'This is for you.' He hands me a phone. 'It only has the number to my burner in it, and that's saved as M. I've put that number on speed dial too, so if you need to contact me, about anything at all, you can.'

He holds out his hand and I take it, following him into the living room. 'You wanna watch a movie or something, to help take your mind off things?'

'Yes, please.'

As he flicks through the DVDs we brought with us, his words from a few nights ago echo back to me.

I don't know how I'm going to be able to provide for you. Yes, I know we're young, but I want a future with you so I will do

everything in my power to be the man you need me to be.

He doesn't need to try.

He's already the man I need him to be.

When he lifts up two movie options, I point to *The Parent Trap* and he pops it in. With another kiss on the head he turns the movie on and heads out.

I pull the throw blanket over myself and cosy into the sofa. The film is the perfect distraction. It's funny and comforting and takes me out of my head; I couldn't have picked a better option myself.

Around twenty minutes later the door unlocks and heavy footsteps sound in the hallway.

Jeez, why is Milosh so heavy footed all of a sudden?

'I remember how much you used to love this film.'

I freeze.

That voice.

The voice that echoes in my memories.

The voice that echoes in my nightmares.

I turn my head to the door and my blood runs cold.

'Mother?'

'Hello, Daphne.'

35

MILOSH

I'm looking around for the organic blueberries when my burner rings.

Major Davis.

'Sir,' I answer.

'Petrov, we just got some intel,' he starts. 'We were able to hack into one of the doorbell cameras of the houses opposite the cottage in France on the day of the break-in. After confirming with Ryan Moore, we know that he wasn't alone that day.'

My blood runs cold.

'He had a partner with him who waited outside and hid just before you came back to the house. He stayed around the side of a neighbouring cottage. When Interpol and the sketch artist showed up he waited until they were inside before leaving his hiding place and putting a tracker under the cars. One of which you took to the safe house. You need to get out now, take another vehicle and go somewhere secure.'

Daphne.

She's at the house.

Alone.

'Sir, I need to call you back.' I end the call without waiting for his response, making my way out of the store while calling Daphne's burner.

I try three times with no answer. Picking up my speed I break into a run just as I see two black SUVs turning onto the road of the safe house.

Running up the street I stop and hide behind a car as I watch four men and one woman with visible holstered handguns get out of their cars and walk up to the house.

They wait at the door for a second before entering, presumably while they pick the lock.

Pulling out my phone I dial Davis back. He picks up after just one ring.

'Write these licence plates down,' I say in a low voice, listing them off one after the other. When I'm finished, I leave the car I'm hidden behind and run to get a better vantage point.

I move to the other side of the road, walk down the driveway of the house opposite Daphne's and hide behind a very conveniently placed bush.

I keep my voice down as I bring my phone back up to my ear. 'Sir, you still there?'

'Yeah, I wrote the licence plates down. Do they need to be run?'

'Yeah,' I bite out, anger building in my veins. I have to focus. That's the only way I'll be able to make sure Daphne's all right. Follow protocol and stick to my training.

'I was out at the shop when you called me so as soon as you told me what happened I raced back,' I start to explain, watching the house vigilantly for any movement. 'But before I could get back I saw two big SUVs parked outside. Four armed men and one woman broke in and entered.'

I hate that I left her by herself. I shouldn't have done it but I didn't know what else to do. Not when she started panicking after realizing there were no blueberries. 'I can't see into the house, but I'm hidden in front of it, so I'll know when there's movement. I don't know if there are any more people in the cars but I'm almost certain these are the same vehicles driven by whoever ransacked the Greens' house a couple of days ago,' I rattle off.

I want to go in there.

I want to storm in there and sort this out. But I know that's an extremely stupid idea.

There's one of me and at least five of them.

Four of them with guns.

Realistically, I know they won't hurt Daphne. They want to use her as collateral and she's no good to them dead.

But that doesn't stop the roar in my ears and how my heart sinks thinking about the fact she's practically defenceless against them.

'I just ran the licence plates and they're all registered to the same fake company,' Davis reports. 'When they start moving, we'll track them. That should take us to a Daveeno base of some sort.'

'Okay—' Before I can finish, the safe house door opens and a woman who looks eerily similar to Daphne steps out.

Wait.

No.

'Sir. Daphne's mother's alive.'

'What?'

'She just walked out of the house, it's definitely her.'

'Well, that explains a lot.'

'What?'

'We had a suspicion that she was a Daveeno agent and faked her own death, but didn't have enough evidence to be sure of it. If she's there, then Daveeno must be getting desperate. They need that formula more than we thought if they're pulling out all the stops, bringing people back to life, just for the chance of getting the location.'

Wait. The formula.

The necklace is still inside Daphne's perfume bottle, but did they find it?

My train of thought falters when the door opens again and the men walk out, one after another.

Three of them are carrying nothing.

One man is holding Daphne.

A very unconscious Daphne.

My vision blurs as my heart plummets and my palms sweat.

'They have Daphne.' My voice is unnaturally calm. So calm it's scaring me.

The fourth man places her in the car, then rounds the back, slipping in the other side as the others also enter the car. Two engines roar to life instantaneously and set off.

'I'll start tracking them now,' says Davis, as I rush back into the house. 'As soon as the cars settle in a location I'll mobilize a unit and we will breach. I want you with them. You know this family better than any of us.'

I rush into the living room only to find our bags practically torn apart, clothes strewn everywhere. A cold weight settles in my heart as I think of one of those grubby men rifling through her intimate things. Disgust burrows into my skin but I damp it down, forcing myself to think.

The perfume.

I need to find the perfume.

I tear through the chaos of mine and Daphne's clothes,

relief surging through me when I spot the perfume bottle still intact.

I stalk into the kitchen and take out a plastic bowl, placing it on the floor. With force I hurl the bottle hard into the bowl, where it cracks on impact. The scent of the perfume fills my nose as I bend down and fish out the necklace. I don't know why Daphne loves this scent so much. Hers is much better.

This one is too much, it gets caught in your throat and it assaults your nose whereas Daphne's wraps around you, the orange blossom and marshmallow mixture soothing your senses.

Grabbing a rag, I dry the necklace off and open it up. The worn picture of Daphne and her mother stares up at me as I remove it. Turning the picture around I see a tiny laminated sheet of paper, which has chemistry symbols scribbled over it.

'Sir, I believe I have eyes on the antidote and toxin formulas.'

'Good. Keep them safe and under no circumstances let them out of your sight. I don't care if it's between the girl's life or the necklace. You will choose the necklace.'

Yeah, that won't be happening, but I'm not gonna start arguing over hypotheticals now.

'I'm going to send you the rendezvous point for the unit. Join them and wait for further instruction.' He hangs up abruptly, and I'm enveloped in silence.

For all those Daveeno people to come and get her something must've gone wrong with the fake drop that should've happened this morning. I walk back into the living room before I leave, just to check if I missed anything, and my eyes settle on a small pink object on the floor.

Bending down, I pick up the birthday present I gave Daphne this morning and check the time before dropping it into my pocket. I need to leave. I need to get to the rendezvous point, and I don't have a car.

Looks like I'm going back into my short-lived life of crime.

It's 4:32 p.m. when I get to the rendezvous point. I arrive at a warehouse, punch the code in the door and walk through.

Snipers, assault rifles, handguns, grenades, bulletproof vests, gas masks and body cams decorate the long tables that run the length of the space. The smell of ammunition and stuffy air, with the addition of the awful artificial lighting, brings me back to when I was on active duty.

'Special Agent Petrov?' a short, blond woman asks as I close the door behind me.

I nod, meeting her outstretched hand in a quick shake. 'Milosh.'

'Lucy Peterson. I'm the commanding officer and I'll be overseeing this breach. Let's get you set up and debriefed.'

After securing my vest and bodycam and picking out

another handgun with some extra rounds, I follow Peterson into a separate room where around fifteen guys are sitting, geared up and ready to go. I take a seat in the empty chair looking over to the board at the front which displays blueprints to a house.

'All right, listen up. For those of you who don't know me, I'm Lucy Peterson and I'll be your commanding officer tonight. We're looking to take out the head of Daveeno, who we now know is currently at this location.' She points to the screen as the slideshow changes and shows a road not twenty minutes from the Greens' house.

'We've been able to hack into their security camera footage and have located seven hostages. There are nine hostages total, so as we proceed, be wary of civilians.'

The two held separately must be Daphne and George.

The slide changes to pictures of the seven staff that were taken, as well as a picture of George and Daphne.

Lucy runs through everyone on the board, giving a basic description.

My jaw tightens as I think about what could be happening to Daphne right now and what she must be feeling knowing her mother's alive.

How a mother could do all of this to her own child is beyond me, but I can't think of that right now. I need to focus.

Lucy rattles off the stations and plan of attack, and what each person is doing. After the first extraction team and the exterior surrounding squad has been allocated, I hear my name.

'Petrov, Cooper and Scott will be the second extraction team. Head for the two other hostages. There will most likely be heavier security around them, so be cautious. Any questions?'

Everyone shakes their heads.

'All right, people. Let's move.'

36

My head feels heavy as the slam of a door jolts me back to consciousness.

'Oh good, you're awake.'

My heart rate increases as my brain struggles to register the cold voice that just spoke. I try to lift my hand to rub my eyes but it's being held down. I go to move it again but I can't. Attempting to move my legs next, I struggle as I feel something holding me in place. With my eyes cast down, I open them fully only to see that my ankles are tied to chair legs and my arms are bound behind me.

I groan as I lift my head, sharp pain ricocheting around the back. The instant I lock eyes with my mother, it dulls.

My very-much-alive mother.

She looks impeccable in a black figure-hugging pencil dress and Louboutin pumps, with the world's most perfect blowout. Her dark skin is pristine and glows with an almost ethereal radiance.

Death apparently suits her.

When I saw her standing there in the safe house, with four large men flanking her, I nearly threw up. It was like time stood still as I stared at her, unbelieving.

'B-but you're dead,' I had said, frozen on the sofa with the film still playing in the background.

'Dead to the world, but still very much alive.'

She looked exactly the same but completely different, strange and powerful. All of her warmth had gone, leaving a frightening lack of emotion.

'Daphne, darling, where's my old necklace?'

I stared at her.

'The necklace,' she bit out. 'Where is it?'

I continued to gape at her.

My mother was alive.

My mother, who I thought had been dead for the last nine years, was alive.

Alive.

As in not dead.

'I don't understand. How are you alive?'

She smiled. Not a warm smile like I remember. A cold, unnerving smile. Kind of like the woman in my nightmare.

Oh my gosh.

The nightmare.

It wasn't a nightmare. It was a memory.

My mother killed someone in our basement.

Bile rises in my mouth and I start gagging, all the while my mother stands there looking completely unphased as if she returns from the dead regularly and often gets this reaction.

To be fair, that's probably spot on.

'It's something akin to sleight of hand, darling,' she answered. 'Now, I really would love to catch up but you have something of mine. Something that I'd like back.'

'What are you talking about?'

'The necklace, Daphne. I need the necklace.'

'I don't have it,' I said, shaking my head.

'Search the room,' she instructed her lackeys. 'You know, your father said the same thing when I asked him.' She made her way over to the sofa, leaning down into my face. 'Like father, like daughter, I guess.'

She nodded to someone behind me but before I could turn around I felt a dull thud against the back of my head and everything went black.

Now, taking in my surroundings, I notice we're in a study very similar to Daddy's, with dark mahogany furniture and a large bookcase taking up the side wall.

I turn to take in more of the room but gasp when I see Daddy in a corner, slumped against a chair. His face is completely swollen to the point it's started changing shape, and he's bleeding. From where, I don't know, but there's a pool of blood by his feet so it's more than likely his.

'Don't worry, he's fine,' sighs my mother, moving over to her desk, leaning against the front of it, her minions following her as she does so. 'He's been given a heavy sedative so there's really no use in trying to wake him up.'

Tears prick at my eyes and I will them away.

If my mother can be cold, then so can I.

I think.

'Why are you doing this? I don't understand.'

'Your father had something, and I wanted it. It's really that simple.'

'Are you talking about the formula?'

She cocks her head. 'Yes. I am. What do you know about the toxin formula?'

'I know that Daveeno wants it but they can't find it.'

'That, unfortunately, is correct.'

I shake my head, still confused by the mere fact my mother is alive, let alone the fact that she's kidnapped me. 'I don't get it. Do you work for Daveeno?'

'Daphne, I am Daveeno.'

My blood curdles and my heart drops.

'What do you mean, you're Daveeno?' I bite out. I can feel the rage bubbling under my skin.

'I mean, your great-grandfather founded the organization. And passed it down to me.'

My mind works overtime trying to connect the dots. 'You were a double agent in MI6, weren't you?'

She smirks. 'Smart girl.'

'You faked your own death,' I continue slowly. 'You faked your own death, so MI6 wouldn't suspect you're a double agent.'

'Very clever.' The fact that she looks genuinely impressed makes me want to jump off a cliff.

'But why? Okay, so you were a double agent, but why bring Daddy into this? Why bring me in?'

'Because my cover wouldn't work otherwise. Before I inherited Daveeno, my grandfather explained to me the art of deception. In order to run the organization, I needed to prove myself; it wasn't good enough that I was blood. So they sent me into MI6. My job was to retrieve as much information as possible, enlist as many people as I could into Daveeno and have them as sleepers in MI6. But in order to do that I had to appear unassuming. And that's where George came in. We met my second year in, when there was a deadly toxin outbreak. George wasn't an active member of MI6 but he was hired as an independent contractor to help work on the antidote. He did such a good job that they kept him on. Because George wasn't a member of MI6 he had to go through a lie detector test every time he went into work, so as long as he didn't know my true identity, every time he took a lie detector test he would be inadvertently maintaining my cover, so I married him. And to keep up appearances, I fell pregnant with you.'

I laugh.

A dry, humourless laugh.

'So that was all fake? All of those memories I have of us as a family, of me and you, you were just faking?'

'No.' She shrugs. 'Even though I didn't want to, I loved you, Daphne. I even grew relatively fond of your father. You made me feel human. You made me feel love.' Her eyes soften, and it's like she turns into a completely different person. The warmth I remember comes rushing back into her face; even her posture relaxes.

She looks familiar. She looks like my mother again.

'I was almost immobilized by guilt when I thought about how my decision to fake my death would impact you. But I didn't have a choice. I kept tabs on you over the years, watched you from afar at your competitions, and I even went to Switzerland for your graduation. And before I "drowned" –' she makes air quotes – 'I left you my necklace. I didn't realize at the time how much of a pain that would be later down the line, but I just wanted you to have something of mine.'

That does explain a lot. My mother never used to take her necklace off. Not in the pool, not in the shower, not even when it didn't match her outfit. She wore it every single day, so I was fully convinced she'd drowned in it too.

'If you're looking for empathy, Mother, you're not going to get it from me. As far as I am concerned, my mother drowned when I was nine years old and that's the end of that.'

She has the audacity to look hurt.

Ha.

Hurt.

How ironic.

'I mourned you,' I spit. 'I mourned you at nine years old and continued to do so for the next nine years, and all the while you were flouncing around living the life you actually wanted to. And you're wrong. You didn't have to fake your own death. You *always* have a choice.'

'That's the thing, though. I didn't. It was either fake my own death or participate in my real one. Nine years ago, MI6 had a huge problem with double agents so they were trying to catch them out. Security checks were more frequent and rules were harsher. As a result of that, some of the Daveeno sleepers started getting nervous. Most were fine after a little *pep talk* but one was more difficult than the rest. He worked with your father and had got a little cagey with his findings. I didn't have time to keep tabs on him so I invited him around for dinner as my men searched his house. They found a lot of incriminating evidence that could take Daveeno down for good and I couldn't have that, so I killed him and framed him for my death, planting his DNA everywhere around the lake, suggesting he killed me. Which, in the eyes of MI6, placed him in Daveeno while I was just an innocent, loving mother and wife, who was tortured for information I simply didn't possess.'

The nightmare.

The basement.

The faceless woman.

'Malcolm.'

Her eyes narrow.

'His name was Malcolm. Wasn't it? I saw you that night. You killed Malcolm, didn't you?'

Her eyes light up. 'I knew you were there! I couldn't be sure but I had a feeling a small pair of eyes were on me.'

'You killed a man, just so you could live?'

'Yes.' She looks at me like I just asked her if grass is green. 'Malcolm was about to ruin everything, not just for me but for you and your father too. If Malcolm came out with his findings, you and your father would've been blacklisted from society. I did you a favour.'

I completely ignore her twisted logic and fire off the next question. 'How did you even come to know about the formula that you're now so desperate for?'

'Malcolm's journals.' She shrugs, like the answer is obvious. 'He kept extensive notes about what he was working on, and because he worked with George the majority of the time, his findings were the most present. He hinted at George making a toxin that was potent, lethal and undetectable but he didn't explain any more. We tried to look around for any evidence suggesting this but found nothing. And with the whole his–wife–just–died thing, George had a lot of eyes on him so we couldn't keep digging. We knew he had something but after my death, he left MI6 for good and kept to himself, so we had no reason to intervene.'

'But why now? It's been nine years?'

She lets out a sigh. 'Love.'

'What?'

'You wanted to smell like me.' She smiles a little, and her face fills with the warmth that I remember. 'You wanted to be close to me so much that you used up all of my perfume. So a few months ago your father started working on recreating that perfume for you, for your birthday. The reason it couldn't be replicated was that your father had mixed his basic antidote starter mix to my perfume to give it more projection, which actually ended up altering the smell. So if he was going to recreate the perfume, he was going to need to remake the antidote starter.' She laughs to herself, glancing over to Daddy in the corner.

'Love is the most potent emotion, Daphne. He knew it was stupid to get the very specific ingredients to make the antidote starter, but he did it anyway. For you. I mean, that man has some serious flaws and he doesn't show his love very well, but when it comes to you and putting a smile on your face, there's nothing he wouldn't do.'

Fine, but none of this explains what happened.

Almost like she can read my mind, she continues.

'The ingredients that you need for an antidote starter like the one your father created are very hard to come by unless you work somewhere like MI6 or Daveeno, but because your father cut ties it wasn't readily available to him so he had to find another way. He reached out to one of his old friends in MI6 asking him to get the stuff for him. What he didn't know is that we'd been monitoring of phones recently and unfortunately the man your father reached out to had one of them. We had a few clues about what was in your father's serums because of an old diary Malcolm kept so we knew he was up to something, we just didn't know what. That's when we sent in Stefan to go and look around his work office. When he found one of George's journals, he brought it back. We went through it and found out that your father did indeed make a toxin but Malcolm told him to get rid of all the evidence because he didn't want Daveeno finding it. George wrote down a riddle to find it in case he ever needed it and that's what we sent Teddy in with.'

'Why do you even want the formula?'

'I like money. And a lot of people will happily pay a handsome fee to get their hands on such a powerful serum.'

That makes sense.

'How did you even know the formulas were in the necklace?'

'Torture, darling. Torture.' She points to Daddy. 'He explained that when I was sleeping he stuck it in the back of the photos, but that's about it. We weren't able to get the location of the necklace out of him. But that's where you come in. Just like me, he has only one weakness. You.'

'I'm sorry,' I laugh, and this laugh is filled with humour. 'I'm a weakness to you? That's the most ridiculous statement I've ever heard. One of your men attacked me in my own home, then two of your people chased me around a mall, trying to kidnap me, then *Teddy* attacked me and *shot* me, and then another man attacked me in the cottage you claimed was your favorite place on earth. Don't patronize me and say I'm your weakness, because the evidence shows that's just not true.'

She looks embarrassed.

'Well, I never said my methods were sound.'

'Your methods didn't even work!' My voice rises in annoyance. 'Why did you bring me here? To use me to threaten Daddy?'

She nods.

'So what's your plan? Threaten Daddy, get the formula, then what? Set us free? Or are you going to kill everyone? The staff that you've locked away as hostages included? Staff that, mind you, you used to know. You loved Josh and Bethany, but now, all because of greed, you have innocent people scared out of their minds. They didn't do anything wrong, yet they're the ones paying the price.'

Before my mother has a chance to answer, the lights turn off.

'What was that?' Mother asks, rounding her desk quickly, opening her laptop.

One of the men pulls out his radio. 'Cole, what

happened to the lights?' He releases the button he was pressing but all he can hear is static. 'Cole, can you hear me?' he tries again, but gets the same result.

'Madam, I think the radios have been scrambled.'

'The CCTV isn't working either,' my mother replies, frowning at her laptop screen before looking back to one of the men behind her. 'Well, go and check it out.'

He shifts, looking uncomfortable for a moment before heading for the door.

'You.' Mother turns around, pointing at another one of the men. 'Stay here and call for an extraction team. You two, haul him and follow me.'

She opens her drawer and pulls out a gun, loading it calmly with deft precision before picking up the knife that was lying on her desk. She makes her way towards me, flicking the knife open, bending down and cutting me free of the cable ties.

'Get up. Let's go.'

I don't move. I don't do anything. Maybe if I stall for long enough whoever's here can find me. My mother moves to do something, but before she can the guy who was on the phone calling for the extraction team speaks up.

'The car will meet you on the other side of the woods, madam,' he says as he pockets his phone.

'Good,' she tells the guy, before turning her attention back to me. 'Now get up.'

When I don't, she cocks her gun in my face, smiling that cold smile. 'Daphne, if you seriously think I won't shoot you, you're sadly mistaken. I have no problem shooting you, or anyone for that matter.' Before I can blink, she moves her gun and shoots the guy who just called the extraction team.

I don't so much as flinch.

Did she kill him?

Will she kill me?

She points the gun at me. 'Get. Up.'

I get up.

The two men who went to haul up my father are now standing with him slumped against them.

Still pointing the gun to my head, my mother looks over to them. 'You ready?' After a curt nod she pushes the barrel of the gun into the back of my head. 'Move.'

With the two guys in front of us we walk towards the bookcase. One of the men presses down on a book and the shelves move. He pushes on them and they open up to reveal a dimly lit hall.

A secret door.

Of course my mother has a secret door.

The men walk through, with me and my mother closely

behind. We descend a set of stairs until we get to a metal door. I can feel the cool evening air rush in as one of the men pushes it open. We walk out into a wooded area.

A very familiar wooded area.

We are in the woods behind my house.

37

MILOSH

We breach strong and hard.

Blinding their security system, scrambling their radios, shutting down their CCTV and cutting off their power so they don't have any mode of communication. They're completely dark.

Thanks to the blueprints we have every exit covered, and from monitoring their CCTV we know where all the security is placed throughout the house.

They have ten men in total.

We have sixteen.

They don't know we're coming.

We're prepared.

We know where to find the hostages and have a good idea where Daphne and George are.

Apart from the bathrooms and one bedroom, the only place without CCTV is the study.

With our earpieces in, we have a constant stream of

communication. I'm not part of the first extraction team, so me, Cooper and Scott head straight for the study. Guns cocked and flashlights on, we walk cautiously through the hall. I hear gunshots, shouts and screams in the background, but I tune them out.

'Seven hostages are secure,' a guy says in my earpiece.

We reach the corner of the hall and turn off our lights. Sticking my head around I see one guy standing in front of the study door. Adjusting my position I signal to Cooper and Scott behind me as we prepare a manoeuvre.

We wait a beat and then all at once cover the hall, turning into the corner, lights back on.

'Hands up!' Cooper shouts as we move in. The guy at the door instantly throws his hands up.

'Slowly drop your weapon.' He complies, dropping it then whipping his hands back up again. We reach him and I kick his gun away, going to open the study door as Cooper cuffs the Daveeno guy.

I move with caution and open the door, speeding to re-secure my gun.

A guy jumps out at us from the side but I quickly dodge him. He stumbles a little, clearly injured, so I take the opportunity to grab him and knee him in the gut. I strike him again, kneeing the groin this time and watch as he slumps to the floor. Retrieving a pair of handcuffs, I quickly restrain him.

Looking around the room I can see it's empty, but I can definitely smell Daphne's mother's perfume that she put on this morning. There's a chair in the middle of the room with severed cable ties lying on the floor and another chair in the corner with a pool of what I assume to be blood underneath.

They were definitely in here. But where are they now?

According to the blueprints there's no way in or out of this room other than the front door, but we would've seen or heard them. The windows are locked, so where did they go?

'Hey.' I kick the Daveeno guy who I now notice is bleeding from his arm. 'Where did they go?'

He starts laughing, but doesn't say anything. I bend down and locate the wound. It looks like he's been shot, and the bullet's still inside his arm. As I press my finger down on his wound, he cries out.

'Where did they go?' I ask again, pressing harder.

'Into the woods,' he cries. 'They went to the woods.'

'Why?' I ask, looking around the room again to figure out how they got out.

'The – the getaway cars,' he pants, my finger still pressing into his arm.

'How did they get out of the house?'

He doesn't answer so I press even harder. 'How did they get out?' I can hear my volume rising as I stare at him. He starts panting through the pain again before answering.

'The bookcase. There's a secret door in the bookcase.'

I stand up and stalk over to the bookcase looking for any abnormalities, then I spot a French travel guidebook amongst the fiction classics. I go to pick it up, but it doesn't budge. Pulling a little harder I hear a click and then a release. I push against the bookcase and the door opens, revealing a dimly lit hallway leading to a set of stairs.

Cooper comes back inside the room, looks from the guy slumped in the corner to me and Scott, and nods.

'I'll take care of him. You two go.'

Me and Scott make our way through the hall and down the stairs, where we push open the door and exit into the woods.

'I need some backup out here,' I say, pressing my earpiece. 'Elizabeth Green has escaped with the last two hostages and they're in the woods.'

'Copy,' Lucy Peterson confirms.

'You keep left, I'll look right,' I instruct Scott as we make our way through the woods. We move silently and carefully, remaining vigilant.

I spot something pink against all the green and brown and narrow my eyes. Five figures come into view in the distance, walking away from us.

'I have eyes on the hostages,' I say quietly into the mouthpiece. Scott looks to me when he hears what I said and comes over.

'Where?'

'Over there.' I point. 'Look for the pink.'

'Got it. What's the plan?'

'We need to get close without them noticing. Let's pick up speed but be careful of any sticks that could crunch under your boots.'

He nods and we keep moving. As we get closer I can see Daphne next to her mother and two men behind them, hauling an unconscious man who I can only presume is George.

'We need to take out the two guys first,' I say just as one of them looks around.

Within seconds bullets go flying.

Scott starts firing back, causing the men to duck and start running, carrying George with them, as we catch up behind them. I don't want to hit George or Daphne, but I'm a pretty good shot and it's still relatively light outside so I shoot back.

My bullet nicks one of the men holding George and he stumbles. The unconscious George slumps against the other guy, who staggers, slowing down.

Ahead of them, Elizabeth pulls out her gun, firing at me and Scott as we get closer.

She hits Scott and he falls.

'The vest caught it.' He coughs when I slow down. 'Keep going, I'm fine.'

I keep shooting at the one remaining guy as I run to reach him and George. His shots, mixed with Elizabeth's, make the journey slower as I dodge bullets while firing my own, but I get a partial break when the man holding George runs out of ammo. He goes to reload but I shoot his hand, then his foot, then his thigh. He screams, falling to the floor, dragging George with him.

I reach them and kick his gun out of the way as Scott joins me, bending down and putting cuffs on the Daveeno guy.

With those two down, Elizabeth is the only one left.

'Milosh?' George stirs on the ground, coming to. I look down at him, just as Elizabeth fires the bullet.

Right through my leg.

38

Click, click, click.

My mother keeps pressing the trigger but nothing comes out.

She has no more bullets.

Before it's too late, I swipe at her legs with as much force as I can, but I don't get both of them. She catches and rights herself quickly – but she's let go of my arm.

I lunge at her, trying to take her down. She falls to the ground beneath me, hitting her head. I don't have enough time to secure her arms and she reaches into her cleavage and pulls out a small knife.

Well, that was unexpected.

She swipes at my face but I dodge the blade just in time. I try to knock it out of her hand but her grip is too strong. I grab her wrists before she can try again, lifting them over her head. We're about the same height so it's a lot easier to pull them taut compared to when I did this with Milosh.

I dig my fingers into her wrists as hard as I can and the knife falls from her grasp. I adjust my position and kneel on her stomach to pin her down.

She whimpers in pain just as four men surround us, pointing their guns right in my face. Somehow Milosh is one of them, shot leg and all.

'Come here, Daphne,' he says. I can see the pain in his eyes as I get up and come to him while the team secures my mother.

He holsters his gun and cups his hands around my jaw. 'Are you okay?'

I nod and fall into him, his arms wrapping around me as he grunts quietly.

'Your leg,' I gasp, pulling out of the embrace to look down at his thigh.

'It was a clean shot,' is all he says before he takes my hand. 'Come on, let's get out of here.'

He's slow in his movements, limping slightly as we make our way back to my mother's house where multiple police cars and ambulances are waiting.

'Petrov,' a short blond lady says, walking up to us. She looks over to me, offering a small smile before she sticks out her hand. 'Miss Green, it's lovely to meet you, I'm

Commander Peterson, but please call me Lucy.'

I shake her hand. 'Hello.'

'I'm glad to see you're out safe. You'll be happy to know that we've got all the hostages out, and they're safe too.'

Relief floods through me.

'With your mother and all the other Daveeno members here tonight in custody, we're well on our way to fully dismantling the organization. I can assure you, they won't be bothering you again.'

'Thank you.' I smile sincerely and look around for Daddy and the other hostages but I can't see them. 'Where's my father?'

'He's been taken to hospital to be treated along with the rest of the hostages. There's an ambulance ready to take you too, just so you can get looked over.' She peers at Milosh's leg. 'You too, Petrov. Scott, you and Daphne ride to the hospital. I'll sort everything out here.'

Milosh nods before reaching into his pocket and taking out the necklace. 'Here.' He hands it to Lucy. 'Major Davis instructed me to give this to you.'

She takes it, tucking it into one of her trouser pockets. 'Yes, he told me you had it. Thank you.'

'What will happen to the formula now?' I ask.

'A select group of scientists will look at the validity of the claims made about it. If it is as bad as your father says it will most likely be destroyed, but there are instances where these serums may be helpful. It's unfortunate, but at least we'll know it's in the right hands.'

'Oh.' Intellectually, I accept that, but I just don't like the thought of it being out there.

Lucy gives me a sympathetic look before walking off.

'Don't worry,' Milosh whispers into my ear. 'I burned the real formula and replaced it with a fake before I left the safe house. Let them come up with their own toxins.'

'You really are as good as they say you are, aren't you?' I murmur, my heart growing tenfold.

He shrugs, smirking. 'Apparently so.'

Gosh, I love this man.

Oh my gosh, I love this man.

Huh.

What a way to end the day.

Three hours later I walk into Milosh's room at the hospital, surprise coasting over me when I open the door to find my Uncle Leo, Uncle Jonathan and Auntie Emily inside.

They all turn as I open the door, relieved at the sight of me.

'Daphne, are you all right?' Auntie Emily asks, walking over to me and giving me a hug.

'Yeah, I'm fine.' I glance between Milosh and them. 'What are you guys doing here?'

'A woman called Lucy contacted me to let me know what's been going on and to tell me that your father's in hospital,' Uncle Jonathan explains. 'I called Emily and Leo and we all came down to see him. He told us the whole story from the beginning and explained how good Milosh was at keeping you safe. We were already thinking of starting up a security division at Greenway, but this situation settles it. George told us that he thinks Milosh should run it, so we all came in here to ask him if he'll accept our offer.'

'I'm sorry, you want Milosh to run a Greenway division?' I ask. Greenway divisions are only run by Greens.

'Yes.' Is his oh-so-simple reply.

'Really?' I start to smile as it all sinks in.

'Daphne, this man saved your life multiple times, has good contacts in the US military and is highly skilled. Which one of your cousins has that resumé?' Uncle Leo chirps.

He's not wrong. All of my cousins are very book-smart but when it comes to strength and agility they are severely lacking.

'Anyway.' Uncle Jonathan looks back over to Milosh who's sitting on a hospital bed, legs swung over the side.

'Give it some thought. No need to give us an answer now, so take your time.'

'Okay,' Milosh responds. 'Thank you for the offer.'

They nod and once they've given me a quick hug they depart, leaving me and Milosh alone.

'Mr Petrov,' I say, walking towards the bed.

'Miss Green.' His eyes soften as they meet mine.

'You just got offered a job, huh?'

'It definitely looks that way.'

'So . . . what are you thinking?' I walk up to him, settling between his open legs.

'I'm thinking that I want to build a life with you,' he answers, his hands landing on my waist, pulling me closer. 'And that this offer could help me give you the life you deserve. What do you think?'

My mouth pulls into a smile. 'I think I love you, Mr Petrov, and I think you love me too.'

'Is that so?' He smirks.

'Mm hmm.' I nod, wrapping my arms around his shoulders.

'You'd be willing to bet money on it?' His hands move and tighten around my hips.

'A significant sum, yes.'

'Well then, I guess you just won big, because I do.' He brings his lips to mine.

'I love you, Miss Green.' He starts dotting kisses across my face and neck. 'I love your face, I love your hair, I love your laugh, I love your smell, I love your mind, I love your voice.' He cups my face in his hands, those beautiful green eyes boring into mine. 'I. Love. You. And I will continue to love you until I have no more breath in my lungs.'

And just like that.

I found my Henry.

EPILOGUE

MILOSH

Five years later

'I delivered three babies today!' Daphne gloats as she dips into the car. I close the door behind her and round the car to sit in the driver's seat.

'Well done, baby,' I praise, placing a chaste kiss on her lips and watching as she slips her engagement ring back on.

'It was two girls and one boy, and they were all healthy with no complications!' She sighs contently, as I start the car and pull out.

It's been six months since Daphne started her new job at the Howard Memorial private hospital and I've yet to fail to pick her up after her shift. I had a meeting with a new client today so I'm in the Tom Ford suit Daphne chose for me the day I accepted the job as CEO of Greenway Security. With Amelia's business, admin and finance background she joined, along with Henry, and, with the support and guidance of the Greens, in the last five years Greenway Security has become the top private security company in England.

While Daphne was training to be a midwife, I attended university part time to get a Business degree so I could do my job to the best of my ability.

Daphne's phone rings and she puts the caller on speakerphone.

'Hi, Daddy, you're on speaker.'

'Hey, Milosh. Hey, Daph, you on your way?'

'Milosh just picked me up. I'm gonna go home, change, and then I'll be right over.'

'All right, but you know this is a surprise baby shower. It won't be much of a surprise if you arrive at the same time as Amelia, will it?'

'Yes, Daddy, I'm aware.' She sighs.

'Okay, well, I'll see you in a bit then. Love you.'

'Love you, bye.'

She hangs up the phone just as we pull into the parking garage of her apartment.

'How did the meeting go?' she asks me as I open her car door.

'It went well. They ended up signing on for three years and they need a lot of security. They're now one of our biggest US clients.'

Once Daphne finished university we decided to move to Chicago so I could be more hands on as we opened up the US division of Green Security. I proposed six months later and immediately bought land to start planning our for ever home. We're getting married in four months and will be back from our honeymoon three weeks later. By then the house will be complete and we can officially start our lives together.

'That's amazing, Milo!' Daphne says as we make our way up in the lift.

'Thank you, Miss Green.'

'You know, one of these days you're going to have to get used to calling me Mrs Petrova?'

'Mrs Petrova does have a nice ring to it. But you'll always be Miss Green to me.'

She smiles, walking into the apartment, heading straight for her dressing room.

I go to the kitchen to get a drink just as my phone starts buzzing.

'Yeah?'

'We have a problem,' Henry's voice says.

'What?'

'We're on our way back now, and not even half the guests are here.'

'Well then, stall her,' I suggest, opening a bottle of water.

'Wow, aren't you a genius,' Henry quips. 'I've already tried that. I'm at a smoothie bar now getting her a drink.'

'Go and look for a pushchair or something then, that'll take ages.'

He pauses, probably mulling over my brilliant idea. 'Okay, that could work. I'll text you when we're on our way.'

I hang up and finish my drink, leaning against the counter and scrolling through my phone answering a few emails and smiling at a picture Susie, George's new wife, sent the group chat of them on their most recent holiday. After the Daveeno case, George completely gutted his house, wanting to be rid of any bad memories, and started over. He hired Susie as the interior decorator, swiftly fell in love – for real this time – and proposed within two years. They got married last year and often go on long holidays, exploring the world together. She sent the photo now to throw off any suspicions Amelia has about the surprise baby shower that's being thrown for her.

Henry and Amelia moved with me and Daphne to Chicago and have the house right next to our soon-to-be home where the surprise party is gonna be held.

'What do you think?'

I look up and Daphne has effortlessly transformed from Midwife Daphne to regular Daphne.

She's wearing a pale pink midi dress with the diamond earrings I bought her as a graduation gift. Her hair is in a curly half-up, half-down style and she's applied a light coating of make-up to her face, just highlighting her beauty.

'I think you look hot, Mrs Petrova.' I walk over to her and grab her waist, my hands costing her soft curves.

'I wasn't going for hot, I was going for classy.' She pouts.

'Fine, then you look regally hot, Mrs Petrova,' I murmur against her neck, dotting soft kisses down her throat.

'Regally hot,' she sighs. 'I like that, you should say it more often.' Her hands find my hair as she directs me where she wants me.

'Will do, Mrs Petrova.' I stop kissing her and look up at her. 'You're right, by the way, Mrs Petrova is better.'

She laughs. 'I never said it was better, I just said you should start calling me that.'

'Well then, *Mrs Petrova*, let's go before we're late.'

'Good idea, *Mr Petrov*.'

She takes me by the hand as she leads me out of the apartment, back to the car.

All I can do is smile.

This girl transformed my black world into one of love, laughter and pink. Every day she finds a new way to amaze me and every day I remind her of that fact.

I stop her short of the door, spinning her around to look at me. 'I love you, Mrs Petrova.'

She smiles softly. 'I love you too, Mr Petrov.'

ACKNOWLEDGEMENTS

Hey, so, BookTok?

Thank you :)

If I could hug each and every one of my TikTok friends I would. But I can't . . . therefore I shan't.

Three years ago, after I finished telling my brother about the plot of a random mafia book I was reading, he suggested I share my delightful opinions with the world so he could get back to his work. And that's exactly what I did.

Three years later, I've grown a lovely group of BookTok friends and I can't begin to tell you how much your love and constant support has blessed me. Without you I would most definitely not have written this book and it would still be a random movie idea that I had in the back of my head. Every like, comment, follow and save has led to *Close Protection* being what it is. So, I thank you!

I hope *Close Protection* lived up to the hype, and I wholeheartedly hope you find your Milosh or Henry for yourself :)

Thank you to Yasmin Morrissey, who is the genius editor and publisher that made all of this happen. Yas, you're most definitely one of my favourite people with your infectious positivity and never-ending ideas. From the moment I pitched this idea to you, you were probably more excited than me (and that's seriously saying something) and since then you've also been the biggest Milosh and Daphne supporter known to man. Thank you for listening to all my random thoughts, from book name ideas to cover designs, you've been so supportive and kind through it all. Thank you for making *Close Protection* a reality.

Andy Darcy Theo, the man you are. Thank you, friend, for answering all my questions, being a huge supporter and listening to my nonsensical voice notes. You've helped me so much through this publishing journey and I can't wait to see you continue to flourish and grow.

Deborah, Deborah, Deborah. You brilliant woman, you. Thank you from the bottom of my heart for all of the time and effort you've put into helping make this book better. You helped me, encouraged me and challenged me. Thank you, you wonderful human being.

To my mother, father, brother and two sisters, you've been the best sounding board for every idea, cover design, name choice and so much more. You read the very first chapter WAY too many times, but your joint opinions have been so helpful.

Thank you to the team at S&S. Each and every one of you are so uniquely talented at what you do and I truly appreciate all the work you've put into this. Jesse and Michelle, thank you for all the effort you put into the cover and designs, and thank you for working with me and getting all the little bits just right, you're both AMAZING!

Millie, I appreciate you and all the hard work you have put into this book. Thank you Rachel, Laura, Ali, Dani, Leanne, David, Alesha, Simi, Kate, Teän, Alice, Sophie, Sorrel and Maud. Without you all there'd be no book! Each and every one of you believed in me, and I thank you for that.

Lastly, thank you Lord Jesus for giving me hands to write and blessing me with a creative mind. There is no way in heaven or earth that I would've been able to complete this book without you. Thank you, Lord, for your grace and mercy and thank you for blessing me with this opportunity.

ABOUT THE AUTHOR

Eden Victoria is an award-winning content creator turned author. She won BookTok Creator of the Year 2023 (@edenvictorria, 700k followers) and also runs a luxury lifestyle, perfume and clothing account on TikTok (@edensslife, 200k followers).

But Eden's interests don't stop there. On top of books, clothes and perfume, Eden is currently training in Musical Theatre with the goal of debuting on the West End.

**DOWNLOAD THE *CLOSE PROTECTION*
EBOOK TO RELIVE DAPHNE AND MILOSH'S
LOVE STORY ANYWHERE, ANYTIME.**

HE'S GUARDING HER LIFE, SHE'S GUARDING HER HEART

CLOSE
protection

EDEN VICTORIA

ON THE GO? DOWNLOAD THE *CLOSE PROTECTION* AUDIOBOOK NOW TO HEAR EDEN VICTORIA VOICE DAPHNE!